The Northern Reach

The Northern Reach

W. S. WINSLOW

FLATIRON
BOOKS
NEW YORK

For my mother

For Max and Grace

And for Frank.
This book is dedicated to
the memory of his maman, Christiane Hodgkins.

THE NORTHERN REACH. Copyright © 2021 by W. S. Winslow. All rights reserved. Printed in the United States of America. For information, address Flatiron Books, 120 Broadway, New York, NY 10271.

www.flatironbooks.com

"Trinity" first appeared in *Bird's Thumb* in October 2018.

"Mother Ship" first appeared in *Yemassee Journal* in Fall 2017.

Book design by Donna Sinisgalli Noetzel

Library of Congress Cataloging-in-Publication Data

Names: Winslow, W. S., author.
Title: The northern reach / W. S. Winslow.
Description: First edition. | New York : Flatiron Books, 2021.
Identifiers: LCCN 2020040975 | ISBN 9781250776488 (hardcover) |
    ISBN 9781250776495 (ebook)
Subjects: LCSH: Maine—Fiction.
Classification: LCC PS3623.I6644 N67 2021 | DDC 813/.6—dc23
LC record available at https://lccn.loc.gov/2020040975

Our books may be purchased in bulk for promotional, educational, or business use. Please contact your local bookseller or the Macmillan Corporate and Premium Sales Department at 1-800-221-7945, extension 5442, or by email at MacmillanSpecialMarkets@macmillan.com.

First Edition: 2021

10 9 8 7 6 5 4 3 2 1

Well you may throw your rock, hide your hand

Workin' in the dark against your fellow man

But as sure as God made black and white

What's done in the dark will be brought to the light

You can run on for a long time

Run on for a long time

Run on for a long time

Sooner or later God'll cut you down

Sooner or later God'll cut you down

—"GOD'S GONNA CUT YOU DOWN,"
AS PERFORMED BY JOHNNY CASH

The Northern Reach

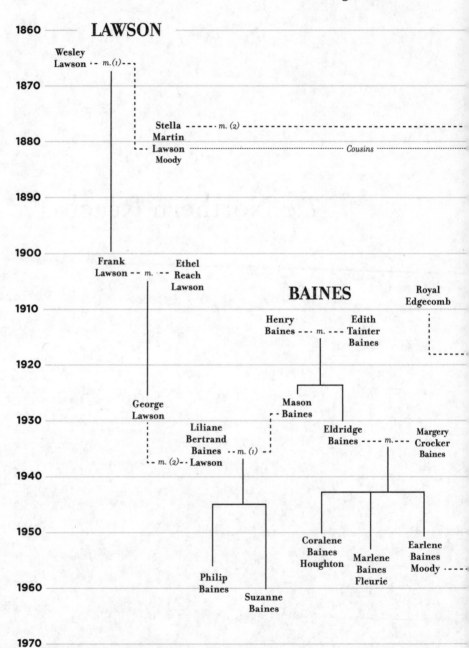

Wellbridge, Maine

LAWSON

1860

Wesley
Lawson · · m. (1) · ·

1870

Stella
Martin · · · · · · m. (2) ·
1880 Lawson
Moody · *Cousins* · · · · · · · · · · · · · · · ·

1890

1900

Frank   Ethel
Lawson · · m. · · Reach
Lawson

BAINES   Royal
Edgecomb

1910

Henry   Edith
Baines · · · m. · · · Tainter
Baines

1920

Mason
George · Baines
Lawson
1930   Eldridge   Margery
Liliane   Baines · · · · m. · · · Crocker
Bertrand   Baines
Baines · · m. (1) · ·
· · m. (2) · · Lawson

1940

Coralene   Earlene
Baines   Marlene   Baines
Houghton   Baines   Moody · · · ·
Fleurie
1950

Philip
Baines
Suzanne
1960   Baines

1970

MOODY

MARTIN

1860

1870

1880

1890

1900

1910

1920

1930

1940

1950

1960

1970

Ray
Moody

Robert
Martin

John
Partridge

Gerry
Moody --- m. --- Fidelia
Partridge
Moody

Myra
Moody

Hake
Moody --- m.

Frenchie
Gagnon
Moody

Ralph
Martin --- m. --- Eleanor
Partridge
Martin

Agnes
(Pug)
Partridge
Juke

--- m. ---

Bucky Levine

m.

Imelda
Martin
Levine

Millhouse
Moody

Tiger
Moody --- m. --- Jessie
Martin
Moody

Albert
Edgecomb

Charmaine
(Chubby)
Moody

--- m. ---

Victoria
Moody

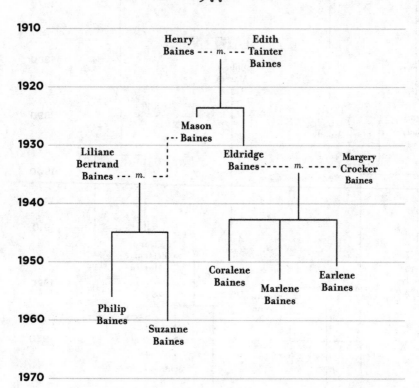

1977

1910 —— Henry   Edith
Baines - - - *m.* - - - Tainter
Baines

1920 ——

Mason
Baines

1930 —— Liliane
Bertrand   Eldridge   Margery
Baines - - - *m.* - - - Baines - - - - - *m.* - - - - - Crocker
Baines

1940 ——

Coralene   Earlene
Baines   Baines
Marlene
Baines

1950 ——

Philip
Baines
Suzanne
Baines

1960 ——

1970 ——

MOTHER SHIP

Edith Baines stares out the living room window at the schooner on the far side of the Northern Reach. It's a traditional boat, big, maybe eighty feet, gaff-rigged with raked masts and some kind of carving on the prow, but in the inky light of the late afternoon she can't make it out. The funny thing is, even though both the mainsail and the mizzen are raised, the boat isn't moving. She squints but can't see an anchor line, or even a buoy through the spitting snow. The current, she knows, is too strong for a mooring over there. Why doesn't the boat drift? Where does it come from? Where is the crew? The questions itch unmercifully in her brain.

Descended from three generations of boatbuilders, Edith has always loved to sail. The summer she was ten—fifty-six years ago it would be now—her father took the family to Mount Desert Island for a weekend parade of tall ships. On a brilliant July morning, they climbed Cadillac Mountain. From a distance, the slopes had looked gentle and smooth like an old marble half-buried in the ground, but up close, on the trail, where the underlying granite pushed through the soil, the stone was brutal, fractured, and dangerous, and Edith imagined that just pulling out one rock might bring the whole mountain down on them. To avoid being buried alive, she walked with her hands in her pockets, kept strictly to the trail, and stepped carefully to avoid dislodging even a pebble.

At the summit, they surveyed her whole world, from the reach she's looking at now, south to the bay, past the islands, and out to sea where the ocean met the sky in soft white surrender. They were so high up Edith imagined she could step off the mountain and onto the clouds. As they slid across the sky, the Porcupine Islands below them seemed to be swimming in the bay, bristled whales breaking the surface but leaving no wake. This, she thought, must be what it felt like to be God, but such blasphemous notions she'd learned to keep to herself. It took days and days to get the soap taste out of her mouth.

That afternoon they drove past the island's rambling summer cottages, half-hidden behind stone walls and tangles of rugosa, and into the town of Bar Harbor to see the tall ships, mostly schooners like this one. Even though she'd grown up around the boatyard, Edith had never seen vessels this big before, and she had to crane her neck to watch the fireworks high above the web of masts and rigging. Edith has forgotten all the boat names but one, the *Fanny Battle*. At the time she thought it was funny to have a boat named after someone's bottom, but Papa said Fanny was a genuine lady's name and told her to stop her deviltry. When she giggled again, he wiped that silly grin off her face, just like he said he would.

Edith presses her fingertips to her cheek, expecting it to feel hot with the slap and the shame, but it's cold, like always. Like everything in winter. Above the reach, low clouds sleepwalk across the February sky. Today they are fibrous, striated, like flesh being slowly torn from bone. It's four in the afternoon and already night has started chewing away the edges of the day. This is winter's waking death: half-light, refracted by gray water and dirty snow, begging the voracious dark to end its misery.

Along her jaw, Edith traces calcified bone bumps like rock beneath her skin. She follows the line from chin to earlobe, wonders when her skin got so loose and thin, thinks maybe if she pinches it hard enough, it might tear away from her skull in shreds like those clouds. Tentatively at first, she tugs at a jowly flap on her jawbone. It's loose all right, and it hurts when she pinches it. The pain cuts through the maddening static in her mind, so she squeezes harder, then rotates her nails into the flesh. If she breaks the skin, will she bleed? Or is she like those hairy moths, the ones with eye markings on their wings that flit around the yellow porch light and explode in clouds of dust when they pass too close? In that last second, she thinks, the light must seem as bright and hot as the sun.

"Mother Baines?" Margery drops her handbag on the floor and skitters over from the doorway. She's wearing her wool coat; wet snow sparkles on her shoulders, almost glamorous. At the sound of her daughter-in-law's voice Edith recoils, as she always does, at the dreadful intimacy of being called mother by someone who is not her child.

Edith looks at her hand. The nails of her thumb and forefinger are red rimmed. She feels a blood drop forming on her chin, but before it can fall into her lap, Margery pushes a lipstick-stained wad of tissue against it, tells Edith to hold it there while she looks for the Mercurochrome. She returns with rubbing alcohol. It'll smart almost as much; the thought makes Edith smile.

"Good Lord, what have you done to yourself this time?" Margery sighs as she replaces the dirty tissue with a stinging cotton ball. Edith doesn't bother with the question, the answer is obvious. Margery puts more pressure on the wound than she needs to, so Edith pushes back with her jaw. When Margery snatches the cotton ball away, the scrum ends in a draw.

"You gonna sit there staring into space all afternoon, Mother?"

"I don't know, Margery, probably," she says. The effort of speaking exhausts her.

Margery leans in to apply a Band-Aid and exhales stale breath past yellow teeth coated in cigarette smoke and saccharine black coffee. Edith turns back to the window.

In a few minutes, Margery emerges from the kitchen wearing an apron over her pantsuit and carrying a packet of egg noodles with a can of cream of celery soup balanced on top. "Tuna casserole or shrimp wiggle?"

When Edith doesn't answer, Margery says more loudly, "For supper, Mother, tonight. Which one?"

Edith waves off the question as if it were one of those moths fluttering around her head.

Margery thinks her mother-in-law is running down, that her interest in life is dwindling along with her stock of words. Edith hasn't said ten things in the past week; before the accident you couldn't shut her up any more than you could slow her down. Now she goes hours without moving or speaking. The silence weighs on Margery, tries her patience.

"I had a nice visit with Earlene today. She asked to be remembered to you," Margery calls from the kitchen, hoping to start a pleasant conversation about her daughter. "She's about to pop with that baby, and still two months to go."

Edith says, "I never thought I'd have a great-grandchild by the name of Moody." It's not meant to be nasty, not entirely anyway. She is genuinely surprised that someone as levelheaded as Earlene would marry into the lowest of Wellbridge's no-'count families.

Ignoring the dig, Margery focuses on being as Christ-like as she can. Since she was born again in Jesus six months ago at the First Light Pentecostal Assembly of Our Lord and Savior—and stopped attending the Congregational church with Edith—her mother-in-law has been nothing but spiteful.

"Heard from Lillian?" Margery asks from the doorway. One of the few things they agree on is Liliane Bertrand Baines, whom both call Lillian, deliberately over-anglicizing the way they pronounce her name in a shared act of righteous denigration.

Edith snorts her reply. She has more important things to think about than that French whore who stole her son, turned him against his family, then sold them all down the river after he died.

"You'd think she'd call," Margery says, persistent. "Today being the anniversary and all."

This day, February 23, marks exactly a year since Edith's husband and two sons went out pulling lobster traps, but only one of them came back: Eldridge, Margery's husband and the younger of Edith's boys. Always the least essential of the three Baines men, he is now the only one.

"I wouldn't think any such thing," Edith says. It occurs to her that no one knows what anybody thinks. It's the lies that hold people together, she believes, the things we never say, the false faces that mask ugly truths.

Here's another thing Edith knows: After twenty years in the merchant marine, Mason was the best waterman in the family. So after the accident, when Eldridge claimed his brother made the decision to try to beat the storm instead of taking shelter at Dogleg Harbor, Edith knew he was lying. It was her husband, Henry, who'd have insisted on running for home. Eldridge always went along with his father; he'd have said anything to outshine Mason, but his need for approval cost everyone plenty. When the coast guard finally plucked Eldridge off the capsized hull, his pelvis was shattered and he was half-dead from exposure. The doctors said he'd be lucky to walk again.

Two days later, Henry's body drifted ashore down Stonington way, his face so bloated and purple his casket had to be closed. Mason never resurfaced. They buried her son's coffin empty, just left his corpse for lobster food at the bottom of the bay. Edith tries not to think about the creatures nibbling away at his eyes and fingers, but the image is never far from her thoughts.

"Well, I *would* think she'd call, if only out of respect for your loss, and to ask after Eldridge of course," Margery says. When she gets no response, she continues, "And since you don't have a preference, we'll go with shrimp. It's Eldridge's favorite."

Margery leaves the living room to see to dinner. After the first pot clangs, Edith reaches into Margery's purse for the pack of Kools, lights one up, and turns her attention back to the schooner. It hasn't so much as drifted.

Since the accident, Eldridge Baines hasn't been able to work. He can barely walk anymore, let alone run a boat or pull traps, so he spends his days limping around the dock, picking things up and putting them down, dreading the boat's return, studying the peeling paint on the office walls, the scabby dock planks, the rusted-out engine parts that litter the yard—anything but that greedy bay. Eldridge doesn't miss lobstering. His lifelong dislike of the water has turned to hate, his fear to terror.

Eight months after the funerals, Mason's widow sold the house he built her to some summer people. They bought Mason's dinky little sailboat, too. Eldridge believes that Liliane deliberately spited his family by selling Mason's shorefront land, her sixty percent of the lobster pound, and the half-wrecked lobster boat to the worst people she could think of: Reynard Fletcher and his harridan wife, Boots. Eldridge's new business partners don't pay much attention to him; they're too busy with each other. Yesterday Boots picked up a chain saw and heaved it right at Reynard's head after he told her to shut her goddamned stupid face. Ten minutes later, Eldridge heard them moaning and grunting in the storeroom. One of them always seems to have a black eye or a fat lip; they both stink of sex. Eldridge gives them a wide berth.

Tonight Margery is late picking him up, and the Fletchers have already gone. They turned down the heat before they left, so Eldridge waits in the cold office, staring at the empty driveway and warming his gloved hands on the metal shade of the desk lamp.

A year ago, he'd have sold his soul for something warm, anything. Though it seemed like days, he was only on the hull for a couple of hours. He sobbed himself dry out there, thought for sure he was a dead man, and prayed to God for the first time in his life, really prayed, for deliverance. At the time it didn't occur to him to put in a word for his brother and father. He worries that it matters.

Because Eldridge didn't die that day, hanging on to the keel of that miserable skeg-built lobster boat of Mason's, he owes God. That's why he goes with Margery to the Holy Ghost Rallies on Wednesday nights and the Miracle Services every Sunday even though he hates being there. The revival tent is in a clearing, but it's surrounded by choke-black woods, the deep kind that could swallow you up in a second, just as fast as that bottomless, icy bay.

Eldridge has been cold ever since the accident, even sitting out in the sun last summer he felt the ache of the Atlantic deep in his belly and bones. He's hoping the pastor at First Light can convince Jesus to warm him up, maybe even get his pecker working again, though the doctors up to Bangor have told him that's not going to happen. The minister says his prayers might work better if, in addition to accepting Jesus Christ as his personal savior, Eldridge were baptized and born again, but Eldridge can't stand the idea of being shoved under the cold water, of being weighed down by his clothes and shoes. Not again.

One Sunday afternoon, he got so desperate he tried to get healed by that TV preacher, Earnest Angely, the one who says to press the afflicted part of your body against the television screen. He stood there with his aching pelvis pushed up to the Motorola for a good five minutes. Nothing happened. Mother saw him but never mentioned it.

Eldridge can't believe the accident was only a year ago. Since then, the days have been endless, droning on, rhythmic and dismal as the tide, coming and going without cease, rising and falling in frigid waves that lap the shore. Every day he tries, and fails, to avoid thinking about that afternoon on the bay, about his brother and father in the pilothouse, fighting each other for control of the wheel. He tries to forget the first wave that came out of nowhere and slammed them back into the second wave, blew out the windows and washed them all overboard, then capsized the boat. He's still not sure how he came to be on top of the hull. Margery says it was the hand of God Himself, a sacred miracle from heaven, but he knows his blessing is his mother's curse, that every time she looks at him, all she sees are the two caskets and wishes it had been him in the empty one. It occurs to Eldridge that his presence makes it even harder for her to bear Mason's absence.

Down on the shore, the crows mob in a sour squall. They always seem to be pecking at each other, screeching and fighting, yet they are either unable or unwilling to separate from the flock. A murder, he thinks, that's what a flock of crows is called. He closes his eyes and shrinks down inside his coat, away from the squawking and the early dark and the tide that never stops. When headlights flash above the hilltop, Eldridge nearly cries with relief.

Edith is sitting at the kitchen table when Margery and Eldridge get home. From the lingering smell of mentholated smoke, Margery concludes that her mother-in-law has been at her cigarettes again and so absolves herself of any guilt she might feel about paying for a new carton from the petty cash drawer at the pound. If only she could find a brand the old lady disliked.

Eldridge greets his mother and pauses behind her chair, wondering how come she is always staring out the window. He doesn't ask, thinks of touching her shoulder, keeps his hand in his pocket; instead, he goes to the living room and turns on the nightly news, plops down in a chair, and pushes the heap of burnt matches to the side of the ashtray with one of Margery's Kents. Why that woman can't settle on one brand he'll never know.

In the kitchen, Margery sets the table and pulls the casserole from the oven. She has been mentally composing her blessing all day. With the three of them seated, she clears her throat to stop Eldridge picking up his fork.

"I'll say grace tonight," she says, as if they say it every night, which they do not.

Given that this is a solemn occasion marking the anniversary of their loss, Margery expects Eldridge and Edith to bow their heads while she fills the room with the presence of the Lord, but Edith says, "No, thank you," and picks up her fork.

She has no appetite and can barely stand the smell of the food but forces herself to spear a few peas, put them in her mouth, and chew. She takes a sip from her glass of milk, then smacks it back down on the table. Her son and his wife stare; Margery's mouth is open, the first syllable of the prayer stalled somewhere around her tonsils.

Edith despises Margery's newfound devotion, her constant Bible-thumping. It reminds her of her father and mother after they took up with that snake of a preacher who came up from New York, bled his flock white, and disappeared when the money ran out. What difference does it make whether Margery is drunk on whiskey or her own righteousness? Like Edith's parents, she is consumed with sanctimony and deluded by false salvation. Like them, she is a fool.

When Eldridge's hand moves toward his fork, Margery smacks her own on top of it in a violence of clasping. "All right, Mother. Eldridge and I will just have a moment of silent remembrance," she says. Edith spears a single greasy noodle and lifts her fork again. Eldridge stares into his lap while Margery moves her lips and tightens her hands in a white-knuckle prayer. When she finishes, she says, "Amen," and both begin eating.

"Needs salt," Edith says. She stands up and retrieves a jelly glass from the dish drainer on her way to the living room, returns with three fingers of Canadian whiskey. She sits down next to the kitchen window, then pushes her plate away and lights the cigarette she has filched from the pack on the coffee table. Margery and Eldridge eat in silence, each checking the other's reflection in the window. Edith steams most of the cigarette in eight hard drags, then stubs out the butt on her plate. The ember sizzles when it hits the cream sauce.

"Don't you think you should put something in your stomach, Mother? At least some bread and butter. I can't remember the last time you ate," Margery says.

"My house, my rules, dear," Edith says, and turns her chair around to face the window. She can just make out the shape of the schooner and its sails against the snarl of evergreens and bare branches on the far shore. In the window, she sees her son and his wife exchange a look. She picks up the book of matches and strikes one, holding on until it nearly burns her fingers, then drops it in the overflowing ashtray next to all the others. The charred stems remind her of burnt bones, ghosts of heat and fire.

Eldridge sips his milk, wishes it were beer. He looks at Edith's drink and feels like he used to at the sight of Margery's ass. Although he has agreed to take the pledge with his wife, he occasionally slips downstairs for a nip when he can't sleep. And then there's the fifth in his desk drawer at work, but that's just for warmth.

Edith watches Eldridge in the window and realizes how it is the whiskey bottle drains itself. "You look like you could use a drink, son," she says to his reflection.

"No thank you, Mother. You know Eldridge and I've quit," Margery answers for him. She seems on the verge of quoting scripture, so Edith makes a hrumphing sound while Eldridge shovels in another mouthful.

Edith watches Margery's reflection take a righteous sip of Tab, then asks, "This local shrimp, Margery?"

She nods.

"Bottom-feeders," Edith says without turning around. "Ever think about that? They're *bottom-feeders*, just like the crabs and the lobsters and all the rest. They eat the shit and the dead things on the bottom of the bay. The bodies." It takes Eldridge a second longer than Margery to get the point, but both drop their forks. Margery covers her mouth with her napkin and runs from the room. The slam of the bathroom door rattles the window frame.

Eldridge stares at the back of his mother's head. She meets his gaze in the glass and would like to ask what he thinks that boat is doing over there but instead presses her lips shut. She won't concede the game of chicken her boat-watch has become. Eldridge pushes his plate away and grabs her glass. He's pale, ghostly even. Everything, she thinks, is at least half-dead here.

It's nearly dawn and the rising sun is starting to push against the fog, but it cannot burn through. So begins the second year of Edith's widowhood. Why, she wonders, is there no name for women who've lost a child? Maybe because those with more than one are still mothers, though they are more changed even than widows. There should be a word for it. Moths, maybe. Abbreviated versions of what they once were, cold and dried up inside, fluttering madly toward any source of light or heat.

She recalls a story Mason told her about seeing a funeral pyre years ago in some foreign country, India maybe. There, he told her, the dead were burned, not buried, and it was customary for the widow to throw herself into the fire with her husband's body. Most had to be dragged, he said. Must have been a rule some man came up with. Who else would decide women should follow their husbands into death, but not their children?

All night long Edith has been propped up in bed, watching the schooner bob and dragging on her cigarettes until the embers warm her fingers. She is parched and her throat burns. In the cold room she pulls up the quilt that has covered her bed since she was first married. It no longer smells of Henry's body. She misses his presence more than Henry himself. In forty-eight years together they were seldom completely miserable; still, she'll never forgive him for losing her son. She'd give anything to have Mason back but knows there's only one way she'll ever be with him again.

Across the room, next to the window, stands the maple chair that used to be pulled up to Mason's desk. Outside, the schooner is still anchored to nothing, crewless and dark under full sail. A phrase floats to the surface of her mind: in irons. The boat must be in irons. She marvels at the cleverness of the image, a boat imprisoned by the nothingness of absent wind, unable to move forward or tack, bobbing and drifting, waiting and waiting.

Why does no one else mention the schooner? Maybe Eldridge and Margery can't bring themselves to look at the water; Edith can't stop.

In the half-light, the fog seems to be rising from the reach, smoke-like, in shifting banks like low clouds. When it thins she sees that the schooner is closer than it was yesterday. She squints at the gray mass of the boat and picks up her glasses. It looks like there are markings on one of the sails. She was sure they were white, but now there are two dark smudges on the main, up near the gaff boom. In a moment of near clarity she sees: there are eyes on the sails, and they are looking at her.

Eldridge's boyhood room can barely accommodate their double bed and is stuffy even on cold nights like this. Margery turns over to face her husband, who groans at being jostled but goes right back to sleep. When he snores, she smells whiskey on his breath and asks God to forgive him for breaking his vow. Quite often she wishes for a drink herself, and this night is no exception. What a horrid thing that was for Edith to say. Margery is trying to think kindly about her mother-in-law, but as always, it's a struggle.

She hates living in Edith's cold, shabby old house, hates Edith for not giving them the money to stay in their trailer when Eldridge couldn't work anymore, hates Liliane for selling everything and running off downstate, even hates poor dead Mason for dragging Eldridge out on that damned lobster boat he was so proud of. Margery's father always said you couldn't trust a skeg-built boat in heavy weather; he swore by the sturdier built-down models and was still pulling traps on his at the age of seventy-three. Mason loved the speed of that boat, the flashiness, and since it was his money that bought the pound and the equipment, he got what he wanted, like always.

Margery had always assumed Mason and Liliane would move away, back to France, after he finished his twenty years in the merchant marine, but instead they stayed in Wellbridge, and right off he started picking through the ledgers, questioning every expense, and swanking around the pound like the lord of the manor. She knows it's wrong to speak ill of the dead, so she keeps her opinion of Saint Mason to herself.

The one person in the Baines family Margery doesn't hate is Eldridge. Truth be told, she prefers this new phase of their marriage in which he relies on her but makes no demands. Freed from the obligation of sex, she can cuddle up to him anytime she likes without fear of starting something. He pays more attention to their children than he used to and even talks to her about them sometimes. When Edith dies, they can sell their share of the pound and this horrible house and buy a place in town. It would be a sin to wish her mother-in-law ill, but she doesn't seem to have much interest in living and there's no commandment says you can't plan ahead.

Edith fails to stare down the schooner and slides low in her bed, eyes squeezed shut as if she's a child playing peekaboo. When she opens them, Mason is sitting on his desk chair; his oilskins drip on the carpet. "Where's my boat?" he asks.

This is not the first time Mason has appeared, but it is the first time he's spoken. Though Edith feels nauseated and barely able to form the words, she manages to ask, "Which one?"

"*Orion.*"

"Your wife sold her."

His anguished keen, like the sound of a dying loon, pierces her chest. *Orion* was their shared passion, a custom-built Dark Harbor 20 just like the ones the summer people race. With a navy hull, teak decking, and tanbark sails, she was distinctive, sleek and low, like a knife through the water. Edith and Mason used to take her out on summer afternoons, just in time to catch the late breeze, then run for home with the wind at their backs. Edith handled the tiller while Mason manned the sails, all the while telling his mother stories of his travels in the merchant marine, bringing her the world she would never see, spooling out the time she thought they'd lost.

She and Mason were the only ones in the family who liked to sail. Henry couldn't be bothered, Eldridge never took to the water, and Mason's wife made it her mission to queer her children on sailing from the cradle.

"Why didn't you keep her?" he asks, staring out the window.

"I can't keep anything," Edith says.

"It's so cold here, Mumma."

Before Edith can answer, her son has gone. Now it's her turn to wail. She stumbles out of bed and over to the window, willing him to come back. The sail's eyes bore into her. The rising sun peeks through a break in the fog and spills its weak light across the water. The schooner is drifting, and its bow has slewed toward shore. Now Edith sees the white skin and red hair of the figurehead on the prow. Suspended over the reach, Fanny Battle leers silently at Mason swimming for the ring buoy just beyond his grasp. Again and again the tide pulls him under. Fanny shifts her gaze to Edith and smiles.

Edith runs downstairs and makes for the back door, desperate to rescue her boy from the cold black water, wanting only to be with him. By the time she steps onto the porch, Mason has made it to the *Fanny Battle* and climbed aboard. He turns to Edith, beckons her from the deck. There is something shining in his hand, almost like he's holding a pinch of the sun. He looks from it to his mother and throws it into the air. Now Edith sees, all around Mason the fog is not fog, but smoke. Above his head the sails ignite, flames scorching away the eyes that have been watching her, consuming the masts and running down the lines to the deck. "Fire! Mason, get off!" she screams, and runs for the water.

The commotion has jerked Margery and Eldridge awake; both assume the house is burning. They race downstairs in robes and slippers and run for the back door, following the sound of Edith's voice, ragged as rusty iron and screaming something about a fire.

Through the mist, Eldridge sees his mother, barefoot and dressed only in her nightgown, running toward the reach on the hard crust of snow that covers the lawn. He and Margery take off but cannot catch her before she reaches the shore. Luckily she loses her footing and falls, giving them time to grab her and pull her out of the water that is so cold it burns. Though he is only ankle deep, Eldridge feels like he is drowning. He, too, is screaming.

Edith kicks and flails at the arms that restrain her, begs them to let her go. She can't see Mason anymore.

"It's burning, the boat, the pyre. Mason lit it. For me. I'm the moth, it's for me. . . ." Together Margery and Eldridge wrestle her to the ground.

"There's no fire, Mumma, there's nothing out there, nothing," Eldridge yells, but Edith doesn't listen. It's only after Margery slaps her, twice, good and hard, that Edith's entreaties turn to whimpers and the fight goes out of her. She embraces the darkness and says no more.

It's early March; several weeks have passed since Edith's first midnight swim and the three attempts that followed. The ground has nearly thawed, with rocks heaved up through the topsoil like bones through skin. What little snow remains has melted into crags of tar-black ice, lurking in shadows and corners that will warm only after the sun has baked the mud to hardpack. In the kitchen of the house on the reach, Eldridge is outlining his plans for this year's garden between bites of peanut-butter toast.

"Mouth full, El," Margery says, waggling her finger, and obedient as a puppy, he stops talking until he has swallowed. He's just begun his explanation of why Mother's Day weekend will be the best time to plant when the phone rings. They both check the clock. Seven-thirty, it could be Earlene's husband calling to say the baby is coming, but by now they both know better than to hope for good news, especially at this hour.

Margery answers. "Not *again* . . . Yes, I understand." She thanks the caller and hangs up.

"The hospital. About Mother. Tried to get out and go swimming in the river last night. Again," she says, and sighs. "That woman is like a moth to a flame around cold water."

Eldridge slumps in his chair.

"El, they said if the drugs were going to work, they would've by now. She's a danger to herself, and she could be to us. That's what the doctor said. You heard him. I can't watch her every minute of every day. Keep her out of the bay and away from the matches. She almost burned the house down that last time. And that business about seeing Mason is just, well, it's crazy, El. At least they can keep her fed and washed."

Eldridge picks at his toast while Margery jabbers. He is thinking about his brother and father, about how they knew the difference between right and wrong, about how blood takes care of blood. His wife can talk all she wants, but it's not up to her.

"The doctor wants to see us," Margery says, and leaves the kitchen.

In preparation for yet another trip to the state hospital, she grabs her handbag. Inside are the involuntary commitment papers Eldridge has so far refused to sign. Margery hands her husband his coat and pats his shirt pocket to make sure he has a pen. He stops in the bathroom on the way out and drops the pen in the trash can.

1904 — 1914

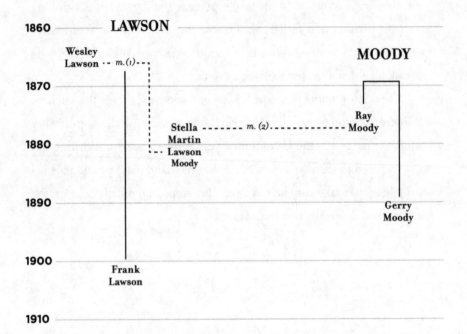

RUNAWAY

―――――

FRANK AND STELLA, 1904

"You brung the boy," Ray Moody said, inclining his head toward Frank, who was standing by the pond. This was not the plan. She and Ray had agreed to leave together, get settled on the farm, and return for her son later, after the new baby came.

"I couldn't leave him, Ray. All alone, with no one but that old . . . witch to look after him." At the thought of her mother-in-law, Stella's fists clenched. The old lady cared for Frank as much as she did anyone, but hers was a cruel, destructive love that twisted people up in knots, made them hard and cold. Stella's husband had proved that—every single night she'd slept alone for the past five years. She could count on one hand the number of times since they were married that Wesley had come to her room; he seldom lingered, never stayed the night, and afterward he avoided her for days.

"He's still your husband. You take his child, he'll come after you."

Stella was afraid to breathe. Even if she could go back to that house, she wouldn't. There was no laughter or music, nothing to read but the Bible and dusty old history books with no pictures or romance. She was carrying a baby that wasn't her husband's. They'd throw her out and keep Frank, who was just four years old, far too young to be away from his mother. She'd rather die than never hold him, or hear his scratchy voice, or smell his neck again.

"I left him a letter just like we said. Under his pillow. Wrote that if he gives me a divorce, he can visit Frank anytime he wants, that I'm going back to my people because a baby's coming and I don't want to shame him. His mother'll say he's well shed of us both, you'll see."

Ray seemed to be thinking it over. After a while, he said, "Another mouth to feed. You know what it's like on a farm."

Stella nodded even though, having grown up in town, she didn't know, not really. She'd visited her cousin's farm in Wellbridge just a few times, had never done much beyond collecting eggs from the henhouse, but she knew she'd be good at it, that she'd be happy out in the country with her new husband and lots more babies to love.

"Hey," Frank called, "want to see me throw a rock?"

Ray nodded, so the boy walked to the shore and picked up a pebble, then sent it sailing to the other side of the pond just like his father had taught him. When it broke the surface of the water, Frank turned to the grown-ups, but they weren't paying attention.

Stella was gazing past her boy and the pond at the boulders and the blueberry scrub, just starting to go red in the October sun. Beyond it, squeezed somewhere between the belching smokestacks and dirty brick warehouses of Bangor, stood her husband's printing company. She was glad it, and the house where they lived, and the gray river that ran through the city, were all too far away to see. That was their old life, even if Frank didn't know it yet. She supposed he'd get over missing his father eventually. Though life with her husband's family suffocated her, it was all her son had ever known. Stella's eyes watered, and she clenched her teeth against the tears.

Ray couldn't back out now. She'd thrown away her good name for a new start with him, risked everything: her future, Frank's, the baby's.

"Pretty good, huh?" Frank shouted.

"Never met a boy who didn't love throwing rocks," Stella said.

"Nope," said Ray.

"He'll be a good big brother."

Ray sighed.

Stella watched Ray walk down the hill toward the pond and motion Frank to join him. He picked up a stone, showed it to the boy, then skipped it across the water in a series of low arcs. Stella counted six bounces. Each produced a perfect ring of ripples, concentric circles moving steadily outward and crossing one another in endless, undulating webs.

"Golly," Frank said. "Can you teach me that?"

"There's a pond out to the farm," Ray said, then led them both up the hill to the wagon.

FRANK, 1914

His real father was a printer, a businessman, that much he knew. And his name, of course: Wesley Francis Lawson. He'd been given his father's middle name but was always called Frank. As he walked across the bridge to Bangor, Frank chanted the name over and over, quietly to himself. *Wesley Francis Lawson. Wesley Francis Lawson.* He liked the rhythm of it, the symmetry. He took a step for each word, adding a single count between repeats, keeping his pace steady and regular. In this way, he would be like his father, steady and regular. Respectable.

Near the end of the bridge, Frank looked up at the brick-and-granite buildings that crowded the riverfront and ran up the hill, gradually giving way to tightly spaced frame houses about halfway to the top. The heavy clouds of late September hovered above the city, almost low enough to snag on the church spires. His eyes traveled back down, from the sky to the river. The banks were choked with nests of weeds and rubbish; an oily film slithered along the surface, making ugly rainbows in the low light. He reached down for a pebble and threw it as far as he could, then waited to hear it hit the water.

Nothing was familiar. Frank couldn't remember living here as a child, but he'd expected to recognize Bangor as home, to have it match the image in his mind of chugging engine clatter, shiny glamour, and gaudy wealth. Instead, the city looked like a bigger, dirtier version of Fairleigh, the market town between here and Wellbridge where he'd spent the last two weeks, picking up odd jobs and sneaking into stables and sheds at night to sleep. Even living rough was better than staying in Wellbridge.

Earlier that morning, in exchange for helping a trapper load up, he'd hitched a ride to Bangor in the back of a wagon full of beaver pelts. They must not have been scraped right because the rancid smell of spoiled fat lingered in his nostrils. He hoped it hadn't seeped into his clothes. He only had the one pair of britches.

It had taken all day to cover the twenty-odd miles to Bangor. The horses clopped along the dusty road, passing low-cut fields, their grasses harvested, dried, and baled for the winter. Here and there were clumps of trees, a few oak and maple with leaves already beginning to catch fire, glowing red and yellow around the edges. There was even the occasional house, hard up against the road, leaning in, eager for news and visitors, which Frank figured were probably rare out that way.

The trapper had taken him as far as the other side of the river and dropped him at the foot of the bridge, tossing him two bits for his work. Frank put the coin in his pocket, adding it to the three dollars he'd saved. A poor-farm boy no more, he was done taking charity. He was a workingman now.

"Boy, if you're smart you'll spend that in a rooming house and not a bawdy house," the driver said, and wished him luck. Frank wondered how old the man thought he was. He'd be fifteen in two months and was just starting to see some ankle between his cuffs and boot tops. Even though he was smallish, Frank was strong and wiry, his face and forearms windburned from working outdoors, which he figured made him look older. He wasn't sure what a *body house* was, guessed it had to do with girls, but Frank hadn't come to Bangor for romance. He'd come for his father, and so he trudged up the hill to look for lodgings.

He passed by several well-kept rooming houses with flowers in the dooryard and kitchen gardens at the side, but he didn't knock until he reached a shabby one on the back side of the hill overlooking the jail, with neither flowers nor grass nor welcome of any kind, just a hand-lettered sign in the front window, "Rooms to Let." Although she seemed unconvinced when Frank claimed to be sixteen and an orphan, Mrs. Dowd offered him the room behind the kitchen for ten cents a night, fifteen with the morning and evening meals.

"Supper's at six. I lock my doors at nine sharp, so if you want to sleep in the room you paid for, you'd best be in it by then," she said, then showed him the privy and the backyard pump.

Even with a full belly, Frank slept fitfully that night. Twice he dreamed of his mother and twice he awoke, sweating and sobbing, grasping for the wisps of her in the unfamiliar dark. At the pump the next morning, he tried to wash away the dream feeling along with the fur stink and the grime of the previous week. He rinsed out his dirty shirt and spare underclothes and hung them on the line to dry. Back in his room, he slipped out of his trousers. Dusty, but they were his only pair, so he shook them out, smoothed the wrinkles, and pulled them back on. His good shirt promised a fresh start; his cap, pulled low, anonymity.

He tried to follow Mrs. Dowd's vague instructions to "go over the hill towards the river, then downstreet past the bank with the clock," and was on the verge of asking for directions when he found what he was looking for, just before midday.

The Lawson printing company occupied a low brick building with double carriage doors painted shiny green and open before a loading bay. To the right was the public entrance, with gold newsprint-style letters stenciled on the window: LAWSON & SONS, PRINTERS, EST. 1860. From his place across the street, Frank faltered for the first time since running away. He reminded himself he was a respectable workingman now. Still, he couldn't bring himself to cross the road, let alone enter the building.

He watched two men wearing aprons and sleeve garters, standing in front of the loading platform, smoking and laughing. Soon they were joined by several others with pipes in their pockets and lunch buckets in their hands. Frank's stomach rumbled. For breakfast, Mrs. Dowd had given him a glass of milk and a slice of brown bread with butter. At the farm, they ate their big meal in the morning, but it seemed city people saved their appetites for supper. If he'd known, he'd have taken a second helping of beans when it was offered the night before.

Thoughts of his belly were interrupted by the sight of a tall blond man in a suit leaving the building. The workers stopped talking and nodded in his direction. Frank heard him say, "Afternoon, fellows," in a clear, reedy voice as he strode past. The men tilted their caps and responded with a chorus of "sirs" and "good days." Frank felt his chest tighten when he picked out an "Afternoon, Mr. Lawson" among the greetings. His memories of his father were hazy, but the man seemed familiar.

Frank shadowed him from the other side of the street, staying well behind and out of sight. In a few blocks the business district gave way to a grid of tidy residential streets, and as they walked, the houses became bigger, the lawns more expansive. Lawson stopped in front of a spare white frame house with neither porch nor shutters nor any ornamentation on either it or the carriage barn that loomed behind. Between the peaked roof and granite foundation, the house's plain face stared unblinking at the street, its run of flaky white clapboards broken only by three smallish windows, one on either side of the black front door and another above it. The grass in the dooryard was half-dead, seared to hay. Frank had imagined his father lived in an elaborate gingerbread house covered in curlicues and cupolas, topped with a widow's walk and surrounded by gardens and fancy iron fencing. But this was nice.

Lawson took the four steps in two strides and disappeared inside the house. He emerged less than an hour later and retraced his path back to the printshop, with Frank leaving his place behind a wide Dutch elm to follow him from across the street. And so it went for the next two days.

On the third day, Lawson stopped at the foot of the dooryard. He turned around to face the elm and called, "Young man, if you have business with me, kindly speak up."

Frank wanted to run but forced himself to step out from behind the tree. He waited for the man to nod before he crossed the street.

When Frank was in front of him, Lawson said, "Yes?"

Out of habit, Frank tipped his cap. "It's me, sir, Frank. Francis John Lawson."

"Is it, then?" Lawson scrutinized him, and Frank wondered what to do. Should he extend his hand, hug his father? He didn't know, so he waited. "What's it been, ten years? Well, I expect it was only a matter of time before you turned up. You'll be wanting to see your father, I presume."

"You're not . . . ? I thought they called you Mr. Lawson. At the printshop."

"I'm William, Wesley's brother. Come inside. I'm sure we've given the neighbors enough to talk about already."

The house was dark and close, the air stale. William Lawson removed his hat and indicated a straight chair. "I'll speak with my brother. You may wait here." He turned down a murky corridor, treading so silently Frank thought he might have disappeared altogether. When he opened a door, a shaft of light pierced the gloom but disappeared as soon as the door rejoined the frame.

Once Frank's eyes adjusted, he looked around. He seemed to recall the chair and the piano in the parlor. Was his father musical like his mother? She hadn't told him much about the Lawsons, except that they were from Bangor and owned a printshop. When he asked why he never saw them, all she said was, "Your father and I didn't see eye-to-eye, and living in that house was awful hard. We're better off on the farm."

Frank hadn't known divorce was a shameful thing until he'd gone to school. One day, when he was about eight years old, Punk Stratton called his mother a whore. He'd heard the word and had a pretty good idea what it meant. So he threw himself at Punk's blubbery middle and managed to land a couple of punches and one good kick before his teacher pulled him off. When she asked for an explanation, Frank refused to speak. Her request for an apology met the same stone wall.

It hadn't taken long for Stella Martin's tawdry story to get around, and soon fights in the schoolyard were a regular part of Frank's day. At first, he tried to avoid them, but eventually he came to accept the inevitability of violence and almost enjoy brawling. Even when he was cut or bruised, he felt clean after a good fight, calm and peaceful. He didn't always win, but he never backed down or failed to land at least one good punch. By the time he was twelve, he stopped going to school, at the teacher's request.

By then, things were bad on the farm. Mumma was always either having a baby or tending one, his sisters were too little to help much, and Ray was drinking up most of the money. So it fell to Frank to run things. He looked after the garden and the animals and fixed the equipment when it broke, but he couldn't pay the taxes they owed. A year later, the Revenue came and took the place. With his mother expecting a sixth child and no family willing to take them in, they ended up on the Wellbridge poor farm, living off what they could grow and the charity the selectmen saw fit to provide.

The poor farm. A string of half-ruined shacks bordering the exhausted fields like broken teeth, it sat high on a wind-whipped hill overlooking the town of Wellbridge, exposed to the elements and visible to the townspeople through a wire fence. One privy for ten families, no running water, freezing in winter, fetid in summer, and crawling with bedbugs and vermin all year round. Frank tried not to think about it, but the humiliation clung to him, covered him in a stink of shame. If he were a real Lawson, it might finally wash away.

He took a step into the darkened parlor and tried to picture his mother there. His sisters would have loved the piano. He hadn't had much to do with them until the oldest brought the measles home from school and he had to take care of them. Mumma wasn't supposed to go near the girls because she was pregnant. But she was softhearted and let the littlest one into her bed when she cried. That last baby, the boy Ray had always wanted, came early and died three hours later. Mumma followed not long after. They were buried together in a single pauper's grave with only a wooden cross to mark their lives.

"It's your fault!" Ray screamed at him. "Good-for-nothing. Should never've let her bring you. Just keep the girls away from her was all you had to do." When Ray swung at him, Frank finally hit back, knocking his whiskey-soaked stepfather to the floor, leaving him sobbing into his chest and crying for his wife.

"Young man, what are you doing down there? I didn't hear the bell."

The voice came from the top of the stairs. It creaked like an old bedspring but still carried weight. Dressed all in black, his grandmother was at first hard to make out in the low light, but he felt a shiver of recognition at her pale face, a parchment-covered skull in a sea of darkness. Hard as a church pew was how his mother had described her; the years didn't appear to have softened her any. He stepped back into the hall.

"I'm Francis, Grandmother. But everyone calls me Frank."

"My goodness," she said, but didn't descend. "Aren't you quite far from home?"

"I'm up here to work."

"Work? At what?"

"Odd jobs so far, but I'm looking for something steady. A trade."

"And you think we might have one for you, is that right?"

Frank had no idea what he should say.

"Perhaps you'd best speak with my son. I presume someone is fetching him?"

Frank nodded.

"Well then." The old woman turned as if to go but stopped and said, "Were you brought up in church?"

"I went to Sunday school, sometimes. Christmas and Easter mostly."

"It must have been a very forgiving congregation. Not Catholic, then?"

"Methodist." It was the only church within walking distance of the farm.

She tilted her head. "You favor your mother. Small, but not quite so swarthy as her people. You should remove your cap in the house."

With a rustle she was gone, and Frank wondered for a moment whether she'd been there at all. He took off his cap and tucked it in his back pocket.

The hallway door opened and William Lawson stepped through. He signaled Frank to come along. The back parlor was bright, overheated by the woodstove that had been jury-rigged into the fireplace, and Frank squinted against the light. The room smelled of liniment and dust. Somewhere in the house a pie was baking, apple by the smell, and Frank's mouth watered. His uncle stepped back through the door and closed it behind him.

Wesley Lawson was a wizened version of his brother, half a head shorter and slightly stooped, nearly bald, the blue of his eyes the same as Frank's, but so faded the irises were nearly clear. Like William, he was dressed in a business suit, but Wesley's seemed to be in the process of swallowing him beneath the afghan draped over his shoulders. Frank was already sweating in the heat. He knew his father was older than Stella by a good bit and had calculated that he must be near fifty. He had the beginnings of that soft, baby look old men got.

Wesley stepped from behind a desk cluttered with books and papers.

"Frank," he said, then repeated the name.

"Hello," Frank said, wondered what he should call him, settled on nothing.

Wesley crossed the room and gave Frank a brief, weak embrace.

"Please come and sit down. Etta will bring some luncheon. You must be hungry. Frank. It's been such a long time. . . ." He pointed to a chair and lowered himself to the settee, sending a cloud of dust motes swirling into a sunbeam.

"You've come from Wellbridge, then?"

Frank nodded. He had dreamed of this meeting for years but now found himself tongue-tied. He took a deep breath.

"Are you not missing school?"

"I work now."

"So you're missing work, then?"

"Nothing steady yet, but I want a trade. Come up to Bangor to find one, I guess." Frank was strung tight as a wire.

"And how is your mother?" Wesley asked.

"Um, she passed. Last year." Saying it always brought it back. Mumma's gray face, her screams as the farm warden's wife pried the tiny dead boy from her arms, the whimpers of his sisters, Ray's rage, and his own endlessly bleeding grief. He turned his face from his father and dragged his sleeve across his eyes.

"I'm sorry, Frank. I hadn't heard. So young. I'm terribly, terribly sorry." Wesley seemed to be waiting for Frank to collect himself. "Is that why you left the farm?"

His father was talking about Ray's place. He thought Frank had left the scraggly patch of rock and dirt his mother and Ray had finally managed to buy, then lose. He couldn't tell his father how low they'd all sunk, so he just nodded.

"Have you a place to stay? Here in town."

"Mrs. Dowd's over on Oak Street."

"I'm not familiar with it. I trust it's satisfactory? Safe and clean?"

Frank nodded again.

A side door to the dining room swung open, and an old woman waddled through it carrying a tray.

"We'll be in presently, Etta. Just leave the things on the table, please."

It was an odd meal: pickled cucumbers and cold ham, no bread or pie. They ate mostly in silence, with Wesley posing questions and Frank providing short answers. Frank watched his father eat. He cut each piece of meat in a perfect square, each cucumber slice into triangles, and chewed slowly.

Before he could stop himself, Frank said, "I thought you were a printer. At the shop."

Wesley swallowed the last of his ham and put his fork down. "I was, but now I prefer to spend my time studying, and on my work at the church. I'm the sexton."

"Studying what?"

"Why, the Good Book, of course. I was once quite interested in history. Still am, but since the . . . in recent years, I've devoted myself to the Lord. Perhaps I'll have a flock of my own one day."

Frank couldn't imagine why anyone would do that when he could go to a nice office and be the boss every day, but he kept it to himself.

After they returned to the parlor, Wesley said, "I wish I could ask you to stay, Frank, but your loss was very trying for your grandmother, and William feels that the strain of being reminded of it, of the scandal, would be too much for her. There'd be talk again. Perhaps he's right. She has spells, you see."

Frank didn't see. The old girl seemed plenty tough to him. He said nothing, and his father hurried on.

"We *can* help you in other ways, though. Financially, with schooling. There are places you could board, academies or homes. You're not even fifteen."

Frank stood. Even with his slight stature he towered over his father, who was hunched in his chair. When he spoke his voice was too loud, but he didn't care. "That's not why I come—for a handout, for charity. I wanted to see you, to find out why you never visited. The farm, to see me. Why?" He wouldn't cry again, not here. He crossed his arms in front of his chest and pinched the skin of his elbow crease to keep the tears at bay. His mother taught him that trick.

There was movement in the hall, and William Lawson stepped through the parlor doorway. "It's all right, Willy. We're fine," Wesley said without moving his gaze from Frank. He had hardly blinked at the outburst. William gave Frank a warning look and backed out of the room.

Wesley closed his eyes and laced his fingers together; he might have been praying. He said, "It was a difficult situation, Frank. A scandal. You're old enough to understand that, I think."

Eyes open, he held Frank in a watery gaze. When he spoke his voice was softer, tinny. "After your mother left, I followed her to Wellbridge and tried to bring you back home. You don't remember? But Stella, well, she was upset, I suppose, frightened, and she said she'd go to court, and the papers, with stories, scandalous untrue things, that would have been, well, they'd have ruined the family name for good. It would have killed Mother. . . ."

"No," Frank said. His body couldn't move, but his mind raced. His father was talking about blackmail. But Mumma would never lie. Wesley was the liar. Frank's hands curled into fists, his nails dug into his palms.

Wesley spoke slowly. "What she did, Frank, whatever her sins, I've forgiven her as our Lord teaches. You see, sometimes love is a selfish thing. Your mother wouldn't be parted from you, even though she knew we could give you a better life, an easier path. She had to live with that, just as I've had to live with my own errors." Wesley looked at his hands. They were cupped in his lap. He seemed to be melting into them.

Feeling like he was back in the schoolyard, boiling with rage, Frank leaned down, grabbed Wesley by the lapels, and pulled him halfway out of his chair. When he spoke he was shouting. "You're the selfish one, not her. You could've gotten me back if you wanted. You could've seen me, but you didn't. Not once. You're the one needs forgiving." Frank dropped his father back into the chair, wrenched open the door, and slammed it behind him. Nearly blind in the dark hall, he felt his way toward the light.

His uncle was waiting for him at the front door and extended his hand toward Frank. Between his thumb and forefinger were two twenty-dollar bills. Frank had never even seen one before. Without looking at William, he took the money and jammed it in his pocket. He hated himself already.

Frank ran back to town and stopped when he reached the river. At the foot of the bridge he picked up a handful of pebbles and walked halfway across. The angle was wrong for skipping, and he was too tired to try, so he dropped them, one after another, into the water and watched the fading sunlight play upon the ripples.

He stood at the rail until the daylight faded to blue, thinking of Mumma and of scandals and of sin and forgiveness. Frank didn't want to believe what his father said about his mother, but if it were true, he figured there was a good reason for what she did. In the end, he thought, Wesley was right about one thing: Your good name matters. His mother never even had that.

A very forgiving congregation. His grandmother's voice scraped the inside of his head. They weren't. No one was, not when they knew your secrets.

The sun was down when Frank turned back toward Bangor. Safe in the empty dark, he wandered the streets until his mind was quiet. At Lawson & Sons, now buttoned up against the night, Frank took his usual position across the street; his fingers followed the grooves in the elm-tree bark while he fingered the crumpled bills in his pocket with the other hand. He bent to pick up a rock. It was heavy, round, and cool in his palm. He tossed it in the air to get a feel for the weight, then stepped back on his right foot, cocked his elbow, and let it fly, just like his father had taught him all those years ago. The plate-glass window in the front door shattered, obliterating the Lawson name. Frank savored the destruction only for a second or two before he walked back up the hill.

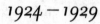

1924 — 1929

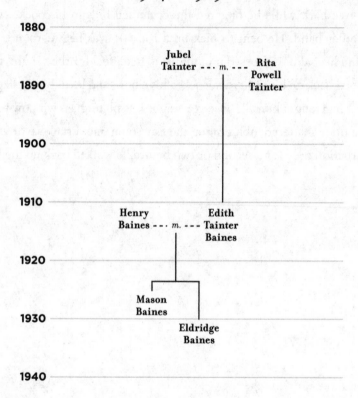

1880

Jubel
Tainter --- *m.* --- Rita
Powell
Tainter

1890

1900

1910

Henry
Baines --- *m.* --- Edith
Tainter
Baines

1920

Mason
Baines

1930

Eldridge
Baines

1940

YIELD

~———~

August 16—In the first-ever daylight march in Downeast Maine, approximately 100 members of the Ku Klux Klan rallied in the town of Wellbridge, sporting white robes and peaked hoods. In the scorching heat of the noonday sun, the Klansmen paraded the length of Main Street, drawing a sizable crowd of onlookers, both for and against. Although such marches have been contentious in other cities and towns around the state, the Wellbridge event was without incident.

Among the participants was Pastor Manfred Bell, minister of the First Church of Christ's Glory and the religious leader, or the Grand Klud so-called, of the local KKK chapter. Mr. Bell traveled down from Wonsqueak Harbor in his runabout to help lead the march, which included members of his family and most of his congregation. An outspoken supporter of the KKK, Mr. Bell proclaimed to this reporter, "Virtually the entire town of Wonsqueak has joined us, and every day we see growing hunger for our message of temperance, 100 percent Americanism, and pure Protestant Christianity in the neighboring towns."

Onlookers included Wellbridge Sheriff Wilfred Titcomb,

who remarked, "It's plain they like to provoke, but we will not stand for violence here." When asked his opinion of the proceedings, the sheriff said, "I think most decent people would disagree with what they say and do, but if a grown man wants to pay ten dollars to join a club so he can prance down Main Street in a white nightdress and a Halloween hood, that's his business."

From beneath the shade of an elm tree, Mrs. Oliver Tunk of Wellbridge asked, "When have Catholics ever done any harm? Deviltry, that's what I call it, just a bunch of hooligans."

The prevailing view of the onlookers was mostly one of agreement with Mrs. Tunk, although there were a goodly number of Klan supporters in the crowd. One of the marchers, who declined to remove his hood but gave his name as Deacon Tainter of Wonsqueak Harbor, stated, "We are not against Catholics or Jews or anyone else so much as we are for the rights of native-born, true Americans and the sovereignty of the King James Bible."

At the registration booth, which was run by the Women of the KKK auxiliary, the line to join stretched down the block. Leaflets distributed at the booth invited all interested parties to attend a "Family Klam Bake" that evening, to be held on the beach adjoining the Edgecomb farm on the East Point Road. When asked about the nature of the event, F. Eugene Farnsworth of Portland, the group's chief in Maine who holds the title King Kleagle, allowed as how there would be picnicking, lemonade, and games for the children as well as speakers and hymn-singing. He refused to say whether there would be a cross-burning, as is common at such events downstate; however, Catholic priests in the area warned their congregations to stay at home after dark, and several local residents reported a large wooden crucifix burned well into the night.

—*DOWNEAST WEEKLY TIMES*

TEMPTATION, 1925

Did she even exist? Since they'd been assigned to the same table in study hall back in September, Royal Edgecomb hadn't seemed to take any notice of Edith Tainter, not when she cleared her throat, not when she rattled the pages of her Latin book. Nor had he spoken to her when she passed him downstreet, standing on the sidewalk outside the Criterion Theatre surrounded by other seniors, mostly girls, and all from the smart set, smoking and laughing before the picture show.

None of them took any notice of Edith, and why would they? She was a skinny freshman in a baggy flour-sack dress that was already unfashionable when her mother made it for her older sister five years before. "Modest," Mumma said. Ugly was what Edith called it, but it was one of the three she owned, so she wore it, once a week, without fail.

Royal told anyone who'd listen, and there were plenty who did, that the minute he graduated he'd be leaving podunk old Wellbridge to enlist in the Army Air Service and become a pilot, see the world. Tall and black-haired, with downcast brown eyes, Royal was born, in Edith's opinion, to wear an aviator's uniform and white silk scarf. No matter that the Great War was over and peace was here to stay, the modern world would always need men patrolling the skies. Anyway, that's what she heard him tell Sylvia Clough, who sat on his right and was his usual conversation partner between shushes from the librarian.

The February morning Royal spoke to Edith, she was anything but prepared, hunched in front of her cubby, struggling to get out of her snow boots, her red tam o' shanter dripping melted snow down her neck. Such was the difficulty of pulling her feet from her too-small overshoes that her glasses had fogged, and though she'd have recognized Royal's voice anywhere, having it tickle her ear from up close gave her a start.

"You're Edith, right?"

Resisting the urge to crawl inside the cubby, she jammed her foot back down into her boot and whipped off her hat and glasses before looking up. Speaking was out of the question.

"Your father was over to our place yesterday, for a meeting, the Klan, you know? And to look at our boat. My pop's thinking of selling it, but only for the right price," he said, puffing up. "It's a sloop, from down Camden way. Built for some summer people."

Jubel Tainter was a terrible snob about boats and wouldn't have been interested in any but a fancy one, a Friendship sloop or the like. Knowing her father, Edith figured he'd tried to get it for a song. She was relieved he hadn't stopped in to see her at Grammie D's house on the way to or from the Edgecombs'.

Unable to come up with any kind of intelligent reply, Edith said, "Oh," and wiped away the sweat that had begun to collect on her upper lip. Her cheeks, she knew, were burning scarlet, but there was nothing to be done about that.

Royal pulled a red apple from his jacket pocket and took a bite, then offered her the unbroken side. She took a ladylike nibble and handed it back. Royal consumed the half with her teeth marks in one bite and wiped the juice from his chin with his shirtsleeve.

"Won't you miss having a boat?" she asked.

Royal swallowed and said, "I don't care about boats one bit, especially sailboats. It's planes I like—cars, motorbikes, anything with an engine." When she didn't respond, he asked, "How come you weren't with him?"

"Um, I stay here, in town. With my grandparents. It's too far to travel every day. From up in Wonsqueak. Where my parents live. There's no high school there."

"Well, come on along next time," he said. "Your pop'll be back."

The bell signaled first period and Royal strolled away, whistling "Hinky Dinky Parlay-Voo" with the squish-squash of his boots keeping time.

That night at supper, when Edith mentioned her father's visit to the Edgecomb place, Grammie D crowed, "Can't you just picture that? The right righteous *Deacon* Jubel Tainter dickering with a rumrunner! For a boat that's soaked up more bathtub gin than salt water, no less."

Grandpa shrugged.

"Wasn't five minutes after they passed the Prohibition that Pete Edgecomb started sneaking Canadian whiskey into town, but since he's married to the sheriff's sister, no one ever bothers him. 'Specially since he pretends to be in that foolish Klan. The Prohis must be on to him if he's selling that sloop, don't you think so, Randolph?"

Grandpa stopped chewing long enough to agree. Grammie D plowed on, "Listen to me, Edie, you stay right away from those Edgecombs. Bad apples, every one, rotten to the core."

"Royal's not rotten. He's going to be an aviator."

Grammie looked at Edith, then at Grandpa, then back at Edith.

"Like that, is it? Well, I don't have to tell you what your father'd do if he thought you was keeping company with any boys, Klan or no. He'd have you out of school and back home like that," Grammie D said, and snapped her fingers. "And nothing I can do to stop him. So unless you want to kiss your education goodbye, you'd best stay right away from that Edgecomb boy."

Her words hung over the table, heavy as thunderheads in the summer sky. The meal continued in silence. When the plates were clean, Grammie said, "I never saw anyone so crazy for sitting in church as your father. He wasn't always that way, you know. The Congregational was plenty good until he started with that cross-burning holy roller Bell and his Ku Klux Klan. Can't say what's gotten into your mother either, she used to be sensible. You ask me, the both of them've got too god-damned much religion."

Edith couldn't argue with her grandmother's assessment of her parents' "awakening," as they called it, but she had no intention of staying away from Royal. She couldn't have cared less about Prohibition, what the Edgecombs drank, or whether they worshipped Jesus Christ, golden idols, or the devil himself. It was a small rebellion, her first ever, a secret flame of sin that flared in Edith's chest and warmed her head to toe.

LUST, 1927

"Holy moley, there's Royal Edgecomb," Silla Trout said right out loud. Luckily she and Edith were beyond his hearing, seated on a hay bale at the Grange Hall Harvest Dance. Edith hadn't seen Royal in the two years since he'd graduated, and certainly not since his accident, but she'd have known him anywhere. He was still himself, just more so, taller and broader, his hair cropped close. The downward tilt of his eyes was more pronounced, and even through his rimless spectacles she could see—no, *feel*—something ferocious in them. It seemed to radiate from him and his new friends, surrounding them in a predatory glow as they surveyed the scene at the dance, which had seemed exciting to Edith before but now looked silly.

In the middle of the hall, a group of teenagers was trying to do the Charleston to "Camptown Races" as rendered by the Fairleigh Ramblers String Band. It was slightly less disastrous than their previous attempt with "Tea for Two." Beefy Gladys Renfrew, who claimed to have done both the Charleston and the turkey trot at tea dances at the Bridge Point Country Club over the summer, was dragging poor Henry Baines, and both his left feet, around the dance floor while some other kids attempted to reproduce the steps from the latest Charley Chase picture. The whole school was mad for modern dancing.

"I hear he almost never leaves the farm anymore," Silla continued, now hissing into Edith's ear. "Since the accident, I mean."

Edith had heard the same thing, that Royal's dreams of flying died in the car crash that crippled his father and killed his little sister, the homely one with the red hair, and since that night he'd kept to himself, working the farm and looking after his parents. Word was, it had been Royal behind the wheel.

"See the scar, Edie? I heard his cheek got sliced right open. They say he hit his head so hard it ruined his eyesight and that's why he couldn't be an aviator."

Edith had heard all of this before. Her parents attended the funeral for the little girl but left the reception scandalized when they realized liquor had been slipped into the cider.

Royal slid along the side wall and wedged himself into a corner, watching the flailing and shimmying on the dance floor and looking, well, *hungry* was the only way Edith could think to describe it.

Her mouth dry, Edith picked her way through the crowd to the punch bowl and lined up for a refill. She was wondering whether Royal would recognize her and trying to figure out how to get his attention when she felt something warm and solid pressing against her back. A voice, smoky and pitch-thick, purred in her ear, "Edith." She could smell liquor and knew she should step away, but instead she turned to face Royal, making sure the breasts she'd developed in the past year grazed him before she stepped back.

"Hello, Royal."

"You want a real drink, I got something better'n punch," he said.

Mrs. Largay filled Edith's cup; Royal waved off the proffered ladle. Up close, she could see his scar, still faintly speckled with stitch marks on either side, like bird tracks in the snow. Some fellows' looks would have been ruined by a mark like that, but Royal's were improved. He could have been a pirate or a gunslinger, and when he grabbed her wrist to lead her away, her skin tingled under his fingers.

He pulled her through the crowd into the Grange Hall kitchen, past the oversize pots and pans that hung from the ceiling, the massive white cookstove, and the jumble of knives and meat grinders.

Once inside the pantry with the door closed, Royal lifted her up and set her on the counter. Edith should have been offended at his presumption, knew better than to stay there, but the heat of him seemed to be melting her, turning her bones to butter. He topped up her drink with whiskey and took a long pull from the flask. "Drink up."

It was Edith's first taste of liquor and she barely managed to choke it down. Even mixed with the sweet red punch it was horrid and burned her throat, but she finished every drop. When Royal smiled at her, that hungry look returned. After refilling her cup, he nodded at her to drink and set the flask on the counter. He put a hand on each of her knees, pushed them apart, and stepped between, watching as she sipped. By itself the liquor was much worse, but she didn't want him to think she was a baby, so she forced herself to swallow. Up close, Royal's features looked distorted, like a photograph that had been torn up and glued together wrong.

"All grown up, aren't you, Edie. What, sixteen? Used to be a scrawny sack of knees and elbows, but look at you now." He ran his index finger down the front of her dress, then back up again, carelessly flicking her nipple on the way to her collarbone. "Built for sin."

Edith's heart was slamming so hard she was afraid Royal would feel it. She was warm all over and knew she should run, or at least push him away and cross her legs; instead, of their own accord, they wrapped themselves around his hips and locked at the ankles. Royal's eyebrows rose in surprise, but instead of kissing her, he laughed. After another drink from the flask, he reached around to his back, separated her ankles, and stepped away.

"A man likes a little sport, you know."

He winked at her, then turned on his heel and returned to the dance, just left her sitting on the counter like a fool.

She was still there a minute later when Henry Baines walked in. They knew each other from school, and he was always trying to start a conversation. Henry was a nice boy, but she couldn't imagine how he'd ever grow into those ears.

"Hiding out from Gladys," he said, "before she breaks *all* my toes." He had a friendly smile, and in any other situation she'd have giggled.

"You okay, Edith? I thought I saw Royal Edgecomb come out of here. That guy's a real rape artist. Just ask Sylvia Clough. I heard he tried to force himself on her, if you know what I mean."

Henry looked away, blushing to the tips of his ears. In a confidential tone he went on, "Pushed her down and ripped her dress 'fore she got away." The story should have horrified her, Edith knew, but instead, the thought of being wanted by Royal, feeling his breath on her neck and his hands on her skin, made her back teeth tingle. And it made her want to beat Sylvia Clough bloody. When Henry extended a hand to help Edith down, she hesitated but took it.

SIN, 1928

Edith hated the Independence Day church service. She saw no connection between the American Revolution and Jesus but knew better than to risk being backhanded, or worse, for questioning it, so she buttoned up her church dress and scuffed into her good shoes. She was hiding the romance paperback she'd borrowed from her friend Silla under the coverlet when her father stepped through the doorway.

"What's that?"

"Nothing, a book," she said.

Jubel Tainter extended his hand for it, palm up, and looked at the cover. "Trash, filth, and sin. That what they taught you at school, girl?" He cocked his elbow and slapped her face with the book, again and again, before he opened it and began tearing out the pages, wadding them up, and dropping them on the floor.

"Clean this up and get out to the car. And for Lord's sake stop your crying."

Chewing her resentment like a cud, her eyes still swollen and burning, Edith settled next to Mumma in the front pew of the First Church of Christ's Glory and thought about her wedding. She and Henry had planned it for next spring, but Edith was trying to figure out how to move it up.

She hated being back under her father's thumb, especially after the freedom she'd had living away from home for four blissful years of high school. Since graduation she'd played her cards right with Henry Baines, and soon enough they'd set up housekeeping in town, safely beyond her father's grasp, finally leaving Wonsqueak behind, along with Pastor Bell and the endless grind of church and more church. At least she wasn't expected to go to the pastor's boring political meetings. Of course if they formed a Klan youth group, like Mother suggested, there'd be no avoiding it.

Edith looked past the minister's jowly face and raw-meat nose to a painting of Adam and Eve, their nudity hidden—and the decency of God's chosen preserved—by some conveniently overgrown shrubs. A clumsy, primitive thing, it was the only decoration in the plain white room. To Edith, it looked like the serpent was about to take a bite out of Adam, while Eve, munching her apple, wore an expression of bemused detachment, blissfully unaware of the damnation, and the agony, that awaited her.

Nodding occasionally to show she was listening, when she was really thinking about what she and Henry might get up to after they spread out their picnic blanket in the back of his truck that evening, Edith considered giving in to Henry's begging.

It was risky. Once he'd had his fun, Henry might call off the wedding and abandon her, and she'd end up ruined and alone like those factory girls in the books from the five-and-dime. He promised he never would, and she wanted to believe him; Henry was nothing if not good-hearted. If she ended up with a baby in her belly, it'd be an awful scandal, but at least she'd get married and away from this suffocating little blot on the coast of nowhere.

"There's more than one way to skin a cat, you know," Henry had told her last time, after she'd refused to take off her underclothes. She was curious to find out what he meant, because she was sure he was a virgin, too. That Henry might actually know something about sex made him seem more interesting.

More interesting than Caleb Bell, anyway. The preacher's son, who as usual was staring at her from the choir loft, probably knew less than nothing about the ways of the flesh. Oh, Caleb was pleasant enough, but his lashless, red-rimmed eyes were always crusty and he smelled of milk; just the thought of having to share a bed with him made her cringe. Her father, she knew, still held out hope she'd marry into the Bell family. If there were a way to force her, and in the process make an in-law of his idol Pastor Bell, he'd find it. The more Edith thought about it, the more inclined she was to let Henry have his way.

"James 1:14," Pastor Bell announced, his sticky baritone oozing through the church. " 'But every man is tempted, when he is drawn away of his own lust, and enticed. Then when lust hath conceived, it bringeth forth sin: and sin, when it is finished, bringeth forth death.' So says James, servant of God and of our Lord Jesus Christ."

Now the preacher was rolling, and it was only a matter of time before he'd find his way to his favorite subjects: demon liquor and its ruination of even the most God-fearing men and women, the filthy ways of

fornicators, and the unholy cataclysm that awaited once the papists succeeded in removing "our own King James Bible from the public schools
paid for with *your* tax money." She stifled a yawn.

Services at the Congregational church in Wellbridge, which her
parents used to attend and Henry's still did, were shorter and cheerier
than this. A couple of hymns, once through the Our Father, a brief talk
about doing unto others or honoring somebody, and you were out the
door before you'd finished digesting breakfast. There was never any
mention of the lake of fire, or the mark of the beast, or avenging angels
of death. No one talked about the pope, let alone called him the Whore
of Babylon. The pews had cushions, and the minister's wife handed out
doughnuts after the service.

Henry's parents, Edith thought, were so much nicer than her own.
They didn't holler or threaten; the doors in their house all locked from
the inside, not the outside; and Henry had never been gagged with a
cloth or had his mouth washed out for blaspheming or just asking a simple question. Henry may not have been her dream man, but the Baineses
were as close to a dream family as she could imagine.

That evening, waiting for the fireworks to start, Edith sat on the
blanket Henry had draped over the tailgate of his father's truck. The
high-summer breeze tickled her bare legs and lifted her skirt. The July
afternoon was finally fading, and the sun had slipped behind the western
trees, spilling shadows across the village green. Overhead the clouds were
stained purple, tender bruises on the sky, and in the gloaming the fireflies
rose from the grass, oblivious to the danger of sticky-faced boys with their
punctured-top jars, bored of torturing frogs and pox-itchy with excitement for the first sulfurous blast of celebration.

Across the green, a fat little towheaded boy with a garter snake
chased a screaming girl. When he couldn't catch her, he flung the creature at her, but his mother was on him in a minute, meting out justice

that was as rough as it was swift. Edith turned away. She'd been on the receiving end of enough slaps, clouts, and kicks to know what punishment looked, and felt, like.

Henry had gone to get a Moxie and should have been back by now. Edith scanned the doorways, but instead of finding Henry's lanky form, her gaze passed over, then went straight back to, a larger, darker one. She didn't need to see his face to know it was Royal Edgecomb leaning against the Grange Hall porch, arms crossed over his threadbare work shirt. As soon as he raised his eyes to hers, Edith looked down at her hands. By the time she looked back, he had moved over to the town hall; again she met his gaze and averted her own. They repeated this dance twice more, until Royal was standing right in front of her. Edith folded her legs underneath herself and tucked her skirt around them.

Royal raised his eyebrows. "Edie Tainter, as I live and breathe." He was mocking her primness, she knew, so she smiled as brightly as she could, just in case anyone was watching.

"How are you, Royal?"

He laughed and leaned so close their noses nearly touched. "Heard you're getting married."

His breath smelled of whiskey, his skin of sweat and earth mixed with something feral that she could neither identify nor breathe deeply enough into her lungs. He settled his right palm on her gingham-wrapped knee and tickled her thigh twice with his finger. His hands were impossibly warm. Edith slid back, just beyond his reach.

"Yup. Next spring. To Henry Baines. My fiancé. He's just gone to fetch a Moxie. Speak of the devil, there he is, right over there by the Rotary Club booth."

Royal didn't bother to look. Two breaths later, when the silence was as heavy as the July heat, he said, "Ain't that swell. You still staying down to your grandmother's?"

"Just for the night. I'm back living in Wonsqueak, till the wedding."
Royal's eyes never left her face.

"You got a sweetheart, Royal?" Edith asked to fill the silence, and immediately wished she could suck the words back in and swallow them whole.

"Ain't the marrying kind."

After waiting just long enough to make her uncomfortable, he said, "I'll leave you to your soda pop and your fella, then. Edie." Her name came out in a sigh, evaporating into the air as Royal slipped away, across the lawn and into the deepest of the lengthening shadows.

"Nice to see you again, Royal. Best to your family," she called after him with exaggerated friendliness, loud enough to be sure Henry heard, but Royal kept moving, didn't wave or even look back, just melted into the oak grove next to the cemetery.

After dismissing Henry's annoyance at her conversation with "an old family friend" and soothing him with a kiss and a cuddle, Edith set the sweating Moxie bottle on the spot where Royal's hand had been to cool the throbbing beneath the fabric of her dress.

Five hours later, her skin was still hot when she looked out her bedroom window and spied Royal standing under the elm tree out back of Grammie D's house. After she'd cleaned the last trace of Henry's fumbling from between her legs, Edith slipped downstairs and out the kitchen door to follow Royal into the woods.

RECKONING, 1929

Edith still held out hope the child would be stillborn. When the contractions started coming fast enough to call the doctor, Grammie D told Henry to run next door and use their telephone. He had been gone a long time, and Edith figured that rather than hurrying, he'd probably wandered over in his usual unheroic way, disappointing her, predictably and again. Lately everything about Henry Baines, even his tenderness—

no, *especially* that—had begun to grate. She knew better but couldn't help it.

Now, flat on her back in the bed they'd shared for the past six months—six and a half if you counted by weeks, seven if you rounded up—Edith's thoughts about her husband came to an abrupt end as the next contraction seized her abdomen, pushing ragged, animal sounds through her gritted teeth. Like all the others, this pain was worse than the one before. When it had mostly faded, she rolled on her side and curled into a ball, squeezing her belly between her thighs and chest.

Grammie D said, "Hurts like hell, don't it? Last time I gave birth—that'd be your angel mother—I bit down so hard I cracked a molar. Eleven and a half pounds Rita was, about tore me in half. 'Course by then I was so stretched out from the first six, I prob'ly could've birthed a normal-size baby with a cough. Didn't know whether to put a diaper on her or a saddle. . . ."

Edith tried to purge from her mind's eye the image of a young Dorothy Powell spread-eagled on the bed tethered to a pony-size infant and with her parts in shreds, but what with it being so disturbing, the thought lingered.

Grammie D mopped Edith's forehead with a cool cloth. Now even between the pains it was nearly impossible to talk, and all Edith could manage were mewling sounds.

"They say you forget the pain after the baby comes, but I never did," the older woman continued. "I imagine it's true for most, though, otherwise nobody'd have more than one. My babies got heavier every time, but don't worry, dear, you're not *awful* big."

To Edith's relief, her grandmother's chatter was cut short by the arrival of Dr. Penney. Henry tried to follow him into the bedroom, but before he could get through the doorway Grammie hustled him back, clucking about birthing rooms being no place for men. Edith heard her say something about women in labor not being in their right minds, but hers had never been clearer. She'd done everything she could think of—starving herself, bumping into things, squeezing into corsets, jumping up and down, even praying—to get rid of this baby, but it had held on and was coming anyway. Payment for "the wages of sin" Pastor Bell was always threatening had finally come due; she saw that now.

The doctor pulled off the sheet and pushed Edith's knees back and apart. Peering into the depths, he was promptly rewarded with a gush of amniotic fluid that sent him reeling into Grammie D, who had just closed the door behind her.

The old lady cackled while the doctor wiped his face. Undaunted, he leaned back in and shoved most of his right hand into Edith, stripping away her final shred of modesty. A drop of her water clung to the doctor's bushy right eyebrow, and when the straw-colored sun caught it just so, it glistened like a diamond, the only beautiful thing in her life. She turned her head to avoid seeing it drop to his lapel and instead looked out at the woods on the other side of the reach. There were a few tattered evergreens, long-needled pine and Christmas tree fir, but most of the trees were deciduous, fleshless skeletons of ash, beech, and oak, wind-raked and gray from the dry-bone crack of winter. In the purgatory of mud season, they remained naked and despairing, oblivious to the promised resurrection of the coming spring.

"Water's broken, no question about that. Nearly ten fingers dilated, too late for ether," he said as if checking things off an imaginary list. Then to Edith, "Looks like it'll be an April Fools' Day baby. You're going to have to push soon, dear... Edith? Do you understand?"

This time the contraction was so intense she screamed. The agony seemed to go on forever, wrenching every muscle, twisting every bone, and as it did, a memory floated up from deep in her mind, growling the same love-pain words she'd heard the night the child was conceived, as she lay on the soggy pine-needle mat with the snaking tree roots digging into her back and her wrists pinned over her head. "I'll do as I please with you, Edie Tainter."

"All right, Dorothy, I think we're going to need your help," the doctor said, then, muttering something about more light, he grabbed Edith by the ankles and gave her a quarter turn so that her legs dangled over the side of the bed. "Prop her up now."

The springs creaked as Grammie D climbed onto the bed, hooked Edith under the arms, and raised her up so that the small of her back rested against the old lady's thighs. Edith's throbbing head settled between her grandmother's breasts. She smelled of camphor and onions.

From far away the doctor's voice asked where Edith's mother was, and across the distance came the snorted response. "At church, of course. Couldn't miss the Sunday service, now they're on a first-name basis with *the Lord*."

If Dr. Penney replied at all, his words were sucked up in a hurricane of pain as Edith's world collapsed into one room, her life to one breath. Now there was nothing but the need to push, to get it out, she bore down once, twice, three times. After that she couldn't count anymore, couldn't even think, but eventually, when she was sure she was dying, a head of dark hair emerged, followed by the white-hot sear of the child's shoulders forcing their way through and tearing her open. And then it was over.

Behind closed eyes, Edith waited for the first cry, frightened and half expecting to see the child blue-faced and limp, with the cord wrapped around its neck like what happened to Silla Trout's baby brother, the one that was born dead. She covered her face with her hands. When no sound came, she peeked between her splayed fingers and saw the doctor holding the tiny boy upside down. Though silent, the baby was alive, his neck unscathed, his face beet red. The doctor gave the child a good whack, and as soon as he brought up the clot of blood that had been clogging his windpipe, her baby took a big breath and let loose an angry wail.

In that moment, with that first cry, Edith was not sorry he was alive, or repentant of the sin of his creation, but happy, and she whispered something so quietly that only her grandmother, arms wrapped around Edith, ear to her cheek, could hear.

"Royal." There was no question in her mind. Finally, he was hers.

LIFE

The first time she sees Henry holding the baby, it isn't love or lust Edith burns with, but shame, its flames licking her face, flushing her cheeks. There is no escaping the truth of this child, or the miracle of him: from her sin and Royal's darkness has come light, immaculate and unfathomable. Nothing else matters.

"He's all you, Edith. Can't see much of me, not yet, anyway," Henry says, gazing at baby Mason, named for his beloved Grandpa Baines. The boy coos in his arms. Outside, a cloud drifts away and a ray of sunlight passes through the window, enfolding her husband and son in the sapling arms of spring.

He lifts the swaddled baby to his face and breathes him in, kisses each downward-tilting eyelid. "Hey there, little man, aren't you lucky you didn't get Daddy's ears." When he looks at Edith, there are tears in his eyes. "Aren't we blessed?"

She cannot speak, so she nods, unwilling to give voice to the lie, acknowledging only the truth, small and sullied though it is. Blessed is exactly what the two of them are.

1945

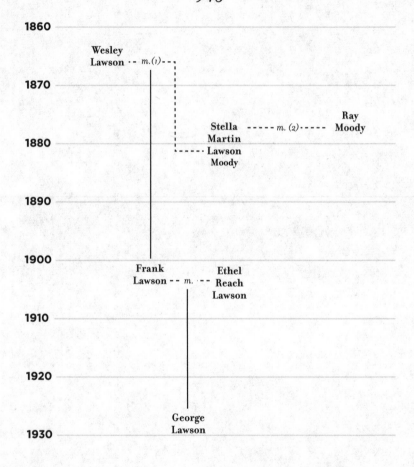

1860	
	Wesley Lawson - - m.(1) - - -
1870	
	Stella - - - - m. (2) - - - - Ray
	Martin Moody
1880	- - - Lawson
	Moody
1890	
1900	
	Frank Lawson - - m. - - Ethel Reach Lawson
1910	
1920	
	George Lawson
1930	

HOME FRONT

~———~

This time it wasn't the usual open hand, but a closed fist, a right cross like a rock to the jaw that George never even saw coming. On the way down he scraped his cheek against the edge of the stove, then landed with his back against the icebox. He felt a warm trickle above his chin. It should have hurt, but it didn't, not yet, anyway. When he tried to get up, his legs were rubbery knees and wet-noodle bones. He stayed put.

Standing over his son, Frank Lawson shook his head, fists curled tight. He looked down at his hands and straightened his fingers, grabbed a dish towel, and dropped it in George's lap. George swatted the towel away and found his feet on the second try.

At the sink Frank left his back unprotected, as if to say, "Go ahead and try it, boy." He reached for his beer glass with his left hand, rather than the one that he had just used on his son. The punch had cost him something; this pleased George.

"I know what I saw," George said. He spread his stance a little wider and lifted his fists waist high. When his father replied, his voice was a low growl. It floated back over his shoulder.

"*Do* you?"

"I seen that woman around, at the mill, down to Hurley's. With lots of guys, but never the same one twice. And not at church either, but maybe she sits up back, huh?"

Frank's right shoulder twitched. Glass in hand, he turned to face his son.

"You don't know a goddamned thing," he said.

"I know you weren't going to Bible study with her at ten o'clock last night."

Frank's voice was lower, harsher. "All you need to know is I put a roof over your head and food on your plate. What I do is none of your business, boy."

"No? What would the other deacons think about your *business*? Or Reverend Quigg? Or Mother?" George's breath was coming fast. With each question his voice rose, turning shrill and thin, and he was ashamed of the sound of it.

Frank snorted. "Christ almighty, almost six feet tall and you're still a little kid. You've got no idea—"

His words were interrupted by the rattle of the bedroom door from the other side of the house. George's head turned toward the sound.

"You leave her out of this," Frank hissed.

Ethel Lawson's fingers emerged from the gloom of the hall and curled around the kitchen doorframe. Once she'd steadied herself, she stepped halfway through and leaned on the jamb, squinting against the midday sun. Her dressing gown was undone; she held it closed with her free hand.

"I can't find my spectacles."

"Right there," George said, and indicated the delicate gold frames on the table.

At the sight of her son's blood-streaked face, Ethel lurched across the kitchen and grabbed for it. Her robe flapped open, revealing a dingy cotton nightgown with an L-shaped tear over her left breast and not much underneath.

"Georgie! What happened? Did you fall?"

The odor of cigarette smoke mixed with talcum powder drifted past George's nose, and he closed his mouth to keep from swallowing it. He shook her hand off his cheek, but Ethel persisted.

"Close your robe, Ethel," Frank muttered from across the room.

She grasped at the garment but couldn't seem to find the belt and gave up. "Not deep but it's messy. It'll leave a scar."

"It's nothing," George said. He was almost seventeen; he didn't need mothering, even the sad scraps Ethel offered.

"Frank, the plasters, do you know where the plasters are?"

"Like he said, Ethel, it's nothing." He ran his free hand through his hair, smoothing it flat to his head, then said, "Boy's getting *ideas*. Thinks he's a big man." Frank didn't seem to be talking to anyone but himself, so George didn't bother to answer.

When Frank passed them on his way to the icebox, George and Ethel both stepped back. Frank took a beer, set it on the table next to his glass, and pulled his jackknife from his pocket, wincing as he used the blade to prize the cap from the bottle. Sallow foam oozed up the bottleneck, over his fist, and onto the floor. He let the cap drop and watched it roll under the stove, then licked the back of his hand.

Ethel didn't admonish him for his carelessness; she hardly seemed to notice. George imagined grabbing his father by the scruff, flinging him to the floor, and forcing him to clean up his mess, then hated himself when he didn't. Just before Frank crossed the threshold, he muttered, "It's me runs things here, and don't you forget it."

Loud enough for his father to hear, George said, "Don't worry, I won't forget." His jaw had begun to ache, but he forced himself not to touch it. He edged away from his mother, shoved his fists into his pockets, and walked out the back door.

———

Outside it was cooler than it had been in the kitchen, but still hot for Maine, even in July. George bent over the garden spigot and splashed his face, drying it on a stained dishrag draped over the porch railing. He flicked a chip of gray paint off the fence post next to the half-dead Victory Garden his mother had planted in a mad rush in the spring, then abandoned a month later, after her mood swung from crazy bright to black.

Depression and mania, Doc Howell told them it was, said it had started after George was born. No one knew the cause, and the only thing for it was shock treatments up to the state hospital, but the old man said no, said she'd come out of it sooner or later, like always. George wasn't so sure. He looked down at the dead leaves and withered vines. A single half-ripe tomato lay nestled in a tangle of dying plants. George's heel crushed it into the soil on the way to the sidewalk.

Kicking pebbles as he wandered, he kept to the shady side of the street and canted his face toward the buildings, relieved not to see any-one he knew. He came to the library. Its granite walls offered respite from the heat; the dark stacks promised refuge. Hiding there meant he'd go back home eventually, but George was as tired of hiding as he was of home, so he continued on, past LaViolette's lunch counter and Hanley's bar, which reeked of stale beer and tobacco from half a block away. Ten doors down, at the end of Main Street, the immaculate whitewashed face of the Methodist church his family went to contemplated the street and its many sins, doors bolted against the unworthy, the week's devotions unsullied and safe behind them.

Until he turned onto Pelham Alley, he hadn't really thought about where he was going. Up ahead, on the unpaved lane that ran behind the courthouse, a paddy wagon kicked up a veil of yellow dust. Across the street, Jimmy O'Connell sat on his rickety front steps, absorbed in a *Superman* comic. He looked up when George flopped down beside him.

"The hell happened to you?"

"Nothing."

"Whole lot of nothing."

"Aw, you know, the old man. Busting my chops."

Jimmy snorted and said, "Pretty crummy."

"Yeah. Can I stay here?"

"Sure." Jimmy folded the comic and stuffed it between the slats of the steps. "So whatcha gonna do?" he asked.

"Don't know. Been thinking about the navy. Get out of town. See the world. Wanna come?" George knew his friend would never bite.

"You kidding? Claudette'd kill me before the Japs ever got a chance. You think your old man's a hard case? My ma's a lot more scarier than any kamikaze."

George grabbed the baseball cap off his friend's head and pulled it low on his own, then set off for downtown. The recruiter would be at the post office until three. He had time.

The next day, while the morning service was going on over at church, George slipped through the back door of his house. The kitchen was just as when he'd left, the surfaces tidy, clean, and respectable. In his pocket were the enlistment papers. The day before, the recruiter had glanced at his face several times but hadn't asked. He said George would need his father's signature to join up, otherwise he'd have to wait thirteen more months until he turned eighteen.

George was surprised to see the blue percolator sputtering on the stove. Next to it, on the floor, sat his father's maple shoeshine box with his unpolished oxfords on top. Every Sunday morning Frank spent half an hour cleaning, blacking, and spit-shining those shoes before church. George's parents seldom missed a service. It was the one event his mother still managed to get up and dress for. She usually dozed through the sermon, but she liked the music.

In the parlor at the end of the hall, George could see his father's head above the back of his easy chair. He was listening to the radio in a haze of smoke so thick he must have been lighting each Camel from the butt end of the last. When the morning news program gave way to an ad for Moxie, the old man's slipper tapped the carpet in time to the jingle.

His mother was probably still asleep. The thought of having to see her in the gloomy rat's-nest bedroom and breathe in her despair made him want to run for the door. Instead George walked up the back stairs to the attic. He had to hunch, and despite his careful steps, they creaked at every tread. In his whitewashed bedroom, it took only a few minutes to pack his clothes and grab his book, a dog-eared collection of Hornblower stories Mother had given him two Christmases ago. She'd been in a bright phase that year and served eggnog and fruitcake after the midnight Mass.

From downstairs came the sound of his father shuffling up the hall to the kitchen. George's stomach turned over. He patted his pocket; the papers crackled. Bag in hand, he drew in a long breath, exhaled hard, and walked back down to the kitchen.

"Where the hell've you been?" Frank asked, closing the flame on the stove. He wore only his undershirt tucked into his trousers; his suspenders hung lifeless below his hips. When his father faced him, George noticed his blue eyes were red-rimmed, his face unshaven.

"Jimmy's."

"That madhouse?" Frank disapproved of the O'Connells. Jimmy's mother had been known to haul her husband off his stool at Hurley's on a Friday night, or worse, join him there. They weren't churchgoers.

"Tell Mother I was here."

"Tell her yourself. She's still abed, she'll want to know you're all right."

Frank seemed to be waiting for a response. When none came, he said, "Oatmeal on the stove. I made extra, but she won't eat. Go ahead."

"I'm not staying. Just come to get my things. I got enlistment papers from the recruiter. Navy. Says you have to sign. 'Cause I'm underage." His voice sounded mechanical and flat in his ears, but at least it wasn't shaking.

Frank lifted his cup to his lips and blew the steam away. A tremor in his hand sent the coffee slopping over the side, and he set the mug down on the counter without drinking.

"What makes you think I'm going to do that?" His tone was mild, as if he were asking George's opinion of a movie.

"Because you don't want me in this house. And even if you did, I wouldn't stay."

"It was just a punch, George. Time you learned to take one. Christ, I was brawling before I was out of knee pants. Got more scars than I can count."

"I'm not sticking around for more."

"No need, 'long as you mind your manners."

"And you mind yours."

"Who the hell do you think you are?" Frank asked.

George dug the form and the pen out of his pocket and set them on the table.

"Just sign the enlistment papers and I'll be on my way."

"For Christ's sake, boy, there's a war on."

"It'll be over before I'm out of basic."

"You'll never get anywhere without a diploma."

George shrugged his response.

"You're only sixteen." Frank presented this information as if it were news.

"Seventeen in three weeks."

"What about your mother?"

George didn't want to think about his mother. This was between him and the old man.

"Just sign the papers, and we'll be done."

Frank picked up his coffee, but instead of drinking it, he dumped it down the drain, then hurled the mug into the pitted slate sink. The cup exploded and the wall above was splattered in oily black. George flinched. His father snatched the pen. When he signed the form, he nearly tore the paper with it.

In the bedroom, his mother's Sunday hat, the dove-colored one with the navy-blue net and two turquoise feathers, lolled on top of the dresser, impaled on a hat pin, affixed to nothing but air. His mother stubbed out her cigarette. She was propped against a couple of rumpled pillows; the drapes were drawn against the day, just as they would be against the night.

When he crossed the room to open them, she protested and switched on the bedside lamp. A pool of light the color of sickly flesh illuminated half of her face, casting the rest in shadow. Another dark day. George couldn't remember the last bright one. She patted the bed near her knees; he sat at her feet.

"I was crazy worried when you didn't come back, Georgie, but now you're home again so everything's all right." The words came in a tumble, followed by an unconvincing smile. Ethel reached for his hand, and he let her take it.

"I'm joining up, Mumma. Navy."

Ethel's grip tightened.

"No." Her voice was barely more than a whisper. "I won't let you."

"He signed the paper."

"He wouldn't, he was so worried about you last night he never slept."

George shook his head.

"No, Georgie, what'll I do?" she asked, eyes closed. She seemed to be melting into the pillows. "Who'll be here with me?"

George clamped his jaws tight and beat back the urge to scream, to haul her the hell out of bed and tell her to get dressed like other mothers, like the one he remembered. Instead, he said, "You'll see, it'll be better this way." He wasn't even trying to be kind.

"Better than what?" Her eyes opened, unfocused and wet. She repeated the phrase in a whisper. Toward the half-open door, she called, "Frank, come tell George he can't go."

There was no reply from the parlor, just the squeak of the swivel chair. Ethel called to him again. George pictured his father padding across the carpet and slipping into a shirt and his old shoes before opening the front door. He heard a soft thunk when it closed. The house was still for a second or two, and then the Goodyear announcer's voice came crackling through the static on the wireless.

"And to our employees in the armed forces, good work in Europe and good luck in the Pacific. Let's keep punching hard till the Japs get theirs."

Ethel released George's hand and slid down in the bed. She rolled over, away from the lamplight and into the shadows. Her low moan rose and built to a stuttering wail he felt in his chest. She was weeping so hard her body shook. He looked over at the poor old hat and tried to think of some way to pull out the knife he'd just driven into his mother. There was only one, but he couldn't bring himself to say he'd stay. So he sat on her bed and tried to recall the smell of the sea. After a while he fetched a glass of water, then slipped away when she turned out the light.

By the time George arrived in the kitchen the next morning, his father was already at work and Ethel, washed and dressed, sat sipping coffee at the table, the paper open to the obituaries. Her eyes were puffy and her hair hung in damp ringlets below her shoulders. It was grayer than he remembered.

She smiled a greeting, and he sat down.

There was a slice of bread with rhubarb jam on the plate before her. She slid it across the table to George, saying she'd already eaten.

"You don't have to go, Georgie, I'm feeling better now."

He knew it wouldn't last and figured she did, too.

"It's him, not you," he said.

"I won't ask what happened, that's between the two of you." She blinked half a dozen times, very fast. "It's natural for boys and their fathers to get cross with each other and even fight sometimes, but I know he wants you to stay, we both do."

"I can't. Just come to say goodbye."

"George, please, no. Every day of this war I've asked God to keep you from it, safe at home with me. I prayed and prayed and I thought I'd saved you from the bombs and the guns, the fires, and those crazy men who crash their planes into the boats." As she spoke she dug at the cuticle of her left thumb with her index finger, gouged it until it bled; the flesh around her nails, which had been chewed to nubs, was torn and raw. Her breaths came fast and shallow.

"You can't. Please, Georgie," Ethel said just before her features crumpled into a tangle of clashing lines and disappeared behind her hands.

George peeled the crust from his bread while she cried, tried to say he'd stay, couldn't force the words. He'd lived in this house, eaten breakfast at this table, slept upstairs under the eaves since he was eight years old. Back then his mother read to him most nights, and his father almost never shouted. Back then, his mother's dark times were less frequent and briefer, usually just a day or two. Back then it hadn't occurred to George that his father somehow blamed him for his mother's illness.

Back then. He tried to imagine what life would be like without the agony of watching her collapse in on herself, without feeling the horrible, addictive pleasure of needling his father.

"I'm sorry," he said. And he was, for all of them.

Later that day, on the way to the train station, George stopped at the baseball field. He gathered up a handful of fresh-cut grass from his spot in center and crushed the blades against his palm to try to force the smell into his skin. Then he walked to first base, Jimmy's position, right in front of the bleachers where the O'Connells watched every game. His mother sat with them sometimes, but his father never came, said he couldn't take off work during the week. George unclenched his fist and raised the wad of grass to his face, then opened his hand and let the breeze blow it clean. His finger traced the cut on his face, still jagged, but crusting over and itchy; it was beginning to heal.

The station was just down the road from the ball field. He stepped to the platform and took a seat on the bench, opened his book but couldn't read. George had only ever ridden a train once, must have been about seven at the time. The lines on the page dissolved and ran together, replaced by memories: the feeling of his hand safe in Mother's firm, kid-gloved one; the excitement of boarding the great, steaming train; the locomotive smell of hot metal and burning oil; the soft, even nap of the velvet seat covers; the anticipation of a visit to Portland, where his father was working on the docks.

Jobs, Mother once told him, had been so scarce after the Crash that his father would take a room wherever he could find work and came home to Augusta once a month. Their trip to see him must have been a holiday, because Frank, whose hair was still shiny black, had spent the whole afternoon with them.

In Portland, they took a streetcar downtown, then walked to a little sand beach at the foot of Munjoy Hill where they watched the boats with their fine white sails tacking back and forth in the harbor. High above them, the gulls glided and swooped, calling to one another in roller-coaster cries. George had never been to the coast before, never seen seashells, smelled salt air, or put his feet in the ocean. He told his mother it was the most beautiful place he'd ever seen. Ethel laughed at her husband's jokes and touched his knee when she spoke. His father told them the names of all the waterbirds, and after lunch he bought George a grape Nehi.

Before they boarded the train home, Frank shook his son's hand, told him to look after his mother. George held her arm the whole ride back, keeping her safe, as the train ran north out of Portland. Through the window, he watched the city thin to country as clusters of tall buildings gave way to barns, fences, and fields dotted with evergreens, boulders, and dairy herds. Then the train jigged inland and followed the river north to the capital. By the time they stepped down to the platform of the Augusta depot, Portland was just a dream.

George opened his eyes when he heard the clang of crossing bells in the distance. A train whistle lowed, the platform vibrated, and a cloud passed overhead, covering George in a reprieve of shade. When he looked up he saw it was not a cloud but a man between him and the sun, his father, dressed in his summer suit, fedora, and dusty dress shoes.

"You talk to your mother?"

It occurred to George that his father must have left his coveralls at the print shop, that he'd never seen him wearing his work clothes. He knew about the coveralls only because Frank brought them home to be washed on Fridays.

George closed his book and grunted in reply, looking past his father to the tracks, where waves of heat shivered up and disappeared into a sky that seemed too high. Before he could speak, Frank said, "She wants me to try and stop you going. Went down to the recruiter after you left this morning. He said you could still change your mind."

George was surprised his mother had left the house. "She better?"

"Probably back in the bed by now."

George stowed his book and stood. He wanted to be eye level with his father but couldn't think of anything to say. Conversation with the old man, such as it was, came a lot easier when they were shouting.

Frank lifted his hat and scratched his head, moving a single gray strand out of place, then smoothing it back. George stared over his father's shoulder to the tracks, wishing the train would pull in, fill the silence and the space.

Frank continued, "She wasn't like that when we got married, you know, sad all the time. It just happened, later, after you were born." He looked up at the sky, down at his shoes, anywhere but at his son, then said, "You didn't tell her about . . ."

George shook his head. The feeling of power over his father was unfamiliar, unsettling. He should have enjoyed it, but it made him feel small and tight.

A gust of hot air jostled him as the train rolled in and screeched to a stop. He hoisted the bag onto his shoulder. A peach bumped him, just below the ribs. That morning, Jimmy's mother had filled his bag with food for the trip. He pushed from his mind the memory of the O'Connell family gathered around him in their tiny front room a few hours before. He'd be damned if he'd cry in front of his father.

The passengers were disembarking, some stretching their legs in the sun, others being gathered up by friends or family.

"Always thought I'd see the world one day," Frank said. He extended an ink-stained hand; it held a brown paper bag. "Got you these for the trip. If you're going to be a navy man, you'd better learn to hold your liquor."

George took the bag and looked inside. Two bottles of ale. He shifted his bag from one shoulder to the other, looked at his shoes.

"You got a church key?" Frank asked.

George shook his head.

"Well, take this, then. It'll do in a pinch and you probably ought to have one anyway. I got others." He held out his pocketknife, but George didn't take it. Frank waved it at him, once, twice, then bridged the gulf between them with his arm and dropped the knife into George's shirt pocket and gave it a tap with his forefinger.

After a moment, he said, "Listen, son, I, uh . . . Drink up." He closed his mouth and cleared his throat. He started to wipe the toe of his shoe on the hem of his trousers but stopped and returned his foot to the platform. He pulled out his handkerchief, tilted his hat back, and mopped his forehead. George thought he might have passed the cloth over his eyes.

The conductor bellowed the all aboard.

George had been wondering if he should extend his hand, but his father's fists were deep in his trouser pockets. Frank said, "Enjoy the beer, George, 'cause it's the last thing you'll get from me."

George walked to his train car and climbed aboard. His fingertips searched for the velvet of the seat cover but found leather instead. As the train pulled out of the station, the last thing George saw was his father's back. Frank Lawson, leaning against the station wall, his hat still on his head with the brim crushed in on one side, looked lost inside his dusty suit. George thought he saw his father's shoulders shake, but he would never be sure.

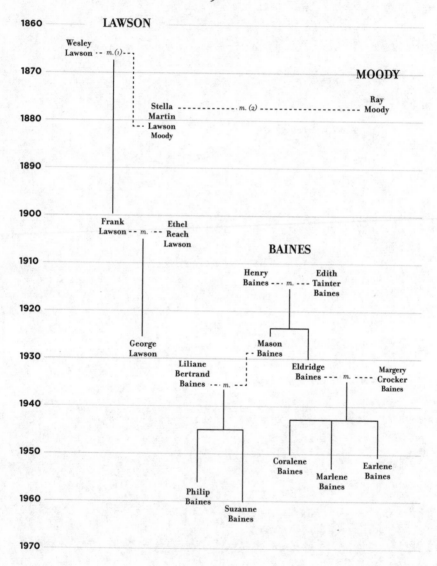

1966

LAWSON

MOODY

BAINES

1860

Wesley
Lawson ·· *m. (1)* ···

1870

Stella ············ *m. (2)* ······················ Ray
Martin   Moody
Lawson
Moody

1880

1890

1900

Frank   Ethel
Lawson ·· *m.* ··   Reach
                     Lawson

1910

Henry   Edith
Baines ··· *m.* ··· Tainter
                     Baines

1920

George   Mason
Lawson   Baines

1930

Liliane   Eldridge   Margery
Bertrand   Baines ··· *m.* ···· Crocker
Baines ·· *m.* ···   Baines

1940

Philip   Coralene   Earlene
Baines   Baines   Baines
                                    Marlene
       Suzanne   Baines
       Baines

1950

1960

1970

STARVATION DIET

Liliane stands in the dark kitchen, staring out the window at the snow and the shallow footprints that skirt the edge of the woods at the back of the house where the door is bolted against the night. Beneath the dense growth of evergreens, there is only a dusting of snow, but from the tree line to the house, in the open space of the backyard, it deepens to more than a foot. There the individual steps of the path merge and cut a trench, leaving a frozen wake where the walker became a wader.

When she left the house earlier in the evening, the snow lay undisturbed, mean jags of sleet bouncing off the icy crust. The sleet turned to snow while she was out, then stopped, and now the sky is clear. The light of the three-quarter moon cloaks her world in shades of blue, from deepest navy to a dreary *bleu celeste*, a lifeless version of the Mediterranean sky before a rain. At the moment, however, Liliane is more concerned with who or what has walked through the woods than with fleeting memories of summer in Antibes. Her gaze flicks from the door to the top of the refrigerator where she keeps the shotgun, while her hand eases open the drawer that holds the shells. She thinks of her children safely asleep at Agnes's house tonight and offers silent thanks to God.

Mason first put the Remington in her hands six years ago, right before he shipped out the first time. Though she'd seen plenty of weapons back in France during the war, she'd never actually held a gun and initially refused to even pick it up. He insisted, though, and showed her how to load it and carry it broken over her forearm. Eventually she'd taken a shot and to her great surprise found she liked the smell of hot metal and burning gunpowder, the weight of the stock snugged into her shoulder, and the kick of the recoil. With the gun in her hands, she feels competent, powerful, less alone. She practices often and seldom misses.

"May I have another lump?" Liliane asked her mother-in-law a week before the night at the window.

"Well of course, dear." Edith Baines pushed the sugar bowl just past the middle of the kitchen table. "Lord almighty, Lillian, I don't know how you stay so thin with all that sugar. I can't stand a sweet drink."

Behind a smile that fooled no one, she thought, If I had anything resembling coffee in this cup, I wouldn't want sugar either. She dropped two lumps into the thin brown swill and watched the chipped blue sugar bowl slide back to the other side of the table. Next time she'd ask for tea.

Liliane said, "*Merci*, Edith," intentionally using the French pronunciation, *AyDEET*. Tit for tat, she told herself. Her mother-in-law had been mispronouncing her name as Lillian since the first day they met, and she believed it was deliberate, an unsubtle way of demeaning her and her foreignness.

Of course, most of the people in Wellbridge had trouble with her name and ended up calling her Lil or Lili instead, which was fine. Her closest friend and three-times-a-week housekeeper, Agnes Juke, tried to French it up by exaggerating the final syllable. The result was something along the lines of *LillyON*, which was even harder on the ear than the version her in-laws used. Still, Liliane appreciated the effort.

After a perfunctory "You're welcome," Edith removed her black cat's-eyes, huffed on each lens, and polished them with the edge of the well-worn yellow tablecloth. Though red-rimmed, her eyes were an astonishing watery blue, nearly translucent. Liliane thought of the wedding photo in the living room. Edith had been such a pretty woman when she was young. Is this what fifty years of gray skies and snow does, she wondered, dry you up, freeze you, chip you to a shard?

Outside, the arthritic tree limbs scratched against the low clouds of the endless Maine winter. Not for the first time that day, Liliane thought longingly of yellow sunlight, café au lait, ripe tomatoes drizzled in olive oil, and the supple give of white sand beneath her feet on the beach at La Garoupe.

To make up for the sigh she was unable to suppress, she said, "On Sunday I take a call from Mason."

"Ship to shore?" Edith asked, straightening in her chair and slipping her glasses back in place. "Where is he?"

"Dakar, in Africa. He has a room in the hotel there while they load up. He will stay for a few days before they gonna ship out to Lisbon. He say the voyage is about—"

"He *says*, Lillian, not he say," Edith interrupted with a smile that could have frozen the churning reach behind the house.

"Ah? Yes, excuse me, Edith. He *says* he will be home in March but he doesn't yet know the day."

While she was speaking, an image came to mind of her handsome husband lying shirtless on an unmade bed with the hot, spice-heavy breeze in his hair. The first time she saw Mason Baines, she knew he was the one. Strong jawed and slim, looking like an American movie star in his merchant marine uniform, he strode through the door of the translation office in Antibes as if he were taking center stage. She'd been passing by the front desk on her way to an Italian transcription assignment but stopped to help the receptionist, who was struggling to understand the peculiar accent of the handsome officer with the wide white smile and the sad brown eyes. English was the weakest of Liliane's languages, and it took several sentences for her to figure out which one he was speaking. At first she thought he might be Scottish—they were always impossible—but he said no.

"Pardon me, but your accent is very, er, unusual," she said. In fact, it was nearly unintelligible, but she wouldn't say that to a potential customer, especially such a good-looking one.

"I'm American, from Maine," he said, speaking slowly and enunciating. "Do you know where that is?"

"No, I'm sorry."

He borrowed a pen from the receptionist, flipped over his business card, and drew the outline of the United States, then colored in the mitten shape that intruded way up into eastern Canada. "Here," he said, smiling at Liliane. "You are going to love it."

And that was it. The afternoon's flirtation led to a dinner date, which stretched well into the next day, then became a monthlong courtship, conducted mostly in his hotel room. When Mason shipped out, she thought she'd never see him or his blend of cocksure arrogance and small-town charm again, but after eight weeks away, he sailed back into port as promised and proposed. Liliane was nearly three months pregnant and worried his family wouldn't approve, but Mason told her that both his mother and sister-in-law had delivered their first child well before the nine-month mark.

"Listen, Lil, I've already got a piece of land. It overlooks a pretty little cove. We'll dig clams and have a garden in summer. My buddy's a builder. He can start on a house next month. It'll be ready by the end of April. What do you say?"

Of course she said yes. In 1958, who wouldn't have wanted to leave shabby old Europe for a sparkling new life in America? She was twenty-two years old and madly in love. He brought her to Maine in the late spring, to the sweet smell of lilacs and the wind's whispered promise of summer. But summer was always an illusion in this place. Fleeting, green, and soft, it was merely a glorious prelude to the main event, the slap of cold, the sting of snow, the agony of winter. And always the absence—of family, of friends, laughter, and the life together her husband had promised.

Liliane managed to swallow an ugly laugh and forced her thoughts away from Mason and back to his mother.

"He's been away long enough, and Lord knows his father could use some help on the boat. Henry's not s'young as he used to be, you know, and those traps don't pull themselves."

The books don't unbalance themselves either, Liliane thought, but instead she forced the corners of her mouth up and said, "Is it not lucky he has Eldridge, then?"

"Oh Lord, Eldridge can't do that kind of work. Last week his back was so bad he could barely get out of bed. 'Course his health's always been iffy, and the way Margery feeds him probably makes him spleenier than normal."

"Maybe he should visit Dr. Norden," Liliane suggested. Or stop drinking and get to work, she thought. Mason's younger brother was a big-pawed puppy of a man who'd been content to drift along in his brother's wake as long as Liliane had been around.

The older woman took a deep drag on her cigarette and leaned back in her chair, folding her arms across the rough brown cardigan that insulated her bony torso. She closed her eyes. Her lips were pulled tight, and it looked like she was using her tongue to extract a scrap of food from her dentures. When she spoke, she formed her words carefully and slowly, as if she were explaining the importance of not running into the street to an idiot child.

"Doctor visits are expensive, dear, and Margery and Eldridge don't have the kind of money coming in that you and Mason do. The pound's their *only* business, you know, and they've got three children to support, not two. They can't just run off to Doc Norden every time they have an ache or a pain."

Liliane murmured, "Um-hm." She didn't bother pointing out that if Eldridge spent less on beer, his family might have more for doctors.

"Looked like you had a nice chat with the doctor at the party," Edith said, referring to the anniversary celebration they'd both attended two days before.

"Yes, he and his wife are very sympathetic. They love to visit in France, you know. In the spring they will go to Paris and Nice."

"Well, la-di-da. Those doctors really rake it in, don't they? I suppose I'll have to hear all about it when I go in for my checkup. Speaking of parties, you remember we're having the potluck on Saturday?"

"A dinner party, no?"

This time Liliane was unable to swallow her sigh. Another grudging, obligatory invitation from her in-laws. Most of the guests would ignore her, and she'd have to keep her back to the wall once Uncle Denton had a few drinks. Edith would make little grunting sounds every time Liliane misspoke, and then there would be her father-in-law. Henry Baines would be tight before anyone arrived and slurring by dessert.

"Ayuh, buffet style, but it's a cocktail, so no kids. Just our family, plus some of Margery's people, a few others, Caspar Titcomb. Have you met his friend? That new caretaker over at the Ridgeback place. What's his name, George?"

"Lawson, no? George Lawson. I met him couple weeks ago. At Caspar's place. He seem very nice—" Edith broke in just as Liliane was about to mention how well this newcomer spoke French.

"Well, I hope Cap doesn't drag him along. Big gaum with a beard—anyway we're starting around six-thirty. Nothing fancy, you know."

And there it was, the inevitable implied criticism: fancy. Fancy was code for French, for your way of doing things, Lillian. For complicated, oddly spiced courses with wine instead of beer or milk next to a single plate of boiled everything. For a relaxed dinner at eight instead of a brief, joyless obligation at five-thirty. For treating food as nourishment for the soul, not just fuel for the tank. For all the ways you are different and all the reasons you think you are better than us, Lillian. *Nothing fancy.*

"What would you like that I make?" Liliane could hear the defeat in her voice.

"We're having casseroles. I'm making my seafood Newburg, and Margery's bringing her pineapple cake so there's a dessert. I don't know, maybe you could do a vegetable? I've got a recipe for green bean casserole that's good for a crowd. People always like creamed spinach or squash. Or maybe a tossed salad? I'm sure we'll like whatever you bring, dear."

"I'll have a look at the Foodland. Maybe Agnes can watch the kids, but I don't know."

"I'm sure you could drop them by Margery's place. Her girls'd love to babysit."

Wasn't their middle daughter, Earlene, running around with that Moody boy? Imagining what went on while Margery and Eldridge were away was even more disturbing than the state her children would be in after four hours in the filthy chaos of their house trailer and a steady diet of Tang and Pop-Tarts, but Liliane knew better than to say anything. Instead, she looked at her watch and excused herself on the pretext of needing to get to the market and relieve the babysitter.

Liliane picked her way across the dirty snow of the driveway. From the yard, there was a clear view of the Northern Reach and the bay beyond with its dreadful, freezing gray water. Days like this, she could almost feel the clouds pressing on her neck and shoulders. She kept her eyes down, watching out for slippery patches in her path.

———

Every trip to the Foodland was a little worse than the last, especially in winter. Droopy carrots, hard tomatoes that never ripened, flavorless iceberg lettuce, no fresh herbs except parsley, and those bitter green peppers the local people put in everything from salad to stews. The produce was wrapped in cellophane and sanitized into tastelessness. The meat was worse, and the pantry items were hopeless—white or apple cider vinegar only, olive oil that smelled like it had leaked from an engine block, and bright yellow mustard that looked, and tasted, like paint. She couldn't even bear to think about the cheese. If not for the fresh garlic and the occasional mushroom, she'd have given up long before.

Liliane palmed a heavy waxed turnip but couldn't bear to put it in her cart. There were beets, but the kids didn't like them, and the delicious greens had been cut off and tossed long ago when they were still fresh. She picked up a packet of spinach and dropped it in her cart, then moved along to the winter squash, trying to think of some way to make it interesting. There was only so much you could do with butter.

"It's quite depressing, isn't it?" came a voice from behind. It washed over her in a warm wave of soothing French, and she turned to find George Lawson pushing a similarly meager cart and shaking his shaggy head.

"Monsieur Lawson, how nice to see you," she said, using the formal *vous*, and felt instantly ridiculous at the pretense no one would notice. She looked around for prying eyes but saw no familiar faces among the shoppers.

"It's George, remember?"

"Certainly, and I am Liliane."

"Of course you are," he said, then suggested switching to the familiar *tu*. "I hate shopping here. How do you manage?"

"Oh, my family bring olive oil and vinegar, charcuterie, cheeses, whatever they can squeeze in the suitcase when they visit. But they only come every other summer. So I use dry herbs, onions, and garlic. I make *frites*. Do you like to cook?"

He picked up a bag of potatoes and dropped it into his cart with a marked lack of enthusiasm. Liliane noticed that although paint-splattered, his hands were by far his best feature, large and strong, but well-formed with long, sensitive fingers and short, perfectly clean nails. His clothing was another matter, ill-fitting and tatty at the cuffs, and he desperately needed a haircut. There was friendliness in his face, but something hard there, too.

"In the navy I tried to learn to cook the local food wherever I was stationed. I met a couple of chefs in Nice; they'd invite me into the kitchen sometimes, but after twenty years of navy food, what I really like is home cooking."

"My husband is like you. When he's home, he refuses to go out for dinner, not that there's any place to go."

"It isn't exactly Paris, is it?"

Not even London, she thought as she picked up, then put down, a green pepper. Liliane made one of those vague French sounds of affirmation that's not really a word and rolled her eyes in agreement. Despite the depressing subject, it was a joy to sink back into her first language and express her thoughts without struggle.

"Do you know there's a real Italian butcher in Portland? Ruggieri his name is, from Siena, I think. He buys from local farmers and to cut the meat himself," George said. She didn't bother correcting his grammar. "A buddy in Portland told me about him. It's a long trip, but every few weeks I drive south for meat—pork, beef, chickens, he makes sausage. If it doesn't snow, I'm going tomorrow. I could get some things for you."

Liliane's mouth watered at the thought of steak tartare and roast pork in garlic and wine. The temptation was too much to refuse. "Well, if you're going anyway . . ."

She scribbled her address on the back of his shopping list. As George headed over to the cash register, she noticed one of Edith's cronies hovering near the citrus, a grapefruit paused in mid-lift, staring openly. Liliane made a mental note to have Agnes at the house when George dropped by.

She arrived home to find her children at the kitchen table, sipping Ovaltine while Agnes put away the last of the lunch dishes.

"Early release today?" Agnes asked from under a single raised eyebrow.

Liliane snorted her response and nodded.

"Best not make a habit of good behavior. They'll think they've got you right where they want you," Agnes said before disappearing inside her hideous green anorak and slamming the back door.

Later, with the children asleep and the dishes drying by the sink, Liliane closed the sunflower-covered drapes against the night and settled on the sofa to watch *The Wild Wild West*. She lit a cigarette, took a deep drag, and swirled the rocks around in her Scotch. The tinkling soothed her. Whenever Mason was out to sea, this was her routine: dinner, bath and bed for the kids, followed by TV and a drink for her. Lately she'd been pouring a second one more often than not. It got dark so early that the night seemed to go on forever, or for two drinks, anyway.

The TV droned on. Though Robert Conrad usually held Liliane's attention, her thoughts wandered away from the program to George Lawson.

He'd been helping Caspar install a new storm door when she stopped by the house with a lemon cake a couple of weeks before. Liliane disliked baking, but Caspar had a sweet tooth, so she made a point of taking him a treat each week. After accepting a kiss on each crepey cheek and taking her hand in both his gnarled ones, Cap introduced his bearded friend as Lieutenant Commander George Lawson. After adding, "Retired, and please call me George," to his title, the man, much to Cap's delight, proceeded to speak in very respectable, well-accented French. Over the years, she had encountered many French speakers in Maine, but they all produced a twangy, oddly inflected Canadian dialect that sounded more like agitated goose honking than her native tongue, and when she had trouble deciphering what they said, they tended to take offense.

In deference to Caspar, they switched back to English after George explained that he had studied French in school and during several tours in Europe. He had, he told her, just retired from the navy and signed on as caretaker at one of the estates out on Bridge Point for a year. Liliane wondered what an officer with a pension was doing working as a caretaker, but she couldn't think of a polite way to ask.

"You're a long way from home, Mrs. Baines. So how is it you ended up in this part of the world?" he asked with what appeared to be genuine interest.

"Please, call me Liliane. My husband, Mason, come from Wellbridge. After we marry in Antibes, we come, no, we *came* here for the children to learn English. Long time ago, Mason buy some land from Caspar over that way, so that's where we build our house," she explained. Her English was usually better than this.

"Antibes? Such a beautiful spot. Did you grow up there?"

"I was born in Saint-Rimay—a very small town in the middle of France. But after the war we return to Antibes to be together with the family of my mother, so that's where I grow—eh!—I *grew* up."

"Saint-Rimay? I can't place it, but I've been to Antibes. I love walking on the seawalls there. I'll bet you miss it, Liliane." She felt a rush of pleasure at hearing her name as it was meant to be said.

"Oh yes, but here we are near the water, and my husband want to be home when he is not at sea. He has a lobster business with his family, so he work at that when he is off the ship."

"I've known Lil's husband, Mason, since he was just a spud, you know," Cap said to his friend. "He was my student up to the Maritime Academy, too. Wasn't enough he was one of the best engineers we ever turned out, but then he went abroad and caught himself the prettiest girl on the Riviera to boot."

Liliane squeezed the old man's arm.

Caspar asked after the children and Mason's current cruise, and as the two friends chatted, George listened attentively. When Liliane spoke, he nodded from time to time but never interrupted.

Liliane could have sat all afternoon chatting in Cap's yellow kitchen but excused herself when she realized she was almost late for school pickup. She was still wondering how George Lawson ended up in Wellbridge when her fingers started to burn. With the filter close to igniting, her third cigarette was spent, so she rubbed it into the ashtray, got up, snapped off the set, and headed for the kitchen, crunching the ice from her drink on the way. No more TV, no more harrowing escapes or whiskeys in the saloon, just sixty more evenings alone until Mason came home.

By the time she got into bed, Philip and Suzanne were already there, having slipped downstairs from their room to hers. In the middle of the mattress, Suzanne was sprawled on her back with her blond curls fanned out across the pillow in a mermaid's mane. Next to her, Philip was curled up with his thumb in his mouth. She knew she should move them back to their own room, but she liked having their warm little bodies close. It was going to be hell trying to get them to stay in their beds when Mason got back, but there would be plenty of long, cold nights to get through until then.

Wednesday evening the butcher's packages beckoned from the kitchen table, each wrapped in brown paper and tied with string just like at home. Next to them sat four fat red peppers George had brought from a corner grocery in Portland's Italian neighborhood.

"I saw these and thought of you and those pitiful green peppers at the Foodland," he said, looking pleased at her response.

Liliane picked up a pepper and sniffed. Sharp but mellow, heavy in her hand. They'd roast beautifully.

George accepted her effusive thanks and seemed to want to linger, but his truck was blocking Agnes's, and as he backed down the drive she followed him out. Just as well. It wouldn't do for people to see a single man leaving her house after dark, even if it was only five-thirty.

Liliane unwrapped each package and inspected the contents, sniffing, fondling, and prodding each item in quiet glee. All were very fine, far better than anything that came on Styrofoam trays from the Foodland. It really was an embarrassment of riches, but in the end she chose the perfectly marbled strip steak, stowed the pork loin for the next day, and rewrapped and froze the remaining packages.

She sharpened the big knife she had brought from France, then divided the steak into two pieces, one to be cooked for the children and the other for her to eat à la tartare. Leaving the children's portion to come to room temperature, she minced her half in precise, tiny cubes and slid them into a glass bowl, then crumbled the yolk of a hard-boiled egg over the top and added a spoonful of finely chopped onion. From the store of supplies her mother had brought from France the summer before, she took a dollop of grainy mustard, some capers and cornichons, and a drizzle of olive oil. She even threw in a handful of parsley and some Worcestershire sauce from the market. After all this was mixed, she lowered her face to the bowl and inhaled before covering the mixture and setting it in the refrigerator.

Liliane sautéed the spinach, fried the potatoes, cooked the meat for the children, and even opened a bottle of Bourgogne from the case Mason had brought home from his last trip. She'd have to drink the whole thing before it went to vinegar, but what pleasure that would be. The smell of the food reminded her of family meals in France. It was sad that it was just the three of them to enjoy this feast. On a whim, she dialed up Caspar and invited him for roast pork the next day.

"And please bring that wonderful friend of yours who find all this treasure for us." They set the time for six-thirty so that the children could join them.

Drawn by the smell of steak and garlic, Philip and Suzanne wandered into the kitchen and took their places at the table without being called. Liliane had never fed them the jars of miracle baby food from the grocery store; it all smelled like dog food. As a result, her children had developed unusually adult food preferences, and while their friends turned up their noses at the sautéed mushrooms and salad she served, her kids happily tucked in.

"Maman, what are you making? Are we having *champignons ce soir?*" Philip asked in the haphazard franglais they used around the house.

"*Champignons*, *steak frites*, and spinach with garlic, *mes anges!*" she singsonged in response, and Suzanne clapped her hands at her mother's tone.

"*Champignons, champignons*, how I love my *champignons*," Philip sang. At the third repeat his sister joined in and eventually all three were singing, accompanied by the sizzle of the meat and the hiss of the oil.

At the table, the children happily popped the mushrooms into their mouths, devoured their steak, and even finished up their spinach with very little nagging. Liliane's tartare was perfect, the beef's coppery richness perfectly complemented by the bite of the mustard and the tang of the pickles. Though tempted to gobble it down in a rush, she forced herself to eat slowly, savoring each bite and even scooping up the meat with her French fries while the children giggled across the table.

Later, happily satisfied for the first time in months, with the feast slowly digesting and the kids tucked into bed, she poured a third glass of wine to sip during *The Dick Van Dyke Show* and hummed along with the boomps-a-daisy theme song. The house felt warmer, the winter at bay.

The next morning, Liliane woke with only a trace of a hangover despite having emptied the bottle. She supposed the heavy dinner had saved her, and she sank back on the pillows, reliving the luxury of the meal. Next to her, Philip produced a delicate little snore and pushed his thumb into his mouth.

She slipped out of bed and into the bathroom. Other than some telltale redness in the eyes, there was no trace of last night's excess. For almost thirty, she mused as she brushed her teeth, she looked pretty good. True, her hair was less blond than it had been under the tender ministrations of the Mediterranean sun, and she could see the beginnings of crow's-feet at the corners of her eyes, but her jaw was firm and she could still get away with nothing more than lipstick when she went out during the day. She ran a comb through her hair. With a little spraying and teasing she'd be able to get another day or two out of her weekly wash and set.

In the kitchen, she made a pot of coffee, rationing a tablespoon of fine black espresso on top of the anemic-looking Maxwell House in the percolator. Coffee was the one item she asked Maman to send from France, and she was going to need more soon.

On impulse, she dialed the overseas operator and placed a call to her mother. It would be lunchtime in Antibes, a good time to talk. After ten rings, the operator asked if she'd like to stay on the line. She declined and pictured her family at one of her aunts' apartments, all squeezed around a table on the terrace, laughing and arguing over the midday meal. For a moment she considered trying to call them but decided against it when she realized she had a lump in her throat. If she cried, her mother would worry, and besides, the children were stirring, so she replaced the receiver and got out the eggs. On the refrigerator door was a note under the magnet. Liliane recognized her own handwriting, though it was messy: Cap 18.30 gâteau choco.

"*Merde,*" she groaned, recalling her invitation and offer of chocolate cake for dessert.

"Maman, naughty word," said Suzanne from the doorway. She was holding her stuffed bunny, Monsieur Mister, by one ear and rubbing her eyes. "I have to make pee pee."

"*D'accord*, you're a big girl, you can do it. *Dépêche-toi*. Then get your robe and come have your *petit déjeuner*. Pip, awake now. Time for school!"

After a cup of coffee and a cigarette, the day felt more comfortable, and Liliane began to plan the dinner party. No one would think twice about having Caspar over, and if he brought George, what of it? Perfectly respectable. She told Suzanne she could wear her party dress and lace anklets and informed Philip he would be the host for the evening. He nodded gravely and ran upstairs to find his clip-on tie.

"Well, hello there, young man!" Caspar croaked as he grabbed Philip under the arms and swung him up into a bear hug. "Lord almighty, you're almost as big as your father. Pretty soon you'll be picking *me* up."

"Uncle Cap!" Suzanne squealed, then skipped across the kitchen floor in the pink ballet slippers she'd insisted on wearing.

"Hello, young lady, and where might Suzy Baines be? You're much too grown-up to be my favorite poppet."

"It's me, Suzy, I'm the poppet!" she said, and held her arms out to be picked up as soon as Philip hit the floor. When Caspar made as if to tickle her, she ran shrieking from the kitchen with the old man loping behind.

"George, this is my son, Philip. Pip, Mr. Lawson."

The boy stepped forward with his right hand extended, a miniature version of his father. "Hello, Mr. Lawson. Welcome to our home," he said, just as Liliane had instructed.

George shook the boy's hand. "Pleasure to meet you, Philip."

"Pip, please take the coats of Mr. Lawson and Uncle Cap and put them on my bed," Liliane said.

"As you're the host this evening, young man, perhaps you'll take the wine we brought for your mother. I can see to the coats."

George's face was as serious as Pip's, and Liliane smiled at her son's evident pleasure at being recognized as the man of the house. She indicated the bedroom on the other side of the kitchen, and George carried the cold things in and laid them across the foot of the bed.

"Is that roast pork I smell?" he called.

"You have a good nose."

"And some kind of potato? Gratin?" he asked, returning to the kitchen.

"And those delicious red peppers you bring us."

"What a feast, eh, Philip?"

"No spinach tonight, and Maman made cake!" Pip said, smiling shyly at the big man who was leaning on the counter.

"Chocolate, I hope."

"Yup. Uncle Cap's favorite."

Liliane handed George a corkscrew and asked her son to get Cap's drink order, though she knew he never took anything but Scotch. From the living room, she could hear the old man reading *My Big Pink Bouncy Bunny* to Suzanne, whose giggling trickled over his gravelly voice and lazy Downeast drawl. This, she thought, was how a home should be all the time.

She turned the pork loin over in the heavy pot and added some wine. It sizzled when it hit the hot fat. George said, switching back to French, "You make the pork on top of the stove? I've never been able to get that right."

He stepped behind her and looked over her shoulder. He smelled of woodsmoke, and his breath was warm on her neck.

"My mother made it this way. Her oven was small and it never worked very well. See, you make the incisions and fill them with sliced garlic, then brown it in the olive oil with onions and add thyme and white wine. Then it cooks slowly, for about half an hour. But of course, you must never overcook it. That's the mistake people make in this country." Liliane was talking faster than usual, a nervous habit.

He inhaled deeply, and when he did his belt buckle grazed her ribs.

"One Scotch on the rocks," Pip announced from the doorway. He stopped when he caught sight of his mother and looked questioningly at George.

"Thank you, sir. I'll get right on it," George said. He crossed the kitchen and opened the bottle on the counter.

Pip delivered the cocktail, then came straight back and took a seat at the kitchen table, sipping his ginger ale until dinner was served in the dining room.

Two hours later dessert was a guilty memory, both wine bottles lay empty, the children were upstairs in bed, and Caspar was dozing by the fire in Mason's favorite armchair, the top button of his pants undone, the occasional snore gurgling up through his open mouth. In the kitchen, George washed the dishes while Liliane dried and put them away. He worked methodically, starting with the glasses, then moving on to the plates and utensils before tackling the pots and pans. Just the way I do it, she thought.

When the dishes were done, he replaced the heavy serving pieces on the top shelf and carried the trash out to the garage. While she rinsed the sink, Liliane watched George walk back to the house. He was even taller than Mason, lanky where her husband was broad, scruffy instead of clean-shaven. Mason was fastidious about his appearance, but George stopped just short of slovenly; she wondered how he'd look with a decent suit and haircut.

Two snifters waited on the kitchen table where she and George sat down to avoid disturbing Caspar. He asked how Mason was related to Cap, apparently confused by the fact that the kids called him uncle. They spoke in low tones, Liliane in French and George slipping back into English when he couldn't find the right word.

"I think it must be a French custom. I can't have them calling him by his first name, but he's like family, so 'Mr. Titcomb' isn't right either. They call him uncle, a compromise."

"He's a good uncle."

"I think Mason decided to build our house here, because he knew Caspar would be near when he was at sea. If you look out the window, you can see the path through the woods that leads to his house. In the winter, when the trees are bare, his porch light shines through at night. See?"

"It must be difficult for you to be alone so much. Annie told me that the happiest day of their marriage was when Cap unpacked his sea bag for the last time."

George was looking at her a little too intently, and she turned away, picking an imaginary piece of lint from her sweater.

"It's hard in winter. Summer, too, I suppose, but not as much. We have a garden, and my family visits, so that helps. I think maybe next summer I'll take the children to France if Mason's away during the school vacation. So they can practice their French, you know?"

Until that moment, Liliane hadn't even considered the possibility, and she was as surprised by the thought as she was by her own words. She said, "I've heard Annie was very sweet. She died just a few years after Cap retired, no?"

"She was and she did."

"How sad. And you never married?" Liliane hadn't intended to ask, but the question seemed to form itself in her mouth and push its way past her teeth all on its own. "Excuse me, that's very personal. I'm sorry."

George sat back in his chair, and in the low light Liliane thought she caught a fleeting glimpse of that hard look again. The navy may have rounded his edges, but there was flint beneath the exterior. He said, "No need to apologize. I was married. Years ago and not for long. My fault. I didn't turn out to be much of a husband. Or father. My daughter's thirteen now. Her mother remarried a long time ago. A teacher. They're down in Connecticut."

"Do you see her often?"

"Not as much as I'd like. You know, I was gone a lot when she was little, and now . . ."

He was looking out the window at Cap's porch light, his right hand on the snifter, stopped in mid-swirl.

"So, you served with Cap?"

He nodded. "He was my first commanding officer, mopping up in the Pacific in '45. I was green as summer grass, so he looked out for me. I was the only other Mainer onboard."

George leaned over to light Liliane's raised cigarette. She wrapped her left palm around his knuckles as he proffered the lighter. His skin was rough, the back of his hand very warm.

"Thank you," she said, and removed her hand.

"I'm looking forward to meeting Mason. When's he due in?"

"Two months, more or less."

"When he gets back, I'll ask Cap to throw a party—my cottage is too small—and I'll make cassoulet. It's my specialty. I'm sure the old coot would host if you'd bring cake."

"That sounds nice. Mason loves cassoulet, but I never make it. Without the duck fat and the sausage, it's not right."

"Well, he's a lucky man, duck fat or no."

The silence hung in the smoke between them. George leaned forward in his chair.

"So, Saint-Rimay. It must have been difficult being in the occupied zone during the war. I found the town on my map, a Nazi command center, right?"

"The Germans took over everything, including my father's garage. By the time they arrived, he was already dead. At the Battle of Sedan, he was a mechanic. . . ."

"Hell of a thing."

"Yes, but we were lucky to have the garage; it was something the Germans wanted. So we ate when others didn't. It was difficult, but it seems long ago. And now here I am in the land of opportunity, where the streets are paved with . . . ice." She forced a smile.

"Funny how things turn out," he said.

She nodded.

"But you couldn't have served during the war. Weren't you too young?" she asked.

"I enlisted just before I turned seventeen. The war in Europe was over and they dropped the bombs on Japan before I finished training. I saw action in Korea, though, on a destroyer at Incheon, some other places."

"It must have been terrible, being there."

His focus seemed to slip. "Yeah, but after a while you get used to the fighting. Familiar with it. Then one day, it's gone and you miss it. Need it. After Korea I started boxing. I wasn't bad, but one day I realized I looked at my gloves the way a drunk looks at a bottle. I never picked them up again. Decided to get out as soon as my twenty years were up."

"Why did you join so young?"

He took a deep breath and stroked his beard, running his index finger along a scar on his cheek. Liliane hadn't noticed it before. He said, "Long story. My parents were . . . well, I don't know what they were, but let's just say there wasn't much keeping me at home. I wanted to see the world, thought it would be like in books. It was, but it wasn't. Do you understand?"

Liliane nodded. "And now here you are. Why Wellbridge?"

"My father grew up here—his mother was a Martin. They go back a ways, to Canadian fur trappers, 1700s I think. I never knew his family, but Cap said there were still lots of Martins around. Guess I wanted to see what he ran away from." He smiled without looking happy. "And of course Cap was here. The man's been like a father to me."

"He's family to us both, then," she said.

George picked up the bottle of cognac, inclined his head to ask if she'd like more. In the living room Caspar gave a huge grating snore. She shook her head.

Neither of them moved; Liliane was barely breathing, waiting. George said, "Well, I should get the old man home before he brings your roof down," but made no move toward the living room.

"Of course, it's late. I'll get the coats."

Liliane exhaled. She felt as if she'd been holding the breath for days. The moment evaporated, and George stood. Without looking at him, Liliane walked to the bedroom. She bent over the bed to collect the anoraks; George passed by the door. He paused only a second, as if he were going to speak, but Liliane turned away and busied herself sorting the scarves and gloves.

Dreading her in-laws' party seemed to make it come around all the faster, and as Liliane finished her face, she entertained idle thoughts of last-minute emergencies, convenient fevers, and dead car batteries. She could see the snow falling in purposeful diagonals outside the bathroom window, and she thought of Mason in some warm-weather port or the middle of the ocean, close enough to the equator to be sunbathing on deck. She wondered why she hadn't heard from him yet. He called almost every Saturday, usually about this time to catch the kids while they were still awake.

She stepped into her dress. The silk lining slid up and the soft navy wool wrapped her in a cozy embrace; it fit perfectly, not too tight. Her mother's dress form was exactly her size, and twice a year Madame Bertrand used it to make something special for her absent daughter, always according to the latest trends from Paris. Liliane hadn't worn this one yet. It arrived at Christmas and would be perfect for dinner. She reached around and pulled the zipper up to the middle of her back. Agnes could finish it when she arrived. Looking in the mirror, she decided the effect was a bit severe, so she added a silver swallow brooch Mason had bought during a stopover in Buenos Aires.

The jangle of the telephone interrupted her reverie, and though she would be happy to hear Mason's voice, she hoped it was Edith calling to cancel at the last minute. When she picked up the receiver, the familiar crackle of the ship-to-shore radio came through the wire.

"Lil, can you hear me?" Mason shouted.

"Yes, Mason! I was thinking of you. Like always. Where are you, chéri?"

"Gulf of Guinea, off Cameroon. About six days out of port. How are you and the kids? Everyone all right?"

"Everybody's fine, but we are wishing for you to be with us."

"I know. I miss you guys, too. Listen, Lil, something's come up. I got offered an extra trip on the end of this one. Perishable cargo—about a month. I hate to tell you we're extending, but the money's good and we could use it for the pound this summer. . . . Lil? You still there?"

In the seconds it had taken Mason to explain, Liliane's posture had slumped from an expectant letter I to a deflated C. Her forehead was pressed against the refrigerator, her eyes closed. She was doing the math. Ninety more days alone under the gray sky with no husband in the house and the children in her bed. Philip's seventh birthday would come and go, the snow would give way to mud, and by Mason's return, she would have spent another empty white winter alone. He had a choice and he made it.

"Liliane, are you okay? Listen, honey, I'll write you with the dates. I'm sorry. Lil, say something."

"Say hello to the kids, Mason. They're waiting for you."

Philip and Suzanne were already standing in the kitchen doorway, bouncing on their toes. Their father's call was their weekly treat. She handed the phone to her son and crossed the kitchen to the sink. With her back turned as if she were looking out the window, she composed her features while the children yammered. Outside, the night was thick and black, the wet snow still coming down, the tree branches bowed under the weight of it.

"Maman, Daddy wants you."

She turned around, smiled at the beaming children, and took the receiver from her daughter's fat little hand.

"I have to go now, Mason. There's a party at your mother house, they are expecting me. I have to go."

"Okay, sweetheart. Kiss the kids for me, and say hi to everybody. I'll call you next week. Have fun at the party. I'm sorry, Lil. I'm sorry. Bye-bye."

The line went dead; the drone of the dial tone replaced the hiss of the radio. Liliane removed the phone from her ear and stood staring at it. To the dead receiver, she muttered, "Have fun, Liliane. Thank you, Mason my love, but I have other plans."

"What did you say, Maman?" Philip asked, his forehead wrinkled under the tumble of curls.

"*Absolument rien.* Nothing. *Alors,* you can finish your show before Agnes will arrive. *Allez, tous les deux.*"

Suzanne trotted back to the living room, but Philip stayed put, staring at Liliane with his father's sad eyes. Twice he asked when Mason would be home. When she didn't answer, he asked a third time, this time whining and stomping his foot. Before she knew what she was doing, Liliane slapped her son, hard, just once across the face.

"Be the man of the house, not the baby," she spat at him.

Tears welled in the boy's eyes, now wide with shock, and he turned and ran from the room. His footsteps pounded up the stairs and his bedroom door slammed. Liliane knew she should follow her son, apologize, and gather him in her arms, but he looked so much like Mason, she couldn't bear to touch him or even look at him.

Ten minutes later, Agnes's truck ground down the drive to pick up the kids. They loved sleeping over at her house because her kitchen had a hard-packed dirt floor. They said it smelled like camping, and she always gave them homemade doughnuts for breakfast. It occurred to Liliane that her children were probably better off at Agnes's place than with her just then, and after muttering something about a tantrum, no mention of whose, she asked Agnes to raise her zipper, then pulled on her snow boots and coat, picked up the dish for the buffet, and stepped into the dark.

Liliane hated driving in the snow and had never gotten used to it. The studded tires made the car awkward to handle, but at least they gave her some sense of security behind the wheel. The melting snow glittered on the windscreen for a split second before it dissolved under the wiper blades. Usually she drove with the radio on for company, but tonight she preferred the silence.

She loved Mason, but she had no illusions about him. He was a good husband and father when he was home, but he was gone half of the year, and what man wouldn't give in to temptation after months at sea? Her husband was above all a physical being, a smooth talker who preferred to avoid deep or difficult subjects, a lover, not a fighter, he liked to say. They'd never discussed it, but there were bound to be women. She'd spent enough time in port cities to know that. And not for the first time, she wondered whether she was anything more to her husband than a shiny souvenir he'd brought home from abroad.

She swung the car into her in-laws' driveway, and her thoughts turned from Mason to his family. As far as they were concerned, he could do no wrong. With his education and big job, Mason was the golden goose whose income propped up the lobster business they'd always wanted. So what if the financial demands of keeping the boats and the pound afloat took him away from his wife and children? In the darkness she laughed at the thought. The wind had picked up, driving daggers of ice into the windscreen. She killed the engine, stubbed out her cigarette, and stepped back out into the sleet.

When Liliane arrived in the living room, the air was chewy with cigarette smoke, body heat, and the anticipation of a second, or in some cases a third, pre-dinner drink. She left her boots in the hall with all the others, stepped into her shoes, picked her way through the crowd of umbrella-shaped, pastel party dresses and skinny ties clipped to sweaty white shirts, and placed her platter of green-bean-and-beet salad on the table next to the vats of sauced meat in warming trays. Because the beans were thick and tough, she'd had to spend an hour frenching them before cooking, and now the tender strands, wound around the bloody slices of beet, looked to her as if they'd been tortured to death, heaped in a mass grave, and left for carrion. Most of the other things on the table looked worse.

From across the room, her sister-in-law, Margery, waved her over, sending a shower of cigarette ash onto the head of Henry Baines.

"Lil, come say hello to Pop!" she called.

Liliane crossed to the sofa where her rheumy-eyed father-in-law was sprawled next to Eldridge, an old-fashioned resting on his paunch.

One look at Eldridge's flushed cheeks told Liliane he and his father had started the party well before the first guest had arrived.

"What a pretty dress, Lillian. It must be from France. I guess hems are going up this year. Is it new?"

"A gift from my mother. And you always look so nice in pink, Margery."

"This old thing? It's hardly fit for scrubbing the floor, but my kids come first, you know."

Over a mock pout Margery complained that her children missed their little cousins and offered her girls' babysitting services, but Liliane knew enough to stay away from the subject of sleepovers; it was a familiar dance. "You are very kind, Margery, but the house is so empty without them—maybe when Mason will get back."

At the mention of his son's name, Henry broke the surface of his stupor.

"Heard you talked with the boy ship to shore last week," he said, slurring only slightly.

Liliane filled him in on the current cruise but couldn't bring herself to mention the extension. She excused herself on the pretext of checking to see if Edith needed a hand.

"She says she's got it under control," Margery said, then stood and dropped her voice to a conspiratorial whisper. "I'll bet she's back there sneaking pepper into everything. She always does. It's a good thing I wrapped my cake, or she'd probably try to spice that up, too."

Liliane made a small cluck and moved away to cut off Margery's complaints.

The kitchen was annexed onto the back of the rambling saltwater farmhouse where the Baines family had lived for more than a hundred years. The only heat came from a small black woodstove that squatted incongruously next to an enormous white electric range. Besides the refrigerator, it was the sole modern convenience. Cold water had to be pumped into the slate sink, there were no cupboards on the mustard-colored walls, and the light glared down from a lone bare bulb on the ceiling. The linoleum floor sat directly on top of hard-packed earth, which gave the room a dank, musty smell. Liliane hated it here; this was Edith's realm.

Her mother-in-law was wrestling with a pot at the stove, a long-ashed Newport dangling precariously from the corner of her mouth. She turned toward the sound of Liliane's tapping heels and with a tilt of her head gestured to her daughter-in-law to remove the cigarette from her lips. To her horror, Liliane saw that the ash was about to drop into the pot, so she grabbed a saucer from the table and slid it under the burning ember before plucking the butt from Edith's fuchsia-colored mouth. Looking into the glutinous contents of the pot, she couldn't tell whether what she thought was pepper might in fact be ash and was glad she'd eaten dinner with the children.

"Thank you, dear. Lord sakes, I almost forgot to add the cheese. I can't think why I'm so scatterbrained today. Must be the crowd."

Must be the gin, Liliane thought as she caught sight of the Tom Collins perspiring on the table. Apparently her husband and son hadn't been celebrating by themselves.

"Here, let me help you, Edith." Together they dumped the seafood stew into a chafing dish.

"Well, there. Don't you look fashionable. Dark colors suit you, dear."

Liliane smiled her thanks as her mother-in-law continued talking. "Now, there ought to be a spot next to the chicken à la king, but I'll go with you to clear a place if we need to."

Liliane hefted the dish and followed her mother-in-law as she tottered down the long dark hall, the orange coal of her cigarette glowing in one hand and the watery remains of her cocktail in the other.

In the living room, Margery was leading Caspar Titcomb over to the makeshift bar. There was no sign of George, and Liliane sighed as she set the dish down where her tray of green beans had been.

"Should we warm that up, Lillian?" Edith asked, pointing to the plate she had just shifted.

"No, Edith, it is a salad."

"Cold string beans and pickled beets? I never heard of such a thing. Well, leave it to you to come up with something original," Edith said. She pushed Liliane's dish to the back of the table, relegating it to the ghetto of pickles and garish Jell-O rings.

"I'll just tuck this back out of the way so those beets won't stain anybody's cuffs," Edith explained. Her smile might have been the product of a gas pain.

From the corner of her eye, Liliane saw George emerge from the hallway. He was carrying a well-used red cassole wrapped in a heavy kitchen towel. For a tall man, she noticed, he moved well. Must have been the boxing.

"Oh my goodness, George, you didn't have to bring anything!" Edith clucked. Clearly the notion of a man cooking was rather mind-boggling. "That looks hot—let me just get a pad for the table," she said, then signaled him to wait and left for the kitchen.

Liliane smiled at the familiar smell. "Cassoulet?"

"I got the confit and sausage from the butcher last week," he said as he lifted the top. "I've had a yen for this since we talked about it, and I even dipped into my store of duck fat since it was a special occasion."

"Oh la la, I don't have cassoulet for years."

Liliane leaned over the crock and inhaled the spicy aroma of duck, beans, and pork. Her eyes closed and her mouth watered, and for one blissful moment she was back with her mother, tossing toasted bread crumbs with duck fat for the top of the dish and helping to slide Maman's heavy crock into the oven. Two people could scarcely move in that little kitchen, but even with the old-fashioned fixtures it had produced years of feasts under her mother's direction. She pictured Maman in one of her flowered dresses and chef's apron, rubbing the big salad bowl with garlic in preparation for the tomatoes and purple-tinged lettuce on the counter.

"Good Lord, Lillian, let the man put that thing down before you fall in," Edith said a bit too loudly and with a possum smile, as she smacked a trivet down on the table.

Yanked back to the frosty present, Liliane straightened up. All around the room, conversations paused and heads turned; she tried to speak but could think of nothing to say, finally closing her mouth as her face began to color.

George registered surprise, then, fleetingly, that jagged look she'd seen before, as if he'd like to strike Edith, but then in a voice as smooth as cream he said, "A well-made cassoulet is nigh on to an art form— French food for the soul, Mrs. Baines. If someone were to drop into this bowl, there could be no higher praise for my cooking." He placed the crock on the table and turned to face Edith. She stepped back.

"I brought along a bottle of wine from the Banyuls to go with it. Can I get you ladies a glass? I think Cap took it to the bar."

"I don't drink wine," Edith replied. Then, because she was apparently still sober enough to realize an effort at graciousness was called for, she added, "But thank you, George, that's awful thoughtful. You've made this quite the feast."

By the time Caspar waved his corkscrew in the air to motion Liliane over to the bar, conversation had returned to normal, and Edith was halfway to the kitchen with Margery in tow. George took a glass of wine and excused himself to mingle, leaving Liliane to chat with Caspar.

The wine was hearty, slightly sweet and spicy. She rolled each peppery mouthful around her tongue and inhaled deeply whenever she lifted the glass to her mouth. Caspar was sipping his usual Scotch and telling her a funny story about tipping cows with Agnes when they were teenagers. George worked his way around the room, chatting, but Liliane caught him looking her way; she took a mouthful of wine and handed her glass to Cap for a refill.

Margery emerged from the kitchen with a dish of creamed spinach and announced that dinner was served. Though she wasn't hungry, Liliane took a portion of cassoulet and small helpings of several other things she had no intention of eating. She slipped off to a wooden chair in the corner to keep her plate out of sight. Over the years she'd become adept at sliding uneaten food into the trash. Her first mouthful included perfectly cooked white beans and tender chunks of duck leg and spicy sausage that could only have been handmade. The crunchy bread crumbs on the top complemented the rich mixture below that was redolent of garlic and spices—maybe a bit too heavy on the cloves for her liking, but only just. She chewed slowly, sipped her wine, and nodded her approval to George's inquiring look from across the room.

The party guests moved around the table and filled, then refilled, their plates. They settled in the living room, perching on chair arms and footstools or standing in small groups with their drinks temporarily set aside.

Uncle Denton and his wife, Doris, took seats on either side of Liliane and asked about Mason and the children between bites.

"My God, these beans are out of this world," Doris said as she mopped up the last of her cassoulet with a slice of buttered bread. "Now, is this a French dish, Lil?"

"Um-hm. It is our tradition for the cold weather."

"I'm gonna get the recipe from that George fella—right after I get just a scrid more," she said before striding toward the table. With Doris out of his hair, Denton shifted his seat closer to Liliane and leaned in close enough to peer down the front of her dress.

"Got a new joke for you, Lil," Henry's brother said with a grin so wide the gap from his missing bicuspid showed. "How does a girl from Wonsqueak Harbor let you know she's done having sex?"

Liliane shrugged.

"She says, 'Get offa me, Daddy, you're crushing my cigarettes!' " Denton guffawed. "Reynard Fletcher told me that one."

"*Cochon,*" Liliane muttered.

"Come again?" Denton smirked, blissfully unaware he'd just been called a pig. "Didn't think it was too funny, huh?"

"Perhaps it lose something in the translation," Liliane said, desperate to get away. She held out her empty glass. "Would you pour me just a little more of this delicious wine, please? *Merci.*"

He took her glass reluctantly, and as soon as he was across the room she stood up with her plate, intending to leave it in the sink.

The weak light from the kitchen trickled into the hallway, and Liliane could hear voices as she got closer.

". . . honestly, you'd think she'd never seen a bowl of beans before. For God's sakes, do all Frenchies make such a fuss over a meal or is it just her?" Margery simpered.

Liliane stopped.

"I couldn't say, but the whole damned family's that way," came the response from Edith. "You know what it's like when they come to visit, eating oysters *raw* and cooking lobsters on a grill. Last time they were here that uncle of hers took a lobster and cut it in half right down the middle—while it was still alive! I couldn't even look at it, let alone eat it after that."

"Well, I suppose her mother made that dress for her. Just as tight as can be and plain as dirt if you ask me. But I'm sure all the men like it just fine."

Liliane's free hand stroked the blue wool, then found its way to the silver swallow brooch over her heart. Her index finger traced the long tail feather and rested on the point at the end.

"I may not know about Paris fashion, but I know a hoochie dress when I see one." Edith continued, "Poor Mason would just die if he saw her falling all over that George and making a fool of herself in front of everyone. The other day Winnie Partridge saw them in the Foodland together. Thick as thieves and practically drooling on each other. I will never know why Mason had to go and waste himself on her when he could've had his pick of the nice girls right here in town. No wonder he stays away as long as he—"

The grope came out of nowhere. Denton must have crept up behind Liliane to deliver her drink and decided to collect his tip in advance. When she felt the unexpected hand on her ass, she jumped and jammed the point of the swallowtail into her finger, dropping her plate in the process. She spun around and shoved Denton hard against the wall, knocking the wine from his hand and sending the glass crashing to the floor on top of the shattered plate.

"Never touch me. Never. Do you understand what I say?" Her voice was an animal snarl, her mouth barely open when she spoke.

Behind her, Edith and Margery were pushing through the narrow kitchen doorway.

"What in God's name?" Edith squawked.

"I just tried to squeeze by. I didn't mean nothing by it, nothing at all," Denton mumbled as he rubbed his shoulder and backed down the hall.

Liliane turned to face the two women.

"Lillian, what's the matter, dear? Are you all right?" Edith asked. Behind her, Margery stood with her hand over her mouth.

Liliane flipped a sliver of plate off her shoe but made no move to clean up the mess at her feet. She said, "We are done now, Edith."

She turned and walked away from the kitchen, through the silent living room, and toward the front door. George stood next to the bar, following her with his eyes, clearly knowing better than to move. Caspar walked her to the foyer and helped her on with her coat.

"Drive you home, Lil?"

"No, thank you, Caspar. I am fine." She leaned in, gave him a quick kiss on the cheek, and walked out the door into the bitter black night. It was still sleeting.

Liliane locked the kitchen door, scuffed into her slippers, and sat down at the table with the Scotch bottle and a glass. The ember of her cigarette was the only light in the house.

"It's very difficult to be the stranger, Liliane."

Maman's words returned to her, years after leaving France with her lovely baby boy and brand-new husband. Like the Baineses, the family of Liliane's father had been less than thrilled when he brought a new bride home from the decadent Riviera to their little town in the middle of nowhere, moving her into the apartment above the garage he ran with his brother. Growing up, Liliane hadn't really been aware of any friction between her father's family and her mother, but after the war, Uncle Jean had been all too willing to shift the well-deserved taint of collaboration from himself to the sister-in-law he'd always resented.

Liliane brushed away a tear and buried her face in her hands as the image of her mother, dragged through the hissing, spitting crowd and into the square to have her head shaved in front of the entire town, replayed itself again in her mind. She'd always believed Maman had done nothing wrong. It had only been the kindness of a German motor-pool officer, the one with the sad smile, whose wife and young daughter were somewhere in Dresden hiding from the bombs, hopefully still alive, that kept them from going hungry. If Maman accepted food, it had been to keep her child, and her husband's family, alive. If she'd taken comfort, who could blame her? The only real collaborator among the Bertrands was Uncle Jean, who'd happily worked on German staff cars and trucks in exchange for the occasional beer or loose cigarette.

That night, nine-year-old Liliane left her stricken mother at the kitchen table, took up her sewing scissors, and cut off her thick blond braid, presenting the yarn-bound plait to her mother, who took one look and shouted, "Foolish girl! Never make yourself a target again. Ever."

Still, they had managed to attach the hair to a head scarf to avoid further abuse on the road and slipped away the next night, heading back to Antibes with nothing but their few clothes, Maman's sewing bag, and a photo of Liliane's father.

Liliane drained her drink down to the ice. She blew her nose, stubbed out her cigarette, squinted at the illuminated face of the clock over the sink. Unable to make out the time, she stood and stepped closer. Ten-thirty. Outside, the heavy night pressed down on the white ground. The evergreen branches sagged under the snow, and the delicate, leafless birches curved earthward with the weight. How long before the thaw? she wondered. Two months? Three?

As Liliane lifts the box of ammunition from the drawer, something stirs in the yard. At first she thinks it might be a bear, but then she sees it's a man, bent low, wading through the snow, too heavy to be Caspar. George Lawson stops three strides from the back steps, looking directly at the kitchen window and cradling a bottle of wine. Can he see her in the dark? She doesn't know whether she wants him to or not.

He waits there like he has all the time in the world. Then he turns and with his free hand grasps the trunks of three bowed birch trees, each in turn, gently shaking off the thick burden of snow. Liliane watches as, one by one, the slender silver trunks straighten and arabesque toward the night sky. She drops the shells in the drawer and flicks on the light.

1989

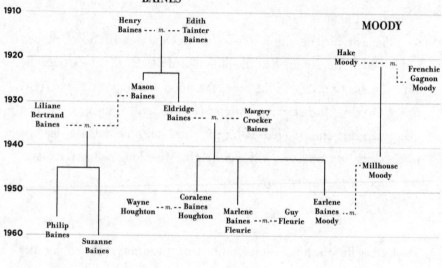

BAINES

MOODY

1910

Henry Baines --- m. --- Edith Tainter Baines

1920

Hake Moody ------ m.

Frenchie Gagnon Moody

Mason Baines

1930

Liliane Bertrand Baines ----- m.

Eldridge Baines --- m. ---- Margery Crocker Baines

1940

Millhouse Moody

1950

Wayne Houghton -- m. -- Coralene Baines Houghton

Marlene Baines Fleurie -- m. -- Guy Fleurie

Earlene Baines Moody -- m.

Philip Baines

1960

Suzanne Baines

1970

TWO-STEP (HIDE YOUR EYES OR LIE)

"Oh, for God's sakes, Marlene, Earlie was *not* having a good time. She only *thought* she was." Cora's voice, snapping through the line, made Marlene feel like she'd been stung, and she jerked her head away from the phone.

Marlene tried to figure out the difference between thinking you were having fun and actually having it, but she couldn't see any. Scarcely pausing to draw breath, Cora continued to criticize the notorious behavior of their sister, who'd been dancing with some of the young people at a wedding reception the night before. As always, Earlie's husband was mostly to blame. ". . . and once she and Millhouse get drinking, I don't even like to think what they get up to, but not a bit of it's good."

Her verdict rendered, Cora turned her attention to the other wedding guests. All seemed to be guilty of something.

Marlene switched the phone to her other ear and pictured Cora thrusting her narrow jaw even farther forward than usual. She imagined Cora's bones grating, like mis-shifted gears in a rusty pickup, the meager upper lip disappearing behind the hard, chapped ridge of the lower one. Strange how little was left of the pretty teenager Cora had been. Could it really be twenty years ago?

Marlene hated it when Cora was cross; it flustered her. She reminded herself to think before she spoke as she watched the tail of the cat clock over the stove swing from side to side. With each tick, its buggy eyes shifted in a knowing leer.

Having ripped the wedding guests to shreds, Cora returned to the subject of their sister and her disgraceful exhibition. When she paused to draw breath, Marlene said, "Earlie was just blowing off steam's all. That's what parties're for. I doubt anyone noticed or cared." She said it even though they both knew most of Wellbridge had seen it, and anyone who wasn't already looking had certainly taken notice when, from the bar at the back of the hall, Millhouse Moody hollered, "Shake it, Mumma!" so loud he nearly drowned out "Super Freak." Marlene smiled at the memory.

"Well, she looked like a damn fool wiggling her fat fanny in front of the whole town."

While Cora enumerated their sister's many personal failings, Marlene thought back to Cora's lurching, joyless fox-trot with her husband. Once the dancing started, but long before the party turned raucous, Wayne had cajoled his wife out onto the floor. From the moment he touched her waist until the last plink of "Jolene" faded, and Dolly finally gave up begging that red-haired hussy not to steal her man, Cora fought to lead, resisting Wayne's direction at every step. It hadn't resembled dancing so much as one of those all-in wrestling matches on TV. At the last chord, Millhouse grinned at Marlene across a tableful of empty glasses and pantomimed striking a bell. "Ding! Three rounds, no decision." Did they even think they were having fun?

"I used to love dancing. Guy was so light on his feet, he could even lead *me*," Marlene said. "I miss him, especially at parties when—"

"Well, I can't believe they played that horrid song at a wedding," Cora interrupted, then went on to attribute the unfortunate preference for filthy music to the groom and his family. The bride was blood.

Marlene swallowed the end of her sentence and allowed herself to think of her husband, dead just over two years in a car crash. Poor Guy. Never anything but a hard worker, he deserved to have a drink from time to time, though of course he shouldn't have been behind the wheel, especially in all that snow and ice. At least he hadn't hurt anyone else, just wrapped his Chevette around a tree and that was it. She ran a corner of her apron over her eyes and reminded herself it was best to concentrate on the good times, like Doc Norden said.

". . . and you'd think Earlie was born a Moody, not just married to one. Well, lie down with dogs and all that. I told her this morning, I says, 'Earlene, you're no kid and even if you were, you warn't ever rhythmic enough to get away with that.' "

"I don't expect she liked *that*, did she?"

"No sir, she did not. Got all huffy. Said if she wanted advice from me, she'd say so."

"She probably had a big head and wasn't in a mood to talk," Marlene offered.

"I guess she did, and Millhouse, too, if you want to know. I can't think what got into her. Our people might take a drink at parties, but those damn Moodys never saw a bottle they wouldn't crawl inside of, day or night. I swear Millhouse was three sheets to the wind before the ceremony even started. Of course that's what you get with an evening wedding—people looking for an excuse to get up to something."

"I imagine people're as likely to carry on in daytime as night. Mostly a question of whether anyone's looking." Marlene shifted on her stool to check the oven timer. Five more minutes.

"I guess everybody got an eyeful once Earlene and Millhouse started that, what do you call it, *Congo line*."

Cora had dragged her husband home shortly after the conga started, sick no doubt of witnessing behavior that would not only sully the Baines family name but also undermine her standing as a deaconess of the First Parish Congregational Church in the town their ancestors helped found. Marlene had always wondered at Cora's inordinate pride in their family's roots, since the truth was most of their relatives were still as dirt-poor as the first Baines had been upon arriving on the coast of Maine two centuries before.

"The bride was at the head of the line, and the groom's father was right behind her, so everyone was guilty there," Marlene said. "I love evening affairs, getting dressed up and mingling. Guy and I loved to go out at night."

"Just an excuse for drunken shenanigans if you ask me. Brings out the worst in people."

From the other end of the line, Marlene heard the scream of a tea-kettle and a thud as her sister's feet hit the floor and plodded across the kitchen to the stove. Though she was a slight woman, Cora had always walked on her heels; even in house slippers she sounded like a moose at half-trot.

"Oh, I don't know about that, Cora. I don't see much difference between drinking at home or out at a party. When Guy's sisters got married, the parties went all night long. Everybody'd start dancing and the supper'd be late, sometimes not till ten o'clock at night! It was an awful lot of fun."

"Lord almighty, those Frenchmen love a spectacle, don't they? They still do that foolish duck dance at weddings?" Cora asked, sounding distracted.

"It's not a spectacle when everyone's having fun, Cora, and the duck dance is just for the kids, you know. Anyway, what's the harm in a little foolishness from time to time?"

"I don't know, you'd have to ask Earlene. Seems to be her specialty these days. That's why we're having the Memorial Day cookout at lunchtime instead of later. My hypoglycemia's acting up, and I can't take that Moody tribe running amok in my house all night long. Hold on a second." Cora smacked the phone down. Marlene heard a cupboard door slam on the other end of the line.

My house. It always rankled. True enough, Cora had been the one to inherit the Baines family farm, but that was only because Mother had signed the entire package, house and land, over to Cora. They said it was so that the property wouldn't have to be sold to pay for a nursing home for Mother, but Margery Baines died at home, never even went to look at the rest home.

After Pop died, Mother had never discussed her will, but Marlene had expected at least to get part of the property. With all that ocean frontage, it was worth more than Marlene would ever see in one place. Earlie didn't seem to care, but then again, she didn't need the money. Cora kept promising to have her sisters' names added to the deed but somehow never got around to it. Last month, she'd gone ahead and sold a piece of land to their cousin Suzanne without even asking anyone's permission or offering to share the money. Actually she sold it to that New York lawyer Suzanne married. He probably paid a ridiculous price. It wasn't fair, but Marlene didn't like to keep bringing it up.

Marlene and Guy had talked about moving back home when Mother got the Parkinson's diagnosis, just ten months after Pop died, it was. They certainly could have used a year or two without rent, but Mother couldn't stand Marlene's Canuck husband, with his greasy mechanic's nails and slippery grip on English. And anyway, it would have been hard to be so far from town with three kids in school and Guy working two jobs.

Between her brood of jug-eared toad killers and that little niece of Millhouse's they'd taken in, Earlene had her hands full, too. No, Cora had been the best choice to see to Mother's care since she didn't have any children, except that one poor baby girl that died. Just stopped breathing for no good reason when she was barely two months old. Margery Rose they'd named her, for Mother. Marlene's throat constricted at the memory of the tiny casket being lowered through the snow into the frigid black ground all those years ago.

After the funeral, Cora never talked about her daughter again, except to say, just once, that there would be no more children. Poor Wayne, Marlene thought, slowly freezing to death in his wife's bed, tangled up with her in the sticky grief of their loss. It was no wonder he was so miserable. And poor Cora, you had to say, too, dragging that empty cold around ever since.

Cora came back on the line.

Marlene pulled her thoughts into the present and said, "Don't worry about Earlie's boys; she'll keep them on a short leash."

"After yesterday's performance, it's not Earlie's *boys* I'm worried about, it's her husband. Millhouse Moody's a drunken fool, and always has been."

Everyone knew Cora never liked Millhouse, and neither had Mother, who couldn't get over him coming from the lowest white-trash clan in town, even after he bought Chet Barker's Chevrolet dealership and started making money hand over fist. No, Millhouse never had a chance with his in-laws, what with being Catholic *and* a Moody.

Cora's husband, on the other hand, had walked on water as far as Mother was concerned. She always referred to Wayne as a "college man" and a "professional" even though he'd barely made it through junior college and never worked anywhere but his father's well-drilling company. Still, Marlene thought, she'd never met a man who smelled as good, and somehow he'd managed to stick with Cora all these years, which had to count for something.

"What time do you want me at the house?" Marlene asked, even though she could see the notation on her kitchen calendar. Three minutes left on the oven timer. A breeze blew in the open window and ruffled the kitchen curtains. Outside, the forsythia she and Norm planted twelve years before waved its yellow arms. The first sign of spring. The lilacs had begun to bud but wouldn't bloom for a couple of weeks yet. Then would come the lupines and the berries, the soft shells and the corn, and before you knew it, the foliage would flame and summer would die. No more long days, no smell of cut grass and rugosa, no tickety-tack of the lawn sprinklers, no more morning heat.

"Half-past eleven, just like I told you yesterday," Cora replied with more than a trace of irritation. "I'm making a pot of beans and potato salad and strawberry shortcake. Earlie's bringing hot dogs and hamburgs, and Mill's tending the grill. I only hope he stays sober enough not to burn the whole place down. Charlotte's going to make her special . . ."

Cora continued to run down the menu, but her recitation was lost in a cacophony of clanking glass.

"I can't hear a word you're saying with all that racket."

"I'm just looking for my bread-and-butter pickles. Wayne'll be hungry when he gets back from the club. I don't know how he works up such an appetite golfing, he rides around in a cart, for God's sake. I can't think where he might be—probably on the nineteenth hole. I called the club, but they couldn't find him." She expelled a wire-brush sigh. "Anyway, when he gets back I'll give him a ham salad sandwich and some pickles to hold him over till supper."

"I thought Wayne hated pickles."

"Now why on earth would you say that, Marlene? He's always loved my bread-and-butters."

"I must be confusing him with someone else. Must be Mill who doesn't like pickles."

"I imagine it probably is."

Marlene knew every croak and squeak that house made, and there was no way Cora was down cellar looking for canned goods. She'd have heard the old steps groan, and the cordless phone would be hissing by now. Instead, through the crystal-clear line, she heard a china mug hit the slate counter, followed by the crack of a bottle cap being twisted for the first time. She tried to recall how much had been left in the fifth of Canadian Mist hidden under Cora's sink when she'd checked it the week before. Marlene pictured her sister adding the first of several bumps to her tea that day.

"So, as I was about to say, if you'll bring the potato chips and dip and the soda, that should about do it. Oh, and if you'd return Mother's punch bowl like I asked, I'd appreciate it. You know, Marlene, I left you a message about this on your answerphone this morning when you didn't pick up. Where were you, anyway? I didn't see you in church."

"This morning? Oh. I went over to Bucksport to go to St. Bernadette's with Guy's sister. You remember Marie, the youngest? We had coffee at her house afterwards. She makes the most delicious banana cake you've ever—"

"You went to Mass? I don't know how you can keep track of all that up and down and answering back. More like an exercise class than a church service if you ask me. Anyway, isn't it a sin to go to the Catholic church if you're not Catholic?"

"I don't know, Cora, it's really all the same, isn't it? Forgive me, Father, for I've sinned, and here's a dollar for the collection plate. Listen, I've got to get along. I said I'd bring a rhubarb pie to the carnival at the high school—for the baseball team fundraiser, you know—and I haven't even rolled out the crust yet."

"Well, you'd best get to it. You always were a last-minute-Lucy, Marlene. Let me scoot. That's the call-waiting, probably Wayne on the other line."

"I doubt it," Marlene said to the cat on the clock after she hung up the phone. Standing in the overheated kitchen with her hand on the receiver, Marlene closed her eyes while the image of a teenage Wayne Houghton sitting in math class came together in her mind. He'd been too lazy to study or do his homework, so he had to repeat algebra, which was how they'd got to know each other in high school even though he was in the class above hers. Marlene was good at math. Sometimes she'd let him copy her answers when the teacher's back was turned. Of course she'd been silly to think he'd invite her to his junior prom—he always went around with older girls—but it had been just plain mean of Cora to ask him to go to the senior dance with her that year. That was Cora all over, never wanted anything until she thought someone else might like to have it.

Marlene's gaze shifted to the tidy blue bedroom she and Guy shared for almost fifteen years. Hanging on the closet door, shrouded once again in the dry cleaner's plastic, was the sea-green party dress that looked so pretty next to the auburn rinse in her hair. Below it, posed with the heels together and one of the toes pointing out like in the magazines, were the matching shoes that made her ankles look so slim. The soles were barely scuffed. At the reception last night, she'd taken a twirl with Millhouse, but no one else asked her to dance.

She ran her hand over her hair. Yesterday's French twist was still good, not too mussed at all. The oven timer pinged. The cat marked time. She turned away from the telephone, then opened the door of the yellow oven, pulled out the pie, and set it on the stove to cool next to Mother's old carrier basket.

"Last-minute-Lucy, my ass," she muttered as she stuffed the oven mitt back in the drawer and gave it a slam. Then she turned to face the silent phone and said in a louder voice, "And for your information, Coralene, Wayne hates your goddamned pickles. And so do I."

Marlene crossed the kitchen to the gray Formica dinette. She picked up the golfing glove she'd found on the floor at Bunker's Fairway Motel that morning and rubbed the soft leather between her thumb and forefinger, slipped it on her left hand along with the wedding band she'd found right next to it. Both were far too big; the ring jiggled on her finger. She lifted her palm to her face and covered her mouth and nose, breathing in the animal smell of cowhide and sweat mixed with cologne and cut grass. The tip of her tongue tasted salt. A tingle ran up her spine. She closed her eyes and swayed to the music in her head. *Marlene, Marlene, Marlene, Mar-LENE, I'm begging of you, please don't take my man* . . . Dolly Parton singing, just for her.

She pulled off the glove and dropped it in her handbag, considered holding on to the ring but instead put it in her change purse. If she hurried, she'd be able to drop them both at the country club on her way to the school, but first she needed a bath. She wanted to change her clothes and get the smell of Old Spice off her neck.

1992

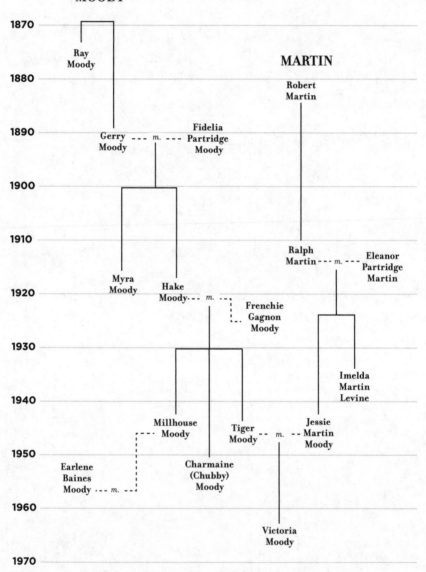

MOODY

1870

Ray
Moody

1880

MARTIN

Robert
Martin

1890

Gerry --- *m.* --- Fidelia
Moody   Partridge
               Moody

1900

1910

Ralph --- *m.* --- Eleanor
Martin   Partridge
                    Martin

Myra   Hake --- *m.*
Moody   Moody

1920

Frenchie
Gagnon
Moody

Imelda
Martin
Levine

1930

1940

Millhouse   Tiger   Jessie
Moody   Moody --- *m.* --- Martin
                                 Moody

Charmaine
(Chubby)
Moody

1950

Earlene
Baines
Moody --- *m.*

1960

Victoria
Moody

1970

PLANTING TIGER

Wake

"Jesus Christ, Merton, look at that. When Chubby walks, her ass looks just like two pigs fightin' in a feed bag."

This was the first thing Victoria Moody heard as she entered her father's wake, and she felt as if God Himself were using her great-uncle Bud's words to remind her why she'd left the town of Wellbridge the day after high school graduation and why, in the ten years since, she'd returned only for command performances like this one. Peering through the gloom of the funeral home, she spied the backside of her aunt Chubby. Victoria had to admit, it *had* expanded pretty spectacularly.

"Well, Vicky, fancy meeting you here," said Bud. He lurched in to give her a one-armed hug. "Been quite a while since we seen you, ain't it, Mert?"

"Ayuh, prob'ly four or five years." For Merton, this was a soliloquy.

"Um-hmm," Victoria replied. "Where's Frenchie?"

"With Millhouse. Right down front there," Bud said, indicating the row closest to the casket where Frenchie Moody rocked slowly, her elder son's arm around her narrow shoulders.

"Your grandmother's a pretty tough bird, but this is an awful hard thing," Bud said. She supposed it was.

At Victoria's approach, Frenchie looked up with ill-concealed surprise and patted an empty chair. Her left hand, nails lacquered as always in Rouge Red, clutched a mascara-smeared lace handkerchief.

"I'm sorry about this," Victoria lied. "Hello, Uncle Mill. How are you holding up, Frenchie?"

Victoria's fiancé had found it odd that she referred to her grandmother as Frenchie, and when he asked what their children would call their great-grandmother, Victoria had opted to fabricate a title rather than admitting that Frenchie was what everyone, including her children, called Magdalene Mere-Marie Gagnon Moody, just one of the many members of Victoria's family she had no intention of ever introducing to any children she might have, let alone her fiancé, Tino. Thank God she'd been able to convince him to stay behind in Portland, three hours away and safely removed from this horror show.

Frenchie blew her nose and in the Quebecois-colored English Victoria hadn't realized she missed said, "I'm okay me, but I don't know about Chubby. She just cry and cry for her brother. You go see your daddy now, Vicky. He look so peaceful. You go and say bye-bye to my Tiger."

There was nothing Victoria wanted less than to approach her father's corpse, but Frenchie had given her a little push out of her seat, and Millhouse nodded, so up she trudged. The casket was wide-open, surrounded by a shrine to Tiger's life: a lurid velvet painting of the Crucifixion she recognized from Frenchie's living room, several childhood photos of her grinning father (including one of him holding a BB gun in one hand and a dead rat by the tail in the other at what appeared to be the town dump), and a massive floral arrangement in the form of a pack of Camel unfiltered. Below lay a smirking Tiger Moody propped at exactly the same angle as when she'd last seen him alive.

Thirteen years before, on Mother's Day, Mill and Earlie had insisted she go with them to visit her grandmother in Moodyville, a dozen swampy, overgrown acres no one else in Wellbridge wanted and which the Moody family had been infesting for generations. Surrounding the brand-new double-wide trailer Mill had just bought Frenchie was a collection of shacks, car parts, campers (both abandoned and inhabited), rusted-out logging equipment, disused outhouses, active outhouses, toolsheds, road signs, gas pumps, dogs, cats, and raccoons, as well as any number of things Victoria would rather not have known or thought about. It was a crap plantation of the first order, like so many others throughout the state, but singular in both its expanse and its decrepitude.

Coming from the place was tough enough to swallow, but the icing on that stale cake of a day was arriving at Frenchie's to find Tiger stretched out on the plastic-covered sofa, watching the wrestling and downing a little hair of the dog. This was her last memory of her father, and it came roaring back at the sight of him in the coffin. Although his Cat Power cap was tatty, the navy cotton turtleneck and flannel shirt he wore looked brand new, and he was cleaner than she'd ever seen him. He looked better dead than alive.

As Victoria dropped to the kneeler, she noticed that someone had tucked a sixteen-ounce can of Colt 45 malt liquor and a battered copy of *Ass Pirate (Seize the backdoor booty!)* into the crook of his arm. "Animals," she said to no one but herself.

Forcing the disgust from her mind, Victoria called upon the Almighty as well as several saints to request leniency in the matter of Tiger Moody's salvation, undeserving though he certainly was. She also put in a personal request for the strength to get through the next twenty-four hours, blessed herself, and headed back down the aisle. She stopped to offer Frenchie an uncomfortable kiss and receive a hug from Uncle Millhouse, who told her where she might find her aunt Earlene.

Eyes downcast, hoping to make it to the next room without having to talk to anyone, Victoria picked her way through the clots of gossiping biddies, low-slung keg bellies, and skanky blondes who could only be Tiger's ex-wives or girlfriends. Though affecting blinders, she was not deaf, and when the familiar chocolate-covered bass came flowing over the hum of the crowd, it seemed to ooze down the back of her neck. She looked up. Over in the corner, talking to his father and standing a full head taller than most of the guests, Dougie Lemay was staring at her. She'd wondered whether he'd be here and half hoped he'd gotten fat or lost some teeth since high school. No luck. When their eyes met, he waved and sent Victoria a Pepsodent smile that raised a low purr in the back of her throat. Dougie's face hadn't changed one bit since the last time she saw it, hovering above her in the bed of his pickup on prom night. She balled her hands into fists to stop them twitching, nodded, and kept moving.

As promised, Uncle Mill's wife, Earlene, was in the side lounge, chatting with her relatives.

"Well howdy, stranger," Earlene said as she folded her niece in a firm embrace. Victoria inhaled her aunt's familiar scent—Jean Naté toilet water mixed with Niagara spray starch. Growing up, Earlene had been the calm center of Victoria's world. Now, each breath filled her with the familiar push-pull of connection and estrangement, the need to burrow and the urge to flee. She exhaled, let go, and stepped back.

Earlene said, "Mill told me you were right out straight with wedding plans and work, but I made up your bed fresh just in case. It's awful about Tiger, of course, but we're always glad to have you home."

Earlene and Mill were among the few members of the family for whom a hug was more natural than a slap, and once again Victoria was overcome with gratitude to them for taking her in and raising her as their own after Tiger went to prison all those years ago. One glance at the crew in the other room reminded her what her life would have become without them.

Victoria made small talk with Earlene's sisters and their husbands: Marlene's new one, who seemed nice enough, and Coralene's husband, Wayne, doused in cologne and sporting his usual vacant smile. The men were the only ones in the building, besides the undertakers, wearing coats and ties. She filled them in on her life down in Portland (very busy) and the plans for her wedding to Tino (very small). If any of them were perturbed at not being invited, they didn't show it.

The Three Lenes. Since she was little, Victoria had thought of the Baines sisters that way. The oldest, Coralene, was too hard, frosty and short as the month of February. Marlene, the youngest, was too soft with her whispery lisp, pink lipstick, and pudgy ankles. Earlene, though, was just right—a handsome woman who was both serious-minded and warmhearted. With three boys of her own, she'd made room for Victoria, given her purpose, pride, and even love. It hadn't erased the burden of having her father in jail for trying to murder her mother, but it had gone a long way toward lightening the load.

Millhouse

Next morning, the first thing Millhouse Moody noticed as he pulled into the parking lot of the Church of Saint Paul the Bleeding Apostle, locally known as Bloody Paul, was his niece on the church steps talking to a tall young fellow in a dress coat and a lumpy scarf, the two of them forming an awkward bas-relief against the church's pocked granite face. The lancet windows on either side of the portal had been boarded up for as long as Mill could remember, and the building's only ornamentation, a soot-covered rose window high above the entry, gave the facade a distinctly cyclopean appearance, a single cataract-clouded eye to watch over God's chosen. Below it, Victoria was gesturing and shifting from side to side like a welterweight, which was a dead giveaway she was het up.

Vicky was certainly a fighter, Millhouse mused, though not always an effective one. She had an unfortunate tendency to lead with her chin and seemed to remember to cover up only after she was down. It occurred to Mill that she'd inherited both tendencies from her father, and at the memory of Tiger, he let out a small sound, somewhere between a sigh and a moan.

"Who that boy there, talking to Vicky? She not happy, her," Frenchie observed from the passenger seat, squinting at her granddaughter through a cloud of cigarette smoke. "*Calvaire*, she look just like my Tiger when she does that, swaying in da breeze. You think maybe she gonna hit him?"

"I expect that's her intended. With that blond hair, he don't really look Italian, but I can't imagine who else it'd be."

"Last night, Vicky tell me he can't come. Too busy at the shop. Look like maybe he get off the day, eh? She think we don't know she is shamed of her father, but I tell her Tiger never want to kill her *maman*. An accident. So what?"

"Well, I don't suppose she wants us gawking at her, and I need to have a word with Father Barbizon to give him some, er, notes. For the eulogy."

Millhouse stepped out of the big sedan and ambled around the front, picking his way across the frozen puddles and crunchy slush. He swung the passenger door open and offered Frenchie his forearm. As she took it, he noticed the flesh had melted away from the backs of her hands, revealing a spiderweb of bones and a lacy tangle of veins where the ashy, mottled skin had collapsed around them.

They arrived inside the church just after Mahlon Thibodeaux, who waved and then continued fussing with the stand for his electronic keyboard in an alcove next to the altar. The full pipe organ would have cost a fortune.

In the nave, the too-clean smell of lemon Pledge nearly overpowered the last traces of incense from the evening Mass, and poor Jesus, battered all to hell with a fat blood tear frozen below his left eye, drooped on his crucifix, looking, Millhouse always thought, like he wished it would all just fucking end.

After settling his mother in a pew next to Chubby, Mill went in search of the priest. As he navigated the hallways and passages he remembered from his brief career as an altar boy, he thought about his niece. Frenchie was right. It was plain Vicky's family embarrassed her, except for himself and Earlene, or so he assumed, but with a father who'd done time for attempted murder and a crazy old whore for a mother, she was certainly entitled. Still, it worried him that she'd hidden things from the boy. If he were worth his salt, he wouldn't care, but there was no telling Vicky that. Of course, the fact that he'd shown up for the funeral might be a good sign, provided it indicated backbone and not a bonehead.

Millhouse followed the lemon-mildew scent downstairs to Father Barbizon's basement office. He knocked softly at the open door to announce his presence.

In his priestly underclothes of black slacks, shirt, and collar, Norman Barbizon looked like a child's drawing: an egg-shaped middle with stick arms and legs, topped by a large square head.

"Good morning, Father," Millhouse said, hovering in the doorway, trying to seem aggrieved and ingratiating at the same time.

"Come in, please, Millhouse. How's your mother?"

"Well, you know she's seen a bit of life, but I don't suppose anything prepares you for something like this. Tiger was her baby, you know." Millhouse had to exert some effort not to tear up. He'd never had any illusions about his brother, but he'd never wished him dead either, and it was all so hard on his mother and sister.

"Well, it does seem unnatural for parents to bury their children, I know, but God's plan is mysterious and not for us to understand, just to believe."

Millhouse was seized with more than a passing urge to knock the smug expression off the priest's big face, but it was important to Frenchie that Tiger be buried in the church, so he nodded, unclenched his fists, and forced what he hoped was a beatific smile. It felt more like a grimace.

"I've got notes for Tiger's eulogy here. I don't know whether anyone else will want to speak, but I'd like to say a few words at some point after you finish. I think Fren . . . ah, my mother, spoke to you about hymns."

"Yes. That's all very helpful. Thank you, Millhouse."

"One last thing, Father. This morning Earlene reminded me we'd been holding on to a donation to the building fund and thought maybe I could just give it to you. That be all right?"

"Of course. How very generous of you both. We so appreciate all you and Earlene do for the parish. Thank you," he said, pocketing the envelope containing a backdated check and a stack of twenties without opening it.

"Happy to help, Father. I'll leave you to your preparations. Oh, by the way, how's that LeSabre working out?" He'd sold the car below cost to the priest, who'd never met an option he didn't covet.

"Quite comfortable for a used car. So nice of you to provide the tape player. Mother loves her Wayne Newton."

"Well, good then." And you're welcome, he thought.

As Millhouse walked through the doorway, he resisted the urge to look back over his shoulder. He didn't need to. Reflected in the glass that covered a painting of Saint Francis, he saw Father Barbizon had pulled the envelope from his pocket and opened it. He was just beginning to thumb through the cash when Millhouse turned the corner.

Tino

He had never been to Wellbridge and had no idea where Victoria's uncle lived, so Tino went straight to the church and waited. As his mother had pointed out, Victoria was bound to show up there eventually. Of course Mamma had been right to insist that he drive up to support his future wife. "Husbands and wives should share everything and have no secrets, son."

Tino had objected to the insinuation that his fiancée was less than transparent. After all, hadn't she just been thinking of his poor father and all the work he'd have to do while they were in Rome for two weeks on their honeymoon? Mamma had to admit that, yes, that was very considerate of Victoria, and of course, Big Tino's health was always on everyone's mind these days, but still a seed of doubt had been planted, and it quickly sprouted into the decision to attend the service despite having told Victoria he would not.

At the garage door, Mrs. Benedetti handed her son a paper bag and a red-plaid thermos, saying, "Make sure to stop at least once to stretch your legs. It should take about three hours to get up there, but you've got plenty of time, so don't speed. I packed a doughnut to go with your coffee and a banana in case your bowels act up. You'll call me after the service, won't you?"

Tino promised to proceed with caution, then waited while his mother scurried back inside the family split-level to get a scarf to go over his topcoat and keep him from freezing to death in the almost certain event of a mechanical breakdown on the highway. He was thinking of Victoria and counting down: three hours to Wellbridge, seventeen days until the ceremony, another eight hours to the wedding night. When his mother returned, he was holding the thermos in front of his fly.

The Happy Couple

Victoria had approached the church at the appointed hour, her over-night bag and camel hair coat (the one Tino had given her last Christ-mas that was a twin to his mother's) thrown on the back seat. The bag was half-zipped, with the arm of her sweater hanging out. It looked like a corpse rolled up in a rug. At the sight of Tino standing out front, she blasted past the church and pulled behind the dumpster of Red Craven's gas station. She weighed her options, fight or flee; there was no choice but to return to Bloody Paul's.

Talking with Tino only made things worse.

"I told you, Victoria, I was worried about you. A good husband is there in time of need," he recited between bites of banana.

These were his mother's words, she knew, and now she'd have to take him to the funeral. Her only hope was to keep Tino outside for as long as possible before the service, then figure out how to get him away fast. She might have to cry, which she almost never did, but by the time they got to the top of the stairs, she was struggling for control.

Once inside the church, Victoria leaned heavily on Tino, steering him toward the oversize pillar she and her cousins always sat behind during Mass because it was the safest spot to nap or read comic books. She gave a low moan and collapsed onto the pew just behind it. Tino followed, and just like that, she'd gotten them settled into the seats with the worst sight lines in the church.

With the vibrato on his Casio cranked up so high the first three pews were quivering, Mahlon was working his way through "What a Friend We Have in Jesus." It sounded vaguely like his version of "Tie a Yellow Ribbon Round the Ole Oak Tree," which he'd played at every wedding reception or anniversary party Victoria had ever attended. She slid low on the pew and scrubbed her face with her palms.

"I knew you were more upset than you let on," Tino said with an approving look. It was disconcerting how much her apparent weakness pleased him, but she decided to worry about that later and gave him the pathetic simper she knew he was looking for, then began roughly kneading his hand for good measure. When he smiled down at her, she took a loud, shuddering breath and buried her face in his shoulder, so that it was nearly impossible for him to turn his head toward anything but the empty aisle to his right. All she had to do was keep him occupied until the Mass began, and she'd be home free.

The hymn closed in an agonized crescendo, but instead of silence, a murmur rippled through the crowd. "Who's that?" Tino whispered. He'd extricated himself from Victoria's grip and twisted around to look past her to the center aisle. With her head now detached from Tino's shoulder, Victoria was able to see.

"No idea," she lied.

Jessie

Jessie Angelique Martin Moody made sure she was the last mourner to enter the church, just before the priest, the pallbearers, and her ex-husband's corpse. She was pleased that most of the congregation witnessed her arrival and that with each step down the center aisle, the buzz grew. She made no effort to hide her limp; rather, she exaggerated it. Hitting her mark at the first empty row of pews she came to, she genuflected lazily, flicked an errant strand of feathered hair off her shoulder, and took a seat ten rows behind the family of the deceased.

She wondered where Victoria was but didn't want to give anyone the satisfaction of seeming interested in the proceedings. She didn't need to check the room to confirm that she was the only funeral-goer in thigh-high boots, a red miniskirt, and a fur jacket.

With nearly everyone in the church giving her the stink eye, it was hard to maintain her invisible safety wall, so Jessie stared at the biggest floral arrangement on the altar and began counting the blossoms. Forty-eight cheesy white carnations, and instead of the regular organist, there was Mahlon Thibodeaux playing his little electric piano. Sounded more like a roller rink than a church, but Tiger's family had always been cheap.

To give her audience something to think about, Jessie made a show of reaching down into the gold disco bag she'd dropped on the kneeler. The only person who saw what she pulled out was old Amos Toothaker, sitting across the aisle and trying to pretend he wasn't watching her.

She palmed the dirty white rabbit's foot, a real one with a single toenail that she'd rubbed shiny over the years, directing her right thumb to the sueded spot where the fur had been worn away, and began tracing the familiar, soothing circles.

"I always said I'd outlive that rat-bastard and wear a red dress to his funeral and spit on his grave," Jessie had told the girls at the Club La Parisienne up in Bangor the night before. Besides a series of black eyes, a persistent case of the clap, and baby Victoria, the rabbit's foot was the only thing Tiger had ever given her in the six years they were together. He'd taken plenty, though: her dreams, every penny she'd saved, and finally two toes from her left foot when he'd gotten drunk, accused her of cheating on him, and tried to run her down with his Ski-Doo. Three years in the state prison hadn't been near enough time, Jessie thought, but in the end there had been more than enough poetic justice to go around. She imagined it was painful to bleed out from the neck like he did. Not bothering to suppress a smile, she slipped the rabbit's foot into her jacket pocket so she'd have it to hand when the time came to bury it with Tiger.

Procession

After her mother's sensational arrival, it took a good few minutes for Victoria to get her breathing under control and pull a plan together. Tino, she remembered halfway through the service, loved a parade, and she realized it would probably be impossible to avoid attending the burial, since it involved being part of an official procession. Throughout the Mass she continued to produce little hiccuping sounds between raggedy, grief-stricken breaths, then afterward told him she needed a minute to collect herself and stayed put in her seat until Jessie was out of the church. As Aunt Earlene passed their pew, she paused to give Victoria a questioning look but continued out the door without speaking.

Figuring that driving would keep Tino occupied, Victoria handed him her keys and crumpled into the passenger seat of her car. She delayed their departure by refusing to put on her seat belt while she rummaged for nonexistent objects in her purse. Among the last to emerge from the church were Dougie Lemay and his father, Spike, who was Tiger's best friend and the only person with him when he died. Victoria scratched an imaginary itch on her scalp and pushed her hair forward to curtain her face as they passed.

Victoria's Corolla crunched across the gravel lot and caboosed the motley train of funeral home vehicles, rusted-out trucks, and ancient sedans held together with Bondo and bumper stickers, including, but not limited to, DOES THIS CAR MAKE MY ASS LOOK FAT? and GUN CONTROL MEANS USING BOTH HANDS.

They drove down Main Street and headed north toward the Catholic cemetery, just over the town line. Once clear of the inhabited part of Wellbridge, the land rolled open and clear down to the reach and the bay beyond. The ground was snow covered, but Victoria remembered it in summer, green with black patches where the blueberry scrub had been burned and dotted with improbable granite boulders abandoned thousands of years before by retreating glaciers. They'd always struck her as looking forlorn, the great rocks, like they were waiting for something, anything, to come along and pick them back up, or at least point them out of town.

The inland side of the road was lined with forest, thickets of needles and leaves, trees and brush, ever advancing, always encroaching, threatening to swallow up the road. Victoria had grown up surrounded by woods, always hated them, couldn't even stand being near them, with their spike-sharp, lichen-scraggle branches, pinching earwigs, snakes, and skunks. As a child, she'd played only in the backyard, well away from the branches' bite and the gloom and the silence. You never knew what lurked in the trees, and you were better off not finding out.

As Tino drove, Victoria finessed her extraction plan.

"How're you doing there, Vic?" Tino asked.

"I just want to get back home," she said, and stared vacantly ahead for effect.

"Okay, we'll get there in time for dinner. Mamma's making meatballs," Tino said as he parked on the side of the cemetery access road. Most of the gravestones were shiny and new and took the form of squat, polished slabs inscribed with life stories told in five words or less, but there was also a smattering of life-size granite archangels and kindly saints to relieve the monotony.

"Meatballs. That's nice," Victoria murmured, having no intention of seeing anybody after this insanity. A hot shower followed by a large glass of Blue Nun would help her put Tiger Moody, this day, and this place behind her once and for all.

Graveside

From her parking place across the cemetery, Jessie watched the burial service attended by a random group of Moodys, friends of Moodys, and Baineses who couldn't avoid coming, but she was too far away to hear anything. What was the point of praying? she wondered. If Tiger was going anywhere other than the cold, black ground, it would be someplace considerably hotter than Maine in February and they all knew it, except maybe Frenchie, but she was his mother and so, Jessie supposed, allowed a little self-delusion.

The graveside service dragged on, but what interested Jessie was her daughter. Vicky was standing to one side of the coffin, looking like she might take off running. Tiger had done the same thing on their wedding day. Somehow he'd made it through "I do," but it was only because her father was standing right behind him with her brother at his side and a Louisville Slugger on the front seat of the family pickup in the parking lot. She was seven months pregnant at the time and foolish enough to think it would all work out once the ring was on her finger. Everyone was stupid at seventeen, she supposed. Automatically, her hand went to her pocket to confirm that the rabbit's foot was still there.

Vicky was twenty-eight now. How could that be? And who was that big blond guy with her? Her boyfriend, maybe even her husband? Jessie hoped not. From behind the bar at the club, she'd seen more of his type than she could count—probably still a virgin, out for a dirty thrill, drunk by the second beer, and giggling at the first pair of tits. Not that she'd ever been any great judge of masculine character—three husbands and three divorces, one uglier than the other. At least Tiger was finally gone. She had no idea where the other two were, probably in jail. Maybe they were dead, too.

"Dare to dream," she muttered.

Vicky looked good, and as Jessie watched her, she remembered the little strawberry-blond child with the iron will and the shrewd green-eyed gaze. She'd almost never regretted letting her go, even though she knew she should. Clearly Vicky had been better off with Earlie and Mill, and the truth was, after five years of motherhood Jessie had had enough and was relieved to be done with it. She'd missed her daughter and thought of her often, but the visits dwindled over time. Not once had she felt even the slightest urge for another baby.

Beneath the darkening clouds, the mourners bowed their heads and appeared to speak in unison one final time. *Peace be with you.*

"Good luck with that," Jessie said. She watched the funeral-goers hurry away from the burial site and back to their cars. Spike Lemay's boy Dougie—how did weedy little Spike ever produce such a good-looking kid?—lagged behind, his eyes locked on Vicky. That was interesting.

Vicky and her blond friend stood in an awkward knot with Earlene, Frenchie, and Millhouse, then Vicky hugged her aunt and grandmother, patted Mill's shoulder, and took off, her startled-looking funeral date trotting behind. "That's right, sweetie, run away, fast as you can," Jessie whispered.

After the casket had been lowered and the morticians had removed both the hydraulics and themselves from the cemetery, Jessie climbed out of her car into the dingy, low-sky afternoon. The clouds were spitting snow in sparse, hard flakes that bounced off the matted tufts of brown grass and frozen mud. Her fishnets provided no protection from the cold sweeping up her thighs as she hurried over to the plot where Winston Fellowes, the town gravedigger, held his shovel.

"Hey there, Win," she said, startling him so that he gave a little squeak.

"By gorry, I thought I was all alone here, 'cept for Tiger. How you been, Jessie?"

He spoke as if they'd just run into each other in the cereal aisle of the IGA. Even though they'd been in the same class in high school, they'd never been friendly, and Jessie was surprised he remembered her after all these years, especially since she'd dropped out so early. Except for being a few teeth short of a full set, Winston hadn't changed much since his teens.

"I'm good, thanks. Just wanted to say goodbye to Tiger if that's okay."

"I s'pose so."

He nodded, started to turn, but stopped and said, "You know, I was just thinkin' about this one time in junior high, Spencer Trout was about to give me a swirly in the boys' bathroom. Usually beat me up after he did that. Tiger come in right when my head was about to hit the water. Grabbed Spencer by the scruff and laid him out, one punch, just like that. Never said a word about it."

After shouldering his shovel, Win said, "I'll just give you a minute, then." And with a grace that both surprised and touched Jessie, he gave a little bow and moved soundlessly away.

Tiger

I'm glad they picked burying instead of burning. Hopefully it's a sign of where I'm going—up rather than down. I'm glad Jessie showed up, too, even if she does still hate me. Which reminds me: I never meant to hit her with that snowmobile, let alone kill her. I was just trying to get her attention, but she was drunk and she stepped right out in front of me in the pitch dark, so whose fault was that? Didn't seem to matter much to the jury, or that bastard judge. Attempted murder, history of domestic violence, danger to the community, bull*shit*. Anyone who lived with Jessie for more than five minutes would've hit her eventually.

By the time I got out of jail, my daughter was settled with Mill and Earlene, and Jessie was gone, already married to some guy up to Bangor. What else could I do except start over? It wasn't like Vicky ever missed me. I know she missed her mother, though. Mill said she cried herself to sleep most nights for the first year she was with them.

Since I didn't seem to be going much of anywhere, up or down, after the service, I followed the procession to the cemetery. It was nice to be near Jessie, just for old times' sake. Forty-five years old and that woman still has an ass you could bounce a quarter off, but that wasn't why I went. It wasn't the only reason, anyway. Tell the truth, I wanted to see whether she'd actually throw that rabbit's foot away.

Meltdown

As she pulled up in front of Mill and Earlie's sprawling green colonial, Jessie was surprised to see her daughter in the driveway with the blond guy. They were standing between two cars, arguing by the look of it, and Vicky seemed to be trying to keep him from going into the house. Jessie parked her Caprice across the street and got out.

At the sight of her mother, the look on Vicky's face was unmistakable—horror followed closely by panic. Jessie wasn't surprised, but it still stung. Vicky grabbed the big guy by the coat sleeve and tried to yank him toward the Toyota parked at the foot of the drive, but he stood rooted to the spot.

"Vicky?" Jessie called as she limped up the driveway.

Victoria Moody froze.

"Victoria?" Now it was Tino speaking. The three of them stood staring at each other until Tino extended his hand.

"Tino Benedetti. I'm Victoria's fiancé."

"Oh, ah, hi. I'm Jessie—Vicky's mother. Pleased to meet you, Tito," Jessie said, wondering what kind of parents named their kid after a member of the Jackson 5, and not even the famous one.

The young man's mouth dropped open. "Sorry, no, not Tito, *Tino.* Short for Valentino." He was looking back and forth between Victoria and her mother, like they were playing tennis. Valentino, Jessie thought, good Christ, that's even worse.

Now Victoria was trying to pull him toward the house, but still Tino would not be moved. Fixing his gaze on Victoria, he said, "You said you didn't know her. You told me your mother was *dead.*"

"She's dead to me."

As if she'd been slapped, Jessie took a step back and put her hand in her pocket. The words came in a rush.

"I just wanted to give you this. It was Tiger's and I thought maybe you'd like to have something from him. He won it throwing balloon darts at the Blue Hill Fair, I don't know, before we was married and anyways he give it to me when you were born. For good luck . . ."

"Good luck? Are you kidding me? *Good luck?* Listen, my luck started the day *you gave me away.* Remember?"

"It was just supposed to be till I found a job. By the time I got set up you were so happy here, and then you were all grown up and . . . I don't know . . . then you were gone."

"I was not *gone.* I was right here. For fourteen years. You hardly ever visited me, not even on my birthday, or at Christmas."

"I didn't want to upset you, make it worse," Jessie lied. "I always sent presents. Didn't you get them?"

"Big deal, Twizzlers and Barbies. Somebody find me an application for Mother of the Year." Jessie took another step back.

"Oh Victoria, don't say that," Tino said.

"Why not, Tino? It's the truth."

The screen door slammed. Earlene Moody hustled from the house, her feet sloshing around in Millhouse's boots, a dish towel slung over her shoulder.

"Jessie."

"I'm not here for trouble, Earlene."

"No you are not."

Jessie could see that the conversation was over, so she pressed the rabbit's foot into Tino's hand, then retreated down the driveway to her car and pulled away. There was no point looking back.

Truth Time

It was hard to pinpoint the exact moment the situation spun completely out of control, Victoria mused later while waiting for Earlene to post her bail. Certainly things took a turn for the worse when her mother showed up at the house. After that, she had no choice but to take Tino inside for the funeral reception.

Hanging on to the last shred of her composure, she'd pushed past Dougie Lemay, to her old bedroom, and locked the door. Tino followed but eventually gave up trying to coax her into opening it and went downstairs, which was when, she supposed, he must have learned that her father had done a stretch in Thomaston for attempted murder by snowmobile.

Victoria finally pulled herself together and wandered back down to the party. She stopped outside the living room, around the corner from where Spike Lemay, with Dougie by his side, was telling Tino the story of Tiger's demise.

"We was up to the Olde Towne Triple X video store in Bangor—I got *Coed Spank Fest* and something else, I forget the title. They let you preview everything, and Tiger brung his flask, so we was there till the well run dry, as it were. Anyways, Tiger was waitin' to pay, and by Jesus, when he saw that meter maid writing him a ticket, he went after her like a raped ape. Poor bastard missed the door and went right through the front window, and that was it. Carotid artery. Bled out in about two minutes. Made a fuckin' mess, lemme tell ya. But at least he spent his last hours doing what he loved."

"Oh my God, Victoria said it was a . . . a . . . heart attack," Tino stammered.

At that point Uncle Bud must have wandered up to the group. Victoria listened in dread as he called Spike a filthy name, introduced himself and his silent shadow, Uncle Mert, and asked Tino how he and Victoria got together.

"We met at church, well, not at Mass. It was an Ave Maria Singles mixer," Tino explained. Victoria braced herself.

"That so? And what do you do at those, the St. Vitus dance?" Bud crowed as the men dissolved in helpless, shit-faced laughter.

Victoria slid past caring. With all the lies she'd told and the repulsive sideshow her family was putting on, she knew she would never become Mrs. Tino Benedetti, never be part of a normal family, never get shed of her trashy name and shameful past. She rounded the corner intending to have done with it; apparently, however, Tino had mellowed after a couple of whiskey sours, because he was giggling along with everyone else.

"Excuse us," she said as she grabbed Tino's arm and pulled him past Dougie into the kitchen, where she took off the engagement ring and held it out. Tino refused. Apparently he'd bonded with Millhouse and even accepted some fatherly advice.

"He told me no family's perfect, and that you must really love me to be so afraid of losing me, and some other stuff, I forget. Did you know he can get me a limited-edition Corvette Grand Sport at cost? Not that it matters. Anyway, Victoria, I love you and I want to get married, so just promise you'll never lie to me again and we'll start over in the morning. I'll call Mamma and tell her not to wait up."

And so for a couple of brief, hopeful hours, it looked like things might just work out for Victoria Moody. Until about three drinks later, when Tino showed Chubby the rabbit's foot.

Earlene

I knew we were in for it when Jessie Martin showed up at Tiger's funeral. It had been at least ten years since I laid eyes on her, but I could see she was still rougher than the back of a ditch. I can't say I was shocked when she walked into the church, but I never expected to see her at my house. When Jessie came limping up the driveway, with her go-go boots and that mop of red hair, and introduced herself to Tino, the look on his face was priceless. I was watching through the kitchen window. Mill told me not to interfere and I didn't, not until Vicky started hollering. She's half Moody after all, and I never met one who didn't like a good fight once in a while.

After I put away the liquor, the funeral crowd disappeared pretty quick. I should've figured something was up when Frenchie asked me for a blanket right before she left. I never saw Mill's sister Chubby go to the toolshed, but I guess that's where she got the pickaxe and the shovel.

We got the call from the gravedigger about five minutes after we turned out the lights. He tried to run the Moodys off the cemetery grounds but gave up after they threatened him with the garden tools. He told us he'd have to call the sheriff because digging up the dead was illegal even if they didn't plan to snatch the body, plus there was no drinking allowed on the premises, or bonfires either, but he figured Millhouse might want to get his mother out of there. I gather she intended to swaddle Tiger against the cold, and Chubby wanted to put a rabbit's foot in his casket. Later, when I asked her why, she said, "Without some goddamned luck, how the hell is he ever going to get to Jesus?" She had a point. What the others intended, beyond boozing and blazing, I still don't know.

The only people in the house sober enough to drive were Vicky and me, but I'd had about as much Moody foolishness as I could stand for one day. It was probably a mistake to let Tino go with Mill and Vicky, but he insisted and I think Vicky wanted to keep an eye on him. He was pretty tight, but he was wide-awake, one of those energetic drunks, and he kept repeating some nonsense about a chubby bunny.

I love Victoria Moody like my own, always have. Three pregnancies I prayed for a girl, and three times God sent me a big wild boy. Vicky was His consolation prize to me, I never doubted it. But I still let her spend that night in the lockup, along with Millhouse and all the rest. After Sheriff Largay arrested everyone but Frenchie—he had his deputy drive her back home owing to her age and bereavement—he called to let me know they'd been taken in. I told him a night in the clink wouldn't hurt any of them one bit after the stunt they pulled, and he agreed. I believe parents these days call it "a teaching moment."

I bailed out my jailbirds the next morning, right after I picked up Tino from the hospital. He didn't remember much about the night before, but he did recall seeing Vicky tussle with the sheriff, who was trying to break up the fight between himself and Chubby. He had no idea why getting that rabbit's foot back was so important to him or even how he got the concussion.

I wouldn't say Vicky is happy being back in Wellbridge, but after her conviction for assaulting an officer, she lost her job down in Portland, and needless to say, the wedding was canceled. She heard Tino took the trip to Rome with his mother.

Between appointments with her probation officer and working at the dealership, Vicky keeps quite busy. Millhouse says she's a whiz with the computer. She set up a slick bookkeeping system for him and is almost done sorting through the paperwork for his tax audit. It's good to have her home. I just wish she'd spend a little more time at church and less with Spike Lemay's boy. That Dougie has never been anything but trouble.

1999

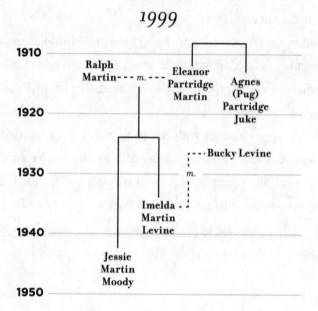

1910

Ralph
Martin - - - *m.* - - - Eleanor
Partridge   Agnes
Martin   (Pug)
                Partridge
1920   Juke

- - - Bucky Levine

1930   *m.*

Imelda -
Martin
Levine
1940

Jessie
Martin
Moody
1950

STRIPTEASE

Imelda Levine was three years old the first time they put her in a strait-jacket. It wasn't because she was crazy; that didn't happen until much later. No, her initial experience with restraints was the result of eating an entire bottle of orange-flavored baby aspirin for breakfast one sleety February morning in 1940. The tablets tasted like candy.

Medication was on Imelda's mind as she crossed the Walmart parking lot with her brand-new prescription. She was remembering how her mother always said she had been saved from the overdose that day not so much by the hospital staff as by her aunt Agnes Juke, whom the family had always called Pug on account of her flat nose and bony calves. It was Pug who rushed Imelda to the doctor while Mumma continued to try (unsuccessfully) to bring up the contents of the child's otherwise empty stomach by ramming her nicotine-stained fingers down Imelda's throat.

What with all the speeding and ramming and screaming, by the time they got little Imelda on the examining table she was too hysterical to thread the stomach pump hose down her throat. Hence the straitjacket. Imelda couldn't recall the event, but Pug had told her the story often enough that the memory had created itself in her imagination, and since then she had occasionally watched it, movie-like, in her mind's eye, which was what she was doing as she approached her car.

Imelda slid into the driver's seat and grunted with the effort of closing the heavy door, then grabbed the family-size bag of Cheez Doodles she'd just bought and shoved it between her stomach and the steering wheel. After undoing the top button on her blouse, she poured out half of her Dunkin' Donuts sweet tea, topped it up with the vodka she kept in the glove compartment, and gave the go-cup a festive swirl before taking a long pull through the straw. "Now that's tea worth drinking," she said to herself as she slipped the cup into the plastic holder that was wedged into the window channel of the driver's-side door.

In 1970, when her butter-yellow convertible DeVille came off the assembly line, it featured an eight-track tape deck, stereophonic sound, white leather seats, power everything, and enough horses to launch a moon shot, but no place to put a drink, which was, in Imelda's opinion, the car's only flaw. She'd taken the Caddie off Edwin Brass after his third DUI, trading him a set of dragoon-size pepperbox revolvers and a bird's-eye maple breakfront of questionable provenance. She missed haggling in her little antiques shop but lacked the stamina to keep it open anymore.

If there was one thing Imelda had always enjoyed, it was the freedom that came with dropping the top on her Caddie and sipping a cocktail while taking a drive on an Indian summer day like this, one that almost made her believe the beautiful lie about how the cruel winter might never come. Might never turn the red and yellow leaves the color of dried blood, then pull them from the trees, leaving them black and slick as they decomposed, like rotting corpses littering the ground below.

Imelda pushed the thought of winter from her mind. What was the point? With the drink safely stowed, she tore open the cellophane and put her hand into the bag. She hadn't had a cheese puff in years. The neon shards raked the roof of her mouth, leaving her palate throbbing and her teeth gummed with a ticky-tacky residue. It was gratifyingly unpleasant. After a couple of handfuls she'd had enough, so she scrunched the bag down and dropped it on the seat. She shook out a yellow pill from the new bottle, chased it with the tea, punched the cigarette lighter, and extracted a Newport menthol ultra light from one of the half-empty boxes on the dash.

Imelda rolled the smoke around in her mouth before pulling it down into her lungs; somehow the nicotine itch was scratched with the first puff, a small miracle. Tilting her head back, she exhaled, releasing the smoke into the open sky. While she waited for the warm wave of nothingness, she took another drag and closed her eyes.

That morning Imelda had been to see Doc Norden for a follow-up visit and prescription refill. Three months before, she'd gone in for a checkup, primarily to put a cork in her husband's nagging but also because she was hoping to get something for the pain in her back and shoulders, figuring it was probably arthritis, at worst a slipped disk. The examination included blood work, which led to tests, which led to biopsies, which indicated surgery was needed to remove a malignant lump in her right breast. But up at the big hospital in Bangor they hadn't cut out anything; instead, they'd had one look inside her chest and sewn her right back up. After suggesting her family "make arrangements," they'd released Imelda with a prescription for Vicodin and the promise of an eventual morphine upgrade. Since then, however, no arrangements had been made, because no one in the Levine family seemed to know how to discuss the situation.

Imelda had at first been angry at the news, but the pills took the edge off, and lately she'd lapsed into a mellower state of regret. Mostly she was sorry she'd missed out on smoking for the past twenty years when, apparently, her health had been shot to shit for some little time. She also regretted not taking the opportunity for a fling with Ellis Titcomb when he came home to bury his father back in '82. And she was disappointed that she would probably not see the dawn of the year 2000 in a few months, when she'd been looking forward to the sparkling new beginning it promised since she first learned to add and subtract and figured out that in 2000 she'd turn sixty-three. At the time, sixty-three seemed impossibly old; now it was just impossible. Imelda sighed and picked up her tea.

"You gonna add a hot-fudge sundae to that wonderful lunch or just keep drinking it?" The voice, soothing as tinfoil between the teeth, was unmistakable, and it snapped her out of her reverie.

"The hell're you doing here, Pug?" Imelda asked her aunt, who'd slipped noiselessly into the passenger seat and was rolling her feet around on top of the empty vodka bottles.

"Same's you, I expect. Sniffing around town, indulging in a touch of self-abuse."

"You can't abuse the dead," Imelda said, and stubbed out her Newport.

"You're not dead yet, are ya?"

"You tell me." When Imelda cocked her head to one side, she felt the fluids around her brain shift. The drugs were starting to kick in, or maybe it was the vodka. "Far as I can tell, no. About halfway, I guess," she said.

"Still half-alive, then. So where're we off to this fine day?" Pug asked.

Imelda had no idea. She hadn't planned that far ahead; these days, she was more of a short-term thinker.

Imelda headed north out of Fairleigh, watching the town, with its half-empty strip mall, tatty thrift shop, and herd of auto parts stores, disappear in her rearview. They were eight miles from Imelda's home in Wellbridge when Pug asked again about their destination. "I don't know, so don't ask me," Imelda snapped. "And if you're going to ride along, would you kindly make yourself useful and hand me a cigarette?"

"Get it yourself. I've got better things to do than help you destroy what's left of your health."

"Ohferchrissakes," Imelda muttered. She pulled into the AutoLube lot, slammed the car into park, and tapped out a cigarette from the pack on the seat. Pug stared off to the east, whistling tunelessly. While she waited for the lighter to pop out, Imelda shoved a tape into the eight-track and was rewarded with the live version of "Cracklin' Rosie," which she cranked up loud enough to startle a delivery-truck driver idling by the loading dock. She'd always had a soft spot for Neil Diamond. Pug hummed along.

Narrowly avoiding the truck's bumper, Imelda swung the Caddie back toward the road. She pulled out in a leisurely fashion but was forced to accelerate by a fully loaded logging truck that was bearing down on her in an urgent duet of horn blasts and Jake brakes. Pug was impressively unconcerned; by now Imelda's husband would have been covering his head with his arms and whimpering. Bucky had never understood the concept of accelerating out of danger. He was more inclined to slow down in a crisis, which in Imelda's experience was usually less effective.

"Goddamned men think they own the road," she said, and stomped on the gas. "And they say women drivers are the problem. Bull. Shit." As the eighteen-wheeler receded from view, Imelda turned her attention away from her passenger and back to the road, swerving into her own lane just in time to avoid an oncoming motorcycle.

"Oopsie poopsie. Sorry, Pug."

"Eyes on the road there, speed racer," was all her aunt had to say. They drove in silence as far as the Wellbridge line. The sun was directly overhead and the wind whipped the ends of the big scarf that was tied around Imelda's up-do. It occurred to her that the only advantage of going straight to stage four was that she wouldn't have to endure chemo and lose what little hair she had. It had always been thin; she'd worn a hairpiece for years.

"I'll make a lovely corpse, you know," she shouted at Pug. "At this rate I'll be at least ten pounds thinner and I'll still have my hair. When Elsie Toothaker died she was bald as an egg. That mortician had to pencil in her eyebrows and glue a wig on her head, remember? She looked like Priscilla Presley on ice."

"Really, Imelda? That's what's on your mind?"

"Yes it is. That is the sum total of what is on my mind at this time, Pug. And thank you for asking."

As they approached the Bridge Point Road, which led to the white farmhouse where she and Bucky lived, Imelda considered turning and even moved her foot over toward the brake, but at the thought of being shut up inside that house, with its low ceilings and too-small windows, she continued north instead. The eight-track clunked over to the next program, and Neil, scratching disconsolately on his guitar, slid into a rather overwrought rendition of "Holly Holy." Imelda snapped the music off.

"Bucky'll be wondering where you've got to. He'll be worried," Pug said.

"About what? That I've run off the road and killed myself?"

"He's quite shook up by all this, you know," her aunt said.

"Not as shook up as I am. And what about you, Pug? You seem to be taking it pretty well."

"Tell the truth, I don't get awful worked up about anything anymore. But it is sad, Imelda, a hard thing to bear. For everyone."

"Seems to me I'm the only one bearing anything, hard or otherwise. Everybody else just goes about their business. 'We're *so sorry*, Imelda. If there's anything we can do, dear, just let us know. Can I get you a pill, Imelda? Should you be driving? How about a nice cup of tea?' Let me

tell you something, Pug, when your life's down to the dregs, the last goddamned thing you want is a goddamned cup of Earl goddamned Grey."

Imelda pushed the accelerator farther down and the Caddie surged
forward, kicking up a shower of dust and pebbles as it fishtailed onto the
shoulder, then back to the blacktop. In a blink they passed through Wellbridge's town center: a prefab building that housed the post office and
town hall: the guano-splattered war monument, the Catholic and Congregational churches glaring at each other from opposite sides of the
road, and Red Craven's single-pump gas station and convenience mart.
Past Red's, the town became the outskirts, and the outskirts dwindled
to country. With every mile the white frame houses came fewer and farther between, their paint getting progressively peelier, their yards more
cluttered. On several properties, pulled up beside the family homestead
was a run-down house trailer, probably occupied by the owner's still
unfledged offspring, living separate, but not apart, from their parents,
pirating Daddy's cable, sharing a cordless phone, and showing up at
Mumma's table most nights for supper and the Wheel.

"Poor Bucky . . ." Pug sighed.

"Poor Bucky! Are you for real?" Imelda sputtered. "Poor *Bucky?*"

Buckminster F. Levine. Even now, Imelda could still recall the exact
moment she decided to marry him. It was their third date; *Georgy Girl*
was playing at the Criterion Theatre. Up to then, they'd kissed only
once, and she still hadn't decided whether there'd be a fourth date, but
as they walked down the center aisle to find a seat, Bucky put his hand—
no, not his hand, it was just the tip ends of his three fingers, now that she
thought of it—on the small of her back in a gentle but proprietary way,
then pressed lightly to signal the turn into the row. He hadn't crowded
her or asked if she'd like to sit there; he'd been just confident enough to
choose a seat without talking at all. It made her like him better.

Imelda saw the form her life would take by the end of the movie,
when Lynn Redgrave did the only intelligent thing and married James

Mason—even though he was a lot older and noticeably peculiar—so that she could keep that cute little baby and live in a nice house and not have to work and be lonely all the time.

In 1967, Imelda married Bucky in a civil ceremony in the front room of his house, where they'd lived ever since. She was a twenty-nine-year-old assistant at the antiques shop in town. He was thirty-eight and had by then been living in Wellbridge and working as a certified public accountant nearly five years. Three people attended: Pug, her husband, Alonzo, and Bucky's widowed father, an aspiring inventor, simmering anarchist, and self-proclaimed "thought innovator" named Melvin Levine (né Levinsky), popularly known as Red Mel.

Imelda had been greatly relieved when, in the summer of 1968, the local planning board, whose members Mel addressed as "Your Imperial Majesties" during the final meeting he attended, rejected his application for a permit to knock down the barn and replace it with an aluminum tepee and peat-moss sweat lodge. The next day, Bucky's father packed up his VW microbus and headed south, then west, eventually landing in New Mexico, where he found a more hospitable environment in a commune of like-minded enemies of the state.

"You know, Pug, marrying me was the best thing that ever happened to Bucky."

Pug inspected her nails.

"It was," Imelda insisted. "Got him out from under his father's thumb."

"And right in under yours."

"Malarkey. Since he retired, he stays shut up in that damned attic all day and night."

"Still building boats in bottles, is he?" Pug asked.

"Friggin' with his riggin'," Imelda muttered. "You know, Pug, I think inhaling all that model glue has affected his mind. Lord's sake, he's only seventy, but he's already an old man."

Pug said, "Maybe he's feeling blue because of your condition, Imelda. Ever think of that?"

Imelda snorted. Bucky was colorless, beige at best. Over the past twelve years, since their daughter left for college, it seemed to Imelda her husband had been gradually disappearing, as if one day he'd slipped inside one of his ship models. Well, she supposed, as she took a sip from her tea, he had his bottles, and she had hers.

"When's Deborah coming?" Pug asked.

"I don't know. You'd have to ask Bucky. He's making her arrangements. Like always."

"He's been a good father, Imelda. You've got to give him that."

Imelda couldn't disagree. In fact, she thought, he'd been nearly perfect—as good a parent as she'd been a failure. When Deborah was little, he'd come home in the evening and feed her and read her to sleep. Most nights he brought his papers and worked at the kitchen table after she went to bed. When Deb got older, he'd help with her homework and take her skating in the winter. They had a bond; she and Imelda never did.

"She does care for you, Imelda," Pug said.

"She tolerates me. When she can be bothered to come home." Imelda's foot had come up from the accelerator as she mused, and the Caddie was drifting along well below the speed limit. She stepped back down.

How had she come to resent her husband and daughter? And when had it become all right to admit it? She supposed it must have started after she gave birth. Postpartum depression, they called it now. Bucky'd had to take care of Deborah almost single-handed those first few months. Pug helped of course, and once Imelda was back on her feet things were pretty good for a couple of years.

It didn't last. The closer father and daughter became, the more they shut her out. Imelda remembered one Sunday, she and Bucky had been fighting for days. Probably it was about money, but it might have been sex or politics, anything that came to mind, really. He had become withdrawn, shambling around the house and mumbling his answers to her questions. Eventually he stopped talking to Imelda at all, even when she made a point of provoking him. But that January morning, with the sky outside so low and snow-heavy it seemed to be sitting right on top of their house and crushing it into the ground, he stood up from the breakfast table, straightened his spine, crossed the living room, and flopped down on the rug with Deborah, who couldn't have been more than three. He spent the whole day with her books and games. Imelda hated to play.

Just that once, Imelda was fooled. Fooled into thinking the darkness would always pass, that the three of them were one family. That night, with Deborah asleep, Imelda waited for Bucky to come upstairs; instead, he sat in his chair, staring out at the snow until it was time to go to work the next morning. That was when she understood how it was and how it would be. Bucky and Deb reserved their happiness for each other and their misery for her, shutting her out, punishing her, she believed, for being who she was. Eventually Imelda spent most of her time in the little shop she'd opened in the barn, distracting herself with her customers and her curiosities, turning her back on her family, rejecting their rejection, disliking them for disliking her.

"You had a right to feel the way you did, Imelda," Pug murmured.

Imelda was about to ask how the hell Pug knew what she was thinking when they came to the Bernville fork: right to stay on the coast road, left to turn inland. She banked left. Pug regarded her from under raised eyebrows.

"You won't find any answers there. He's sick, emphysema. Got one lung and a hole in his throat, with no wife to look after him," her aunt said.

"Good," Imelda said.

She'd heard about her father's condition the week before from her baby sister, Jessie. Six months after Imelda's mother died, their father remarried for the first time, ultimately adding a passel of half- and stepsiblings to the five he already had in a series of short marriages and haphazard relationships.

Imelda had been thinking about her mother a lot lately, wondering if she'd see her on the other side, or if there even was another side. She'd never been much for church and Bucky was an avowed atheist, but the idea that all death offered was slow rot in a pine box under the freezing ground seemed to suck the air from her lungs, made her feel like she was suffocating, even in broad daylight, under the September sun.

The pain between Imelda's shoulders flared and she pulled over.

"Five kids in ten years Mumma had. Can you imagine? He might just as well've killed her himself," Imelda said.

"But he didn't," Pug replied, a deep sigh pushing the words across the bench seat and into Imelda's ear.

"The hell's that supposed to mean?" Imelda asked. Bile rose in her throat, but she forced it back.

"She had an anxiety condition, Imelda. Least that's what they called it. After she had Jessie, she couldn't bounce back, just sank deeper and deeper. You know that, you've always known. That's why we were so worried after you had Deborah. You were nervous, too. Like your mother."

"Is that so, Auntie? That the *diagnosis* they gave you up to the state hospital? 'Imelda's quite *nervous*, so what we'll do is just tie her up in this lovely white jacket and run enough electricity through her brain to light up the midway at the state fair. That ought to steady her out. Make her into a right perfect little wife and mother, and if it doesn't, we can always try it again.' Was it you that signed those papers, Pug, or my loving husband?"

"You were so sick, Imelda. We were afraid you'd hurt yourself, or the baby. They said it was the only way to make the depression go away.

You didn't eat or sleep. You couldn't be left alone, not even a minute. For a whole month after Deb was born, you wouldn't feed her or pick her up. You remember."

Imelda's head and neck were throbbing. She rummaged in her purse for the Vicodin but couldn't extract a pill, so she dumped some in her lap. With a shaking hand she shoved three in her mouth, then took a gulp of tea, barely managing to choke it down.

There was so much she'd lost after the shock treatments, huge chunks of her life that had been blown to scraps, experiences and feelings she knew she'd had but could never find again. Even so, she was drowning in the flood of memory, recalling the things she couldn't forget even when she tried, and now the worst ones came gurgling up like stinking black dregs from a clogged sink pipe.

She remembered Mumma crying more and more as her belly got bigger that last time, then later, when Imelda was almost ten—in the fall, just a few weeks after Jessie was born—finding her mother in the woods behind their ramshackle pile of a house, red rivers from the gashes on her wrists pooling on the yellow leaves that littered the ground on either side of her, one shoe on and the other next to her poor cold foot. It seemed so wrong, her lying there all uncovered, that Imelda stooped down to put her shoe back on even as she screamed. Now all she wanted was to pull the plug on that memory, wash it away once and for all, down the drain with her mother's blood.

Imelda clenched her jaw and rubbed her eyes, then put the car in gear. She jerked it back onto the road and had just reached cruising speed when she noticed party lights in her rearview mirror.

"Good God almighty, what now?"

Imelda replaced her scowl with a plastic used-car salesman grin and said, "Well, well, as I live and breathe, it's Stumpy LaVallee. Seems like the deputy wants to chat."

Pug suggested pulling over, which Imelda did, so abruptly that

Stumpy's cruiser nearly rear-ended the Caddie. With the blue lights flashing, he stalked up to Imelda's side of the car.

"Well, hello there, Stumpy. Might want to get those brakes looked at. Damn near stove in my rear end," she said, then winked to show she was willing to be a good sport about it.

"Mrs. Levine, have you been drinking?"

"Yup, smoking, too."

"I think you'll need to get out of the car."

"Why would you think that?"

"Step out, please."

"No need to get stroppy, dear. If I was speeding, you can just write me a ticket and I'll be on my way." Feeling parched, she took a delicate sip of her tea.

"You will not. Mrs. Levine, I'll need your license and registration right now, and you will step away from the vehicle. I can smell the liquor in that drink from here." He pointed at the vodka on the front seat. "And that bottle has been opened." Stumpy's voice rose with each word, the last one came out just shy of a squeak. He grabbed at the cup in her hand, which Imelda thought was awfully rude.

"If you'd like a drink, Deputy, all you've got to do is ask," she said, firmly but not unpleasantly, holding the cup beyond his reach.

"I do not. Now put down that alcoholic beverage and remove those keys and step out of that car. I'm not going to tell you again, Mrs. Levine. I don't want to take you in, but I will."

Imelda considered the possibility of being bound up again, this time in handcuffs, locked away in a tiny cell, just sitting in the dark, and rejected it. "Listen, Stumpy, enough is enough. I'm a sick woman and I don't have time for this foolishness. You just go ahead and drop that ticket by the house," Imelda said as she took her foot off the brake and stamped on the gas. Over the squeal of the tires, she called back, "Bucky'll take care of it. Bucky takes care of everything."

The deputy scrambled back to his car. When he pulled out behind her, he added a siren to the lights.

"Oh, stop your noise," Imelda said, and accelerated to put some distance between them.

"Poor Stumpy, always a bridesmaid," Imelda said to Pug, who'd sat silently through the altercation. "Sheriff Largay'll never retire, you know. Told me once he planned to die with his boots on. More likely he'll be wearing orthopedic shoes and a truss."

Her aunt shrugged.

Stumpy was closing, clearly intending to lock her up, so Imelda picked up the vodka bottle and tossed it over her shoulder. The deputy swerved to avoid it. The tails of Imelda's head scarf were slapping her face, so she loosened it with her free hand, letting the oversize square of pink-and-green silk flutter away. It settled right on Stumpy's windshield, which forced him to slow down. The Cheez Doodles created a garish orange snowstorm as she shook out the bag.

Imelda watched in the rearview mirror as Stumpy tried to push the scarf aside with the wipers, but before he could clear his view, she'd pulled off her hairpiece and let that go, too. Then she slipped out of her cardigan and flung it back at Stumpy's car. Only when she was down to her bra and skirt did she stop undressing and look behind her again. The wiglet and assorted garments were snarled in the cruiser's wiper blades. Stumpy stopped, jumped out of the car, and pulled at the tangled mess.

The whine of the siren receded into the distance. The sun was warm on Imelda's skin, and her unpinned hair blew back from her face. Up ahead, just past the next rise, was the turnoff for Skunk Pond. She took it faster than advisable, but the big car hugged the road.

"How's that for problem solving, Pug?" she asked as they clattered down the dirt track.

"A problem delayed is not a problem solved. You know as well as I do."

"Is that so, Dear Abby?" Imelda shot back.

"Ayuh. And where do you think you're going?"

"You know as well as I do," Imelda singsonged back.

The prowler's siren rose and fell as Stumpy blew by the turnoff to the dirt road. Imelda stopped the car. She remembered being twelve years old and bumping along this very stretch in Pug and Alonzo's old truck, the same one that had rushed her to the emergency room when she was three. That second trip, Pug had driven out to Skunk Pond to collect her niece, the one with the sassy mouth who looked so much like her dead mother that neither her father nor his brand-new wife could stand her, or her back talk, one minute more.

Ralph Martin had been drunk the day he threw his eldest daughter out of the house, like most every day since he'd lost his wife. Even so, he'd had room in his heart for the other kids. But not Imelda.

"Why, Pug?" she whispered.

"I don't know, maybe he loved your mother too much to be reminded of her, or maybe he didn't love her at all. I never could tell."

Imelda had cried to leave Jessie and her brothers, cried for the loss of her mother and for the father who didn't love her anymore, or maybe never had. But Pug had loved her, and in his way maybe Bucky had, too, even if she'd never been able to love him, or Deborah, or herself, quite right. She was crying still, but now she felt strangely light, as if the past were dissolving, like blood drops in puddles.

Imelda sat for some time just past the second bend in the Skunk Pond road, a mile from the place where she was born, surrounded by the smell of pine sap mixed with the sweet rot of dead leaves and wet bark. The sun peeped through the branches overhead and kissed her upturned face. The September breeze blew her eyes dry and caught the wisps of her hair as it rippled over her head and shoulders, caressing the arms folded across her chest and the hands that gripped her shoulders.

Pug was whispering in her ear. "It's all right, Mellie. I took you home once and I always will. Remember?" She hadn't been called Mellie in such a long time, not since she was a girl.

"I remember," Imelda said. She took a deep breath, uncrossed her arms, and raised them to the sky, unfettered and free.

When Stumpy LaVallee finally retraced his route and headed toward Skunk Pond, he found Imelda Levine, all alone, just as she had been when he pulled her over, seated behind the wheel of her yellow Cadillac, barely cold and still as winter night, smiling softly to herself.

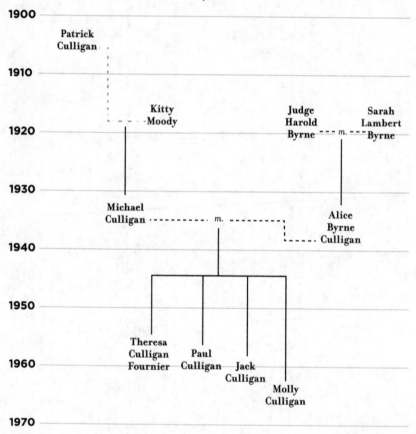

2003

1900

Patrick
Culligan

1910

Kitty
Moody

Judge
Harold
Byrne — m. — Sarah
Lambert
Byrne

1920

1930

Michael
Culligan — — — m. — — — Alice
Byrne
Culligan

1940

1950

Theresa
Culligan
Fournier

Paul
Culligan

Jack
Culligan

1960

Molly
Culligan

1970

SMOKE SIGNALS IN THE AFTERTIME

Alice Culligan died feeling she'd been goaded into it. She was long past hope and ready for the end, but once the visiting nurse slid the needle into her arm and the morphine began to flow, she'd have been content to drift forever in velvet limbo. Her children, however, had other ideas. They'd convened at her house with a funeral to stage and grieving to do, and her continued existence kept them from getting on with either.

Day and night they hovered, disrupting her peace with their squawking and their relentless, pecking care. At first their voices were low, their conversations hard to follow and full of odd pauses, which Alice assumed were filled by gestures that conveyed what they didn't want her to hear. Later though, as the days wore on, the chatter became louder and looser.

Every few hours, when the morphine's hold began to slip and Alice became twitchy and agitated, they'd quiet down for a while. Sometimes she whimpered in pain, other times in frustration. She discovered that the more she moaned and thrashed, the sooner the drug was dispatched down the tube to plump her flaccid vein.

One day her daughters argued about how much to give her. Theresa, the eldest child, fretted their mother was getting too much.

"Jesus Christ, T," her younger daughter, Molly, spat. "An over-dose'd be a gift from God. *That* is not living."

Oh, but it was. For the first time in her adult life, Alice was completely relaxed, her mind free to wander wherever and for as long as she liked. Confined to her bed, with nothing left to hide and no one else to worry about, she felt finally, truly free.

As she lay there, cast-off memories came drifting back, flotsam and jetsam on the opium tide. She recalled the Christmas tree lights twinkling in the darkened living room of her parents' house, the aching cold of Penobscot Bay in summer, and her first real party dress, a lemon chiffon confection with a midnight-blue silk sash that she and her mother had bought in a fancy dress shop down in Portland, Ducharme's Couture it was called. They served Mother champagne in a long-stemmed lily pad while Alice modeled dress after dress. The day ended with a steak dinner at the Fessenden Club, served by ancient men in white mess jackets and Bing cherry bow ties. In the smoky, candlelit dining room, with her father ordering for the three of them, Alice sipped a Shirley Temple from her own delicate stem; it was one of the few times she could remember her mother laughing.

As her thoughts unspooled, Alice lost all sense of time. Still she was tormented by hands, familiar ones that held hers and stroked her forehead and strange ones that tore at her parchment-skin, cruelly shifted her from one side to the other, and casually groped the most private parts of her body like greasy mechanics manhandling rusty car parts.

Voices besieged her, too. They demanded her attention, asking, "Mum, can you hear me?"

"We're all with you, Mumma," they informed her. "We're right here."

Well of course you are, you goddamned fools, she thought. I'm dying, for Christ's sake. Where the hell else would you be?

Eventually Alice was worn thin, too tired even for her memories.

More than anything, she wished to be left in peace, floating serenely to oblivion on the great rolling river of dope.

The last straw was a visit from Father Barbizon. The thought that he'd be anointing her with his white woman-hands and speaking the sacred last rites with his rosy, too-moist mouth was more than she could stand, even with the drugs.

That ridiculous old fool, she thought. I don't know whose ass he had to kiss to get Bloody Paul's, but if he thinks he's going to be the one to give me absolution, he is very much mistaken.

And so, before the priest could open his Bible or uncork the holy water, Alice Byrne Culligan rolled the dice on eternal salvation and let go of her life. To hell with it, she thought, I've had enough. Let this be the end.

It wasn't.

The dying was easy, simple release, no pain, no fear, but no heavenly host either, and this surprised Alice. For a moment she worried she might be headed for hell, which was not a possibility she had ever entertained. But no, she wasn't suffering, nor could she detect anything like the sulfurous flames of eternal damnation the Sisters of Mercy had so often threatened her with in school; this was a relief. Though she was clearly no longer in her body, neither did she appear to be going much of anywhere, and at least for the nonce, she remained in her rambling shingled cottage way out on the tip end of Bridge Point, where the reach met the bay.

Her thoughts became unusually clear, the morphine's blur replaced by bright, sharp consciousness unencumbered by flesh. At first she was aware only of relief at being released from that dreadful, decaying prison. All her life Alice had been proud of her appearance, vain even, but the ravages of the last year had stripped away her cool, blond beauty and, with it, what remained of her dignity and patience.

She gazed down at her discarded corpse but felt no attachment; it no longer interested her in the least. The nurse with the brutal touch removed her sausage fingers from Alice's wrist and looked away from her watch. When she spoke, there was a palpable wave of shock in the room. After murmuring some canned words of condolence, she slipped away. It was the only graceful thing Alice could recall her doing.

The family was ringed around the hospital bed that had replaced her four-poster when she could no longer get up on her own. At her right shoulder stood a startled-looking Norman Barbizon, Bible in hand, gob half-open, and she was pleased to have shoved his absolution back down his throat. Alice regarded her children with regret, the priest with something very like pleasure.

Having overcome his initial shock, Father Barbizon flipped from last rites to prayers for the dead, his flustered fingers rattling the pages of the holy book until he found the appropriate selection and was able to get to work.

"To You, O Lord, we commend the soul of Your servant Alice Byrne Culligan," intoned the priest. "Being dead to this world, may she live unto You. In Your most merciful goodness forgive whatever sins she has committed in this life through human weakness: through Christ our Lord."

Theresa sagged in the armchair next to the priest with her face in her hands. Her closed-mouth keening sliced through the drone of the sacrament like a siren in a traffic jam. No one seemed to notice.

Alice's attention shifted to her elder son; she was anxious to witness his devastation. Tall, fair, and patrician in a beautifully cut gray flannel suit, Paul stood stock-still, staring at his mother's vacant body; he blinked twice. Only the thin, rigid line of his mouth betrayed any hint of unexpressed emotion. His right arm was wrapped around his younger sister, Molly, as she sobbed into his shoulder. Alice was surprised that her daughter, a journalist whose unblinking accounts of atrocities from hellholes around the world had built her reputation for toughness, would be so shaken. She and Molly hadn't really ever been close.

The priest droned on.

Alice's fourth child, Jack, was stationed at the end of the bed, white-knuckling the footboard, silent tears rolling down his cheeks and dripping from his chin to splatter the leaping black stag on his tatty old high-school sweatshirt, making it look as if the animal had been tommy-gunned in midstride. Alice wondered where he'd found that old rag. Must have been rummaging around in the attic again, she thought. Jack made no sound as he wept and looked off into the middle distance rather than at the desiccated shell that had, until recently, been his mother. He didn't seem to notice his nose had started to run.

Next to him, Ina Coltrane, who'd been with the family for more than forty years, stood with one hand on Jack's shoulder. With the other, she tapped his arm and handed him a tissue from her apron pocket. Her gray eyes never moved from Alice's face. She appeared to be waiting for a surreptitious breath or telltale flutter of the eyelids, but they did not come.

"Let us pray together. Please respond with *Lord, have mercy on her.*"

Like Pavlov's puppies, Alice's four children bowed their heads and responded to the priest's words as they'd been trained to do since they first learned to talk. Mrs. Coltrane lowered her eyes, but her lips did not move.

As the repetitive call-and-response rolled on, Alice watched her family. Normally, emotional displays embarrassed her, but she was gratified at being properly mourned, and by the fact that the loathsome priest was witness to her family's grief.

She could see that Jack and the girls were stricken, but Paul puzzled her. Still handsome at forty-five, he was the only one of her children to inherit her looks and had, she could now admit, always been her fa-vorite. She had expected him to feel her loss much more deeply than the others and was perplexed to see him standing dry-eyed next to her corpse, an island of buttoned-up composure in a roiling sea of emotion. His stoicism could have passed for strength, and that was probably how the others would see it, but Alice wasn't so sure.

With the children's final call for mercy on their mother's soul, Father Barbizon made the sign of the cross. "The Lord be with you," said the priest, signaling the end of the proceedings.

"And also with you," came the rote chorus.

The priest bent forward, closed Alice's eyes, and pulled the sheet over her ghastly face. The family seemed to emit a collective sigh of relief.

At this, Alice expected she might finally feel the pull from on high or at the very least see the bright light she'd heard about on *Oprah*, but still she lingered, even as everyone began to file from the room and the priest packed up his paraphernalia and folded his stole.

Turning to leave, he placed his small hand on Theresa's shoulder and murmured, "I'm so sorry for your family's loss, Theresa, but we can all take comfort in the certainty that your mother's earthly suffering is over and that she's with God now."

Theresa, now alone with the priest and the corpse, her swollen eyes narrowed like gun slits in the mottled fortress of her face, said some-thing Alice never would have expected from her.

"I doubt it."

And with that she rose from her chair and walked from the room, leaving the priest standing next to Alice's body with his shiny red mouth hanging open for the second time that day.

Alice would not have been surprised to hear such a remark from Molly. Her relationship with her youngest child had always been contentious, and Molly had embraced her role as the family heretic early on. At sixteen she'd announced that she would no longer be bound by "some life-denying rules made up by a bunch of power-mad hypocrites and closeted old queens just so they could push everybody else around." She had become, she told anyone who would listen, an existentialist. When Alice inquired as to what that might entail, Molly said, "God does not exist, so everything is permitted. I am my own project."

Alice let it drop, figuring age and experience would eventually lead her youngest back to the one true Church. They had not, and Alice still regretted letting Molly switch from Latin to French in the eighth grade.

Her eldest child was a different story. Often, but never kindly, referred to as "Mother Theresa" by her younger siblings, Theresa had never shown any sign of being other than a rock of silent Catholic rectitude, the living embodiment of familial devotion. Or as Alice's husband had remarked, long before Mr. Alzheimer stole his mind and convinced him he'd been elected governor of Maine, "Theresa wouldn't say shit if she had a mouthful."

Apparently, Alice thought as she trailed her family out of the death room and down to the first floor, she's had a bellyful.

It was here that she first noticed the smoke. Not sooty black chimney smoke, but wispy, vaporous strands like spiderwebs that seemed somehow attached to her nothingness. Although Alice could see the smoke, she couldn't quite make out where it began or ended, which gave her the sensation of being tethered, like a balloon in the Thanksgiving Day parade, unable to control her position and unsure of where she was going or who was handling the lines, floating just above the crowd at the base of the stairs.

Paul was shaking Father Barbizon's hand and thanking him. "I'm sure she knew you were here and was comforted by the presence of the Church," Paul said with apparent sincerity, even though he had broken his promise to have Monsignor Kennedy attend his mother. Jack stood awkwardly by, making small, fidgety movements with his hands. Molly drifted out of the foyer and over to the drinks table in the living room, next to where Theresa had dropped into Alice's favorite chintz armchair and was staring intently out at the milky winter afternoon and the whitecaps on the bay.

The priest declined Paul's offer of refreshment and excused himself. Once the front door clunked shut, Jack suggested that a cocktail was in order. Molly's glass was already half-empty. Refusing a drink, Paul moved in the other direction, down the hall toward his father's study. Mrs. Coltrane headed for the kitchen.

While Molly and Jack drank Irish whiskey from her husband's heavy crystal tumblers, Theresa chose one of Alice's delicate little thimble glasses for the Scotch her mother always preferred. "Just a halfsie," Alice would say when Mike offered her a refill, and she'd hand her husband the little glass for a drink that didn't really count as a drink at all.

Theresa's tears had left dry, chalky tracks on her cheeks, and her short dark hair, with its liberal sprinkling of wiry grays, was choppier than usual, looking, as it always did, like she'd cut it herself. In her uniform of colorless twinset, wool skirt, silver crucifix, and low-heeled pumps, Theresa might have been taken for a nun, but in Alice's view it was the tough, unyielding set of her jaw that made her a dead ringer for a Bride of Christ. Straight-backed and disconcertingly still, her ankles crossed against the faded roses of her chair, Theresa stared unblinking out the window at the dreary ocean where a lone cormorant swooped low and glided above the surface, neck craned, prospecting, its reflection distorted in the ripples. Apparently satisfied that there was nothing for it in the water, the bird pumped its wings and ascended, flapping high and out of sight.

When did Theresa get so old? Alice wondered. Good Lord, she's only forty-seven.

Jack asked after Theresa's twin daughters and was told they were on their way home from college in New York. "They really loved Mum," Jack said, unconvincing in his lie.

"They did not," Alice said aloud. Apparently no one heard, so she went on, pleased at no longer having to censor herself. "Truth be told, I suppose it was mutual. Oh, Theresa, I know it broke your heart when you couldn't have children, but why did you have to go all the way to Korea to get some? I never understood that. Surely the Church could've found a baby here, or in Ireland. God knows there are plenty of bastards around. It would have been so much easier if they'd looked just a little bit like you or—"

Alice was interrupted by a loud blowing sound. Molly wiped her nose and got up from the sofa to get another drink. Her daughter's brown curls needed washing and there were ugly purple half-moons under her blue eyes.

"I can't believe she's gone, that it's all over. What do we do now?" Molly said. She looked small, diminished by her doubt.

"Paul's taking care of things with Mr. Fell," Theresa said.

Molly shuddered. "Jesus, Mary, and Joseph, not another fucking family jamboree at Toothaker and Fell. I hate that place—it smells like old man, and that puky green ladies' room is always freezing."

Jack grunted, shoved his tissue in his pocket, and plunked down on an ottoman in front of the fire, tumbler in hand. He was shivering despite the heat on his back.

"Why there?" Molly asked.

"Mum wanted it there. She left very detailed instructions about everything. Thought they had the nicest rooms, and Fell's the only undertaker who lets you set up a bar at the wake," Theresa replied without moving her gaze from the water.

"She always hated a dry event," Jack said with half a grin. "And really, when do you need a drink more than at a funeral? Good thinking. Thanks, Mum." And he raised his glass in toast.

"You're welcome, dear," Alice said.

Molly's eyes snapped open, and Alice thought she might have heard her speak. "Oh Jesus, they're coming to get her. Shouldn't we do something, you know, put a dress on her or pull out the IV? Oh God, what about the catheter? The nurse is gone. We can't let the funeral guys see that. Can you imagine what she'd say about being taken out of the house in a hospital johnny?"

Jack raised one eyebrow and looked at his sister. "You can go rummage around for urinary clamps if you want to, Mol, but there's no way I'm having that end of Mum be my last memory of her."

"Take that mess and throw it in the bay for all I care. Just keep the damned casket closed," Alice muttered.

Molly started to cry. "Urinary clamps," she said, looking at Jack. Then she laughed right out loud and covered her mouth. The more she tried to stop, the worse it got, and soon both brother and sister were consumed by an unsettling mix of frantic giggles and wretched sobs.

"A little respect?" Paul said from the doorway.

It took a good few seconds for Molly to muster sufficient control to speak. "I'm sorry," she gasped. "It's just the thought . . . of the . . . Mr. Fell . . . with his toupee . . . " And here she let out a sound somewhere between a howl and a screech. "His head under the sheets . . . oh God, I can't. Sorry . . . so sorry."

This wasn't the first time Molly had been felled by inappropriate laughter. More than once the nuns had had to rap her knuckles to stop her disrupting classes or, worse, chapel with her silliness; of course Alice had quickly put paid to that. You couldn't have people, holy orders or not, striking your children. Still, she was surprised to see it happening now, and she was even more startled that Jack was joining in. He'd always been devoted to her.

Glass in hand, Molly fled the room, leaving Jack shaking in silent hysteria on the receiving end of his brother's obvious disapproval. Only Theresa, seated off by herself, seemed unfazed by the scene. She calmly raised the tiny glass to her lips and sipped, wrinkling her nose at the taste.

After Molly left, Alice noticed she felt a bit less tightly bound by the smoke. She could still see it, but not as clearly as before. There was a sort of looseness to her movements, as if the bonds had been elasticized.

Without his sister to egg him on, Jack's outburst subsided and the living room became quiet again. He got to his feet and moved toward the kitchen, mumbling apologies as he went. Paul motioned for him to wait and then outlined the sequence of events to come, starting with the funeral home pickup (Mr. Fell was on his way) and ending with a Mass and burial in three days' time.

"I'm going to Fell's tomorrow to pick out a casket. If you want to come, you're welcome, but no pressure," he said. "We'll need flowers for the wake and the service. What do you think Mum would want?"

Again Theresa roused herself, this time rising from her chair and pushing wordlessly past her brothers toward the den. When she returned, she handed a piece of Alice's heavy ecru stationery to Paul. On it were the instructions Alice had written out three months previous. Paul skimmed it and nodded curtly.

"Trust Alice to run the show right to the bitter end and beyond," he murmured, then said, "Fine, I'll pass this to Mr. Fell. Thanks, T."

You'd think he was handling a difficult client, Alice thought. "I just wanted to make it easier, so you knew what I intended," she explained, wishing they could hear.

"Where's Molly?" Paul asked.

In response Theresa shrugged, so Jack volunteered to find her and fill her in. He gave his older brother a manly pat on the shoulder, then continued toward the kitchen, pulling Alice along in the sticky cobwebs.

In the oak-beamed kitchen, Mrs. Coltrane was making sandwiches. "A plate of sandwiches and a pot of tea, the Irish response to every crisis," Alice said. "That or hot whiskey." Jack had grabbed a sandwich off the platter and was torturing it as he sat hunched in his usual chair at the old pine table in the corner.

As she watched the hired woman methodically assemble first egg salad, then ham and cheese, Alice wondered about the inscrutable Ina Coltrane.

"Coltrane, you are an odd duck. The kids love you, and God knows how I'd have managed without you, but after all this time you're still a mystery. What makes you tick, Ina Coltrane?"

Alice thought back to the bleak February morning Coltrane had come to them. With a newborn, Jack, three-year-old Paul, and Theresa, not yet five, all at home, Alice had been careening toward a nervous breakdown, there was no denying it.

Her own mother was more interested in tennis and shopping than her grandchildren, who, Alice suspected, made her feel old. The one thing she had done for Alice was make inquiries about domestic help at the church. As it happened, Father O'Neill knew an Irishwoman who, having recently fled her abusive American husband up north, was looking for a live-in work situation somewhere her seven-year-old son could go to a good school. Alice was skeptical at first, but the priest reassured her, saying, "She's Irish off the boat, but the woman's teetotal, so she can be trusted to stay away from the liquor. She says she's willing to

look after the children and get the meals, just see to things generally."
And so the deal was struck without any further input from Alice.

Five days later Mrs. Coltrane arrived with her son, two suitcases,
a teapot, one book, and a teddy bear. She quickly settled into the
caretaker's apartment above the garage, which Alice's mother had had
painted, cleaned, and furnished with castoffs from her rambling, fre-
quently redecorated home in Fairleigh. Though emotionally chary,
Sarah Byrne was generous with a dollar.

If Ina Coltrane was happy living on Bridge Point, she never let on.
With her long copper-colored braid, now shot through with gray, and
imperturbable demeanor, she initially put Alice in mind of a statue. She
tended to be terse, though her speech was laced with an Irish accent,
which lent it a lilting, musical quality that everyone, Alice included,
seemed to find soothing.

Mrs. Coltrane soon became the calm center of the Culligan house.
When Molly came along quite unexpectedly four years later, it was Colie, as Jack had nicknamed her, who took the baby in hand while Alice
stayed in bed with an extended case of postpartum pip.

Alice's reverie was interrupted by Jack asking Mrs. Coltrane where
Molly was.

"She'll be down presently, I expect. Just upstairs washing her face."
As if summoned, Molly slipped down the stairs and took a seat at the
table. Without a word, Mrs. Coltrane placed a sandwich and a cup of tea
before her and nodded her instruction to eat.

"Egg salad?" Molly asked.

"Um-hm."

"Not too hungry, but thanks, Colie." Molly wrapped her hands
around the cup and lifted it to her face.

"Molly Culligan, you should be ashamed," said Alice to her unhear-
ing child. Ina Coltrane looked up from her cutting board, then quickly
back down.

"Sorry about . . . you know, in there," Molly said to Jack, glancing toward the living room. Seated together like that, the two of them could have been twins. They shared the same coloring and features; even their expressions and posture were similar. Jack, however, was tall and rangy like his father, while Molly was built more along Alice's lines, below average height and about half a club sandwich past skinny.

"Shit happens, Mol. Don't worry about Paul, such a tight-ass."

"I can't believe I did that," she said. "Last time it happened I was in a bunker in Tora Bora, and my producer got so freaked, she sent me to an army field shrink. Happened in New York, too, 9/11. I just could not stop. He said it's a common reaction to trauma or stress, but sometimes it just comes on because you know you shouldn't do it."

"Oh yeah?"

"Um-hmm. Remember Dawn Pendleton from high school? I did the same thing at her wedding to Freddy Houghton. He stood up and read this really horrible, sticky love poem he wrote and I just lost it, had to leave. Someone said the maid of honor played 'Leather and Lace' on a recorder right after. I'd've had to *crawl* out of Bloody Paul if I'd heard that. Alice was pissed, but Dad thought it was a hoot. Dawn never spoke to me again. Whatever, I couldn't stand that girl."

Molly sighed, and Alice thought she detected a trace of a smirk on Coltrane's face.

"Dawn Pendleton? I did her," Jack said without a trace of embarrassment. "Guess that's why she didn't invite me to the wedding, huh?"

"Ew Jack, that is so gross," Molly said. "When?"

As Jack described the encounter, Alice wondered, Are these my children? Do they always talk this way? And in front of Coltrane? Alice wasn't so much startled at Jack's conquest as she was disgusted by the discussion. It didn't surprise her that the Pendleton girl had been loose. All you had to do was take one look at the mother to realize how the acorn from that tree would sprout. And although Alice had never been bothered by colorful language—she very much enjoyed swearing—the subject of sex had always made her distinctly uncomfortable.

"Really," Alice said to no one in particular. "There hasn't been so much dirty talk in this house since Jack threw a petting party in high school, little bastard."

Behind Mrs. Coltrane, Alice found herself being drawn back up the stairs. Paul had asked Molly to help prepare the body for the undertakers, who were due momentarily, but seeing the look of horror on Molly's face, Colie had volunteered to go instead. Alice was surprised her daughter would be so squeamish. She must have seen hundreds of dead bodies in the course of her work.

With Alice floating along, Mrs. Coltrane entered the bedroom to find Theresa rummaging through the dresser drawers.

"I need a scarf," Theresa said. She held a white cotton slip and a pair of stockings and looked dangerously close to tears.

Mrs. Coltrane crossed to the hulking Queen Anne wardrobe, her steps soundless on the Oriental rug. "Here, I know where she keeps them. Now won't this be just the thing, duckie? It was one of her favorites." Alice was flabbergasted; she hadn't heard Coltrane speak this way since the kids were babies.

After shaking out the white silk square with intertwined gold chains and navy ropes, Mrs. Coltrane adeptly folded it into a triangle and approached the hospital bed. "Now, Theresa, you'll have to help me if you can, dear. It would never do for anyone to see your mother like this, would it?" Her voice was low and soft, calming as milky tea. Theresa nodded.

"Good girl. Now I'll just roll back the sheet and you'll need to lift her head. Are you ready, dear? . . . That's it, good."

Alice watched in fascination as Coltrane removed the white fleece cap from her poor bald head. I looked like a rotted fetus by the end, she thought. After her hair fell out she couldn't bear to look in the mirror anymore. Though it seemed a long time ago, Alice could still recall the agony of her bones poking through her skin, which had become so thin it hurt to have anything rub against it. Theresa had sewn the cap with the seams on the outside so they wouldn't irritate her. What a relief it had been to have warm ears. She watched Mrs. Coltrane expertly wind the scarf, turban style, around her abandoned head, knotting it securely at the base of her neck.

"That's better," Theresa murmured as she gently eased her mother back to the pillow.

Together the two women removed the tubes from her arm and the catheter from below the sheet and disposed of the bags and needles. After taking a pair of white silk pajama pants from the dresser and a navy robe from the closet, they set about easing Alice's corpse into them, gently, as if she could still feel it. The final step was to slide a pair of fleecy ballet slippers over her blue feet. Much to Alice's surprise, all this Coltrane did with gentle matter-of-factness, saying when they'd finished, "Now, isn't that better?"

For the first time since her passing, Alice was touched by the events surrounding it, and when Mrs. Coltrane took Theresa's hand and said, "It's time for us to say goodbye now, dear," she was overcome with gratitude to this woman she'd given so little thought to for the past forty years.

"She never really loved me, you know," Theresa blurted out. "If I'd been pretty like her or successful like Molly and Paul, or popular like Jack, maybe it would have been different, but I was just one disappointment after another to her. An embarrassment." The emotion returned to Theresa's voice, and as she spoke, she again began to sob, this time silently, her body shaking with the intensity.

It was true she'd expected more from Theresa than a teenage marriage and endless service to the Church. She'd been convinced that her first child, the one she miscarried just a few weeks after marrying Michael, had been a boy, and during her second pregnancy she'd been desperate for another one, only to deliver a plain, stern-faced girl who looked for all the world exactly like Michael and not a bit like herself. It wasn't easy feeling connected to a child like that. She'd tried to be good to Theresa, and all her children, had always given them the best of everything. Didn't that count at all?

Once again, Alice felt the suffocating pull of the smoke as she watched Coltrane slip an arm around Theresa. "It wasn't you, dear, truly it wasn't. She loved you as much as she could love anyone. No, I think it was herself your mother didn't care for. She was an unhappy woman, and I suppose that was the reason for the drinking."

"The drinking? *The* drinking! Why do you say it like that, Coltrane? And what're you talking about, anyway?" In the silence of the room, Alice's voice rose to a shriek. "The drinking!" The directness of the statement and the clear acknowledgment that both Theresa and Coltrane had talked about it catapulted Alice from tenderness to fury. Not only was Coltrane implying she'd had a problem, she was acting as if it had been a known fact that everyone, including the help, was entitled to discuss.

"That's rich coming from you, Ina Coltrane," she raged, "a twelve-stepping charity case from the slums of Limerick. That's right, I know all about you. Well, let me tell you something, if you'd grown up with a cold bitch for a mother, got landed with a whoremongering dullard of a husband, and been stranded at home with four screaming children instead of having a career and a life outside Nowheresville, Maine, you might have occasionally dipped into the whiskey and wandered off the path of righteousness yourself!"

In the still room, Alice thrashed and raged unnoticed. Theresa drew a shuddering breath and pulled the white sheet back over her mother's face. As she did, Coltrane lifted her eyes from the corpse and turned her gaze toward the big mirror over the dresser where Alice had been hovering. There was a question mark between her eyebrows, but she turned away at the sound of a car door slamming. Below in the driveway, the long black hearse containing Mr. Fell and his minions had just pulled up.

While the morticians plied their gruesome trade, Alice careened around the bedroom, her thoughts, like a sack of civets, hissing and clawing and spitting, too closely confined with no possibility of escape. The work of loading her corpse into the body bag and onto the stretcher went on methodically below, with Coltrane and Theresa looking on in silence. Theresa dabbed at her eyes and blew her nose; Coltrane scarcely blinked.

The two women brought up the rear of the procession as Alice's body was taken down the stairs, past the assembled family members, and out of the house. Again Alice was yanked along by the smoky gray strands, now tighter and more constricting than ever.

The family spilled out the front door and watched the gurney roll along the walkway to the waiting hearse. In the cold blue light of the dying December day, old Mr. Nadler from around the corner was passing with his shambling white-muzzled retriever, Gerald, on a leash. At the site of Fell and his cargo, he stopped and signaled the old dog to sit, just shy of the mailbox that anchored the front walk. He removed his battered Red Sox cap and placed it over his heart, standing in solitary recognition of the family's grief until the tailgate was closed and the car lumbered away. As the taillights receded down the Bridge Point Road, he gave a small, melancholy nod toward the house, replaced his cap and continued on his way, looking a little more stooped than before.

The gesture calmed Alice, and she began to wonder if she'd ever be released from this unholy limbo and the suffocating, smoky bonds. It was all getting to be too much; she yearned for relief. Then it occurred to her that maybe this was all there ever would be, that instead of healing lights, heavenly splendor, and the restoring warmth of almighty forgiveness, she was destined to spend eternity as a shadow, listening to conversations she didn't want to hear, being hauled around like a helium-filled house trailer, and eventually fading from memory as her family returned to the business of living.

So preoccupied was she by this new line of thought, Alice didn't realize she'd been pulled to Michael's den, where Paul was sitting at his father's mahogany desk, the telephone to his ear. From his tone, Alice assumed he was talking with his wife. She watched him tap his silver pen on the leather frame of a photo of herself and the kids that Mike had taken at Christmastime back in the early seventies, the last year the kids could be wrestled into matching holiday outfits. In front of the thickly tinseled tree, Alice was perched sidesaddle on an ottoman with Molly on her lap and Jack hunched on the corner, hands tucked between his knees. Paul, who must have been about eleven, stood behind her right shoulder, chest out, his hands clasped behind his back. Next to him, a teenage Theresa stood with one arm crossed over her middle, grasping the other elbow. They were all smiling, but no one looked happy. How was it she'd never noticed what a miserable photo it was?

Alice pushed the question from her mind and listened while Paul reeled off the sequence of recent events. He spoke with the easy intimacy of the long married, and as the conversation went on, Alice was relieved to be in the soothing presence of her handsome son.

"I'm fine, hon. Now that they've taken her body away, it's a relief—for everyone, I think." He took a deep breath, dropped the pen, ran his free hand through his thinning blond hair, loosened his tie. "Okay . . . yup . . . I will. Love you, too. Bye-bye."

Paul put down the phone and exhaled deeply, letting his head fall forward into his upturned palms, then sat motionless. Was he weeping finally? Alice hoped so; however, when Paul lifted his head in response to a rap on the door, his fine, sharp features were arranged into the usual mask, his eyes dry.

Jack walked in balancing a tray with tea things and a sandwich on one hand.

"Colie sent this," he said, gesturing to the china pot with his chin. "Said you hadn't eaten all day and dinner won't be for a few hours. She's making meat loaf, says we need a regular meal before people start bringing over food and we're all living on casseroles and banana bread. She looks beat, but says she'd rather stay busy."

After placing the tray on the desk, Jack asked, "Talk to Connie? Kids okay?"

Paul nodded as he poured out a cup of tea and laced it liberally with milk and sugar. "Bump?" Jack asked, producing a flask from his back pocket.

"Thanks, Jacko."

Staring down into the cup, Paul asked, "What about your girlfriend, she coming to the funeral?"

"Nah, we're not on family-crisis terms. Besides, she's covering my shifts till I get back."

Paul sipped with a thoughtful expression on his face. "You work together, huh? Dad ever tell you not to shit where you eat, Jack? No? He told me. More of a 'do as I say' rule, I guess."

So Paul knew. Here it was, then, the final humiliation. Not surprising really, Alice thought. Apparently there were no secrets at Byrne, Pocket, Randall, and Culligan. Especially if your name was on the letterhead.

"Who was it?" Jack asked, though he didn't look like he wanted to know.

"Who was it?" Paul repeated. "Who *wasn't* it, Jack?"

"Jesus Christ, Paul, how'd you find out?"

"The tawdrier, the more shameful, the dirtier the story, the worse people want to tell it, my boy. It's fun."

Jack closed his eyes. Alice could almost see his illusions crumbling, a brick wall suddenly stripped of mortar. He slid from the arm of the green leather chair down onto the seat, nodding and cringing in one motion.

"Well, one day about, I don't know, ten, twelve years ago, Theresa called me in hysterics. One of her friends had an aunt who was a secretary at the firm. Back in '68 the aunt got pregnant and had to go 'tend a sick relative' in Boston for a few months. She wouldn't say who the father was, but the family assumed he was a coworker, married. The friend put two and two together because the kid looked so much like Theresa and, by extension, Dad.

"Anyway, when the secretary got back from her 'sabbatical,' the firm bought her a little house in Augusta and set her up with a job in a partnership down there. She couldn't get by on the salary, though, and so she asked for support, threatened to go to Mum and the papers if she didn't get it. Anyway, long story short, Mum found out about it while she was pregnant with you and about had a nervous breakdown. So Nana hired Colie."

"How do you know for sure?" Jack asked.

"Good question. Thank you for asking," Alice said. Though she was horrified at the airing of their dirty laundry, she was mesmerized by the scene playing out before her.

"I asked Dad."

"What'd he say?"

"He said, 'Don't ever shit where you eat, son.' I told you."

"That was it?"

"He told me the story, or a version of it anyway. The rest I got from Arthur Pocket. Artie was a regular washerwoman."

"Arthur Pocket, that son of a whore," Alice said. "He always did like to talk. So self-righteous, with that bucktoothed lump of a wife and all those cats instead of kids. And a summer cottage in Provincetown, thank you very much—who did he think he was kidding? Probably had his own little secret life."

"So you're telling me we've got a random half-brother out there someplace?"

"I imagine there's probably more than one, but he's the only one I know about," Paul said, looking every minute of his forty-five years.

"So that's why Mum was such an unholy bitch to Dad for all those years? Why she drank? How come she didn't divorce him?"

"We're Catholic," said Theresa from the doorway, where she'd been standing unnoticed. "Besides, I think she'd've died before she ever admitted anything to anyone, and it was probably more gratifying to torment Daddy than throw him out."

"Not exactly, dear," Alice murmured. "Close, but no cigar, as they say."

"Oh dear, I am sorry," Sarah Byrne said without a trace of regret. Then without missing a beat she went on, "But look on the bright side, Alice, no one even knew you were pregnant, though I'm sure there was plenty of talk. God has a plan, you'll see. Pretty soon you'll be nothing but relieved. It'll give you time to settle in with Michael. That'll be fun."

And so, after Alice miscarried her first child less than a month after her wedding day, that was all she got from her mother by way of comfort. It was no more or less than she'd expected.

Certainly her marriage had caused talk. In 1953, you got married before college graduation for one reason, and if people hadn't put two and two together based on the timing of the union, they certainly figured it out when Alice and Michael held the ceremony on a Friday afternoon in the church sanctuary, attended only by Father O'Neill, their parents, and the two friends who stood up with them.

The few photos from the day showed Alice in the trim gray silk suit and matching hat she'd bought for the junior year in Rome she'd never get to have, and Michael, tall and dark in his one and only business suit, looking like a deer the moment before it was jacked.

"If he'd known what he was getting into, I suppose he'd have been well within his rights to refuse to go through with it," Alice murmured, but in those days you didn't, and certainly not when you were a dirt-poor third-year law student from the wrong side of the swamp, and the girl you'd gotten in trouble was the only child of the most powerful lawyer in your hometown. If her uncle just happened to be the chief of police, well, you might as well grin and bear it because there was only one way it was going to go.

As Alice's thoughts drifted back over the years, she had to admit that she and Mike weren't in love then; they never really had been. They were both young and beautiful, which helped, but lust took you only so far in a marriage, and they'd quickly discovered the limits of physical attraction in the years following the makeshift September wedding.

Of course, later there were the children, and with each one Alice hoped things might change. Her feelings, his feelings, anything really. It wasn't so much that she loved her husband; she hadn't, not in any profound sense. It was more that she wanted him to love her. After all, she'd given up everything: her long-anticipated, carefully planned year in Rome, her friends at Mount Holyoke, the glamorous career in Boston or New York that her art history degree would have made possible. Everything.

For Michael, it was different. The marriage gave him all the things he'd been working for: social standing, a partner-track job in one of the state's biggest firms, plenty of money, and eventually his name on the brass plate of the office door in Fairleigh. "He had a good run for a fatherless boy from Moodyville," Alice said to herself. "And look at him now, poor bastard, a mind like mashed potato and a heart that'll never quit."

The day she found the note from that whore of a secretary in Michael's suit pocket, Alice had no one to turn to. Eight months pregnant with her third child, and the first two not even in school yet, she felt cornered. I should have had it out with Michael then and there. Maybe we'd have ended up getting divorced, or maybe he'd have straightened out. Who knows? One thing's for certain, following Mother's advice didn't do much good.

"We'll get you some help. After the baby's born, you can start playing tennis again. It'll give you your figure back. You know, dear, you need to get out and do more, maybe volunteer work or a bridge club— make yourself interesting," she said.

Then in a confidential tone Mother added, "Alice, all married men *think* about straying, and most of them do. It'll pass. Enough said. I'll talk to Father O'Neill tomorrow and we'll find someone to live in. Isn't there an apartment over the garage? Perfect. Just leave it to me."

So Alice said nothing to anyone, chasing the bitter pill of betrayal with anything she could find in the liquor cabinet. When Mrs. Coltrane arrived, Alice simply handed over the children and the house and slowly retreated into her daily routine of wine with lunch, sherry before dinner and whiskey after, except on tennis afternoons, when she held herself to one blameless beer in public with the girls.

"And that was my life," Alice said. "No, Theresa, you're wrong. I took no pleasure in tormenting your father. There was no pleasure at all, just the oblivion of the drink. Then, when Michael got that diagnosis, when they told me his mind would be gone in a few years, all I could think of was getting him into a home so I could finally be shed of him and his filthy ways. Can you blame me? Can any of you?"

Alice thought back to the last time she visited her husband at the nursing home, the time he took her for a secretary, called her tootsie, and pointedly beckoned her toward his lap to "take some dick-tation." She was mortified, but the smiling nurse's aide told her, "He says that to everyone, even the nuns." Consistent to the last, she'd thought.

Alice's memories were interrupted by the familiar sound of Paul's measured tones. "She held all the cards, Jack," he explained with more patience than he probably felt. "Look, Dad was a shanty Irish bastard from Moodyville, about to become a partner in one of the biggest firms in the state, which just happened to be headed by his father-in-law. He couldn't leave."

"So what makes you think there were others?" Jack asked.

"Oh, Jack," Theresa said with a sigh, "Fairleigh's a small pond, and people saw him around. Someone ran into him in Bangor with a blonde a couple of times, and once when Molly was home from college, she saw him going into the Holiday Inn. On a Saturday afternoon when he was supposed to be golfing in Bar Harbor. It was no secret."

"Well, it's news to *me*. So Molly knows, too? How come no one ever told me?"

Theresa and Paul exchanged weary glances. Finally Paul shrugged and said, "I don't know, you weren't around much. And you and Dad were so tight. You were always his favorite," he said pointedly. "He went on and on about how you *did your own thing*, didn't care what anybody thought. He envied you. Anyway, it's not exactly the kind of thing you just mention over Christmas dinner."

"Christ almighty," Jack exploded. "I was in Kingfield, not Siberia. It's *two hours* away! You could've picked up the fucking phone."

Paul's voice rose to meet his brother's.

"Yeah? And what would you've done, Jack? Huh? What? Blasted home for the day and straightened everybody out? Anyway, I didn't, okay? I didn't. I had a wife and kids to take care of, clients, Mum and Dad on my hands, and unbelievable as this may be, you and your . . . priorities . . . were not always top of mind." He paused and seemed to consider withdrawing, but instead he pushed on.

"You're a smart boy, Jacko. You could've figured it out if you wanted to. Or if you'd given a sweet shit." Alice watched in horror as Paul's lawyerly cool shattered and years of resentment and frustration splintered his meticulous veneer of self-possession. He stood, but instead of rising along with him, his voice fell to a menacing baritone, sarcasm dripping from every syllable. He was pointing down at his brother with two fingers and stabbing the air between them.

"You were too busy *helicopter skiing* and delivering *sailboats* and tending to your *many* responsibilities behind the *bar* to worry about what was going on with Mum or Dad, or me, or *anyone but yourself*. Not when Alice's drinking got completely out of hand, not when we found out Dad had Alzheimer's, not when she got cancer. Never."

"Oh no, oh no, Paul, please stop. Stop it now before it can't be fixed, please stop it, please," Alice beseeched as her panicked thoughts tore at her consciousness. The anger built in the room beneath her, and she felt as though the smoke tendrils were pulling her in a dozen directions at once. The boys' rage and anguish washed over her; it was unbearable. "This isn't how it was supposed to be. All those years, just so you wouldn't see how things were, so no one would."

Paul continued, clearly unable to stop the torrent. "So don't you think, not for one—fucking—*second*, you ungrateful little prick, don't you even *think* about giving me a hard time about how I chose to handle the shit show that landed in my lap. We don't all have the luxury of staying seventeen forever," he said.

Alice was stunned to hear Paul swear, and the shock of seeing him lose control seemed to freeze everyone in place. Molly was standing behind Theresa in the doorway, peeking around her sister's shoulder like a child who'd walked in on her parents in the middle of a drunken brawl. Once again Theresa had withdrawn behind the impassive, expressionless facade. Above them, Alice felt as if she were being wrenched apart by the rapidly darkening, tacky strands that threatened to consume her. The angrier her children became, the thicker the smoke turned, the more violently it shook her.

Now Jack, too, was on his feet, and he leaned over the desk until his face was inches from his brother's. "You bet your ass it's wonderful, *Paul*. Every day's a blissful fucking Soma holiday—it's all blow jobs and rainbows and unicorns for Jack. That what you think?" he shouted.

His brother said nothing, his teeth so tightly clenched his jaw trembled.

"Seventeen? Yeah? So what?" Jack continued. "I'll never be you, Paul, never be Mr. Perfect, Mr. Georgetown, with a perfect wife, perfect kids, perfect life. Shit, I barely graduated on the five-year plan and the best I could manage was a sociology degree, for Christ's sake. That make you happy, buddy? No? Well, Mum and Dad didn't like it much either."

Jack's words echoed in the stillness of the room. Just inches apart, the two men stared at each other like cats preparing to spring, each daring the other to blink. No one moved, no one spoke. Above it all, their mother hovered, thrashing in the vapory tethers as her sons seethed below.

The overhead light clicked on, chasing away the gloom. Molly stood with her hand on the switch plate, then pushed past her sister. Her voice cut the silence.

"That's enough. Idiots. Sit down now, the both of you." She gestured for her brothers to sit. Alice half expected her daughter to pull out a microphone, so complete was the transformation to her TV self. She'd always been a great one for the headlong charge, and Alice was relieved to see Molly return to her more familiar persona.

"Look, Dad was easy to love, when he was around. Mum, not so much. But she's gone and he might as well be, and we're all we've got.

"So yes, Jack," she continued, "I knew he fooled around, but you know, that was between the two of them and . . . God, or the universe or whatever. Daddy was a skirt chaser; Mum was a frustrated, selfish alcoholic who probably never should have had children in the first place. Fine. If you want to shove 'em into little boxes with tidy labels, have at it. "

And there it was. After all the years of protecting them and pretending, Alice reflected, she hadn't fooled anyone.

Theresa moved from the doorway to the fireplace. Jack and Paul stood down, slumping into their chairs and breathing deeply, almost in unison. With each exhale, Alice saw the smoke lighten and felt the pulling and tearing ease.

Theresa spoke first. "Jacko, remember when that big lummox of a girl—what was her name, Standish, Stanley?—whatever, anyway remember how she'd wait for you after school every day and beat you up? What were you in, third grade, fourth?"

"Misty Stanley, yeah, I remember. She'd wait outside the schoolyard and follow me home, then thump me. I couldn't hit her because she was a girl. Plus she was a lot bigger than me. So what?"

"Didn't you ever wonder why she stopped?" Theresa asked.

"I figured Dad took care of it," he said with a shrug.

"Nope. Mum heard about it, but the principal said they couldn't do anything because it was off school property, so she had your teacher keep you after school the next day, and she went looking for the kid. She told her if she ever so much as glanced in your direction again, she'd beat the hell out of her, then have Uncle George arrest her, and her father, Judge Byrne, would send her to reform school. Colie told me about it a few years ago."

Alice recalled the incident. When she'd told Mike about it, he'd said only, "Jesus Christ, Alice, he's getting his ass handed to him by a little girl. He needs to toughen up. I'm not going to interfere and make him more of a mama's boy than he already is."

What choice did she have but to take matters into her own hands?

She wasn't proud of threatening that unfortunate child, but she'd had no choice.

"Alice did that? To Manly Stanley? Well, fuck me. Alice could be tough, but it's hard to imagine her threatening anyone with an ass-kicking."

Alice wondered at his reaction. She'd done what any mother would have; surely he understood. Jack shook his head as if to clear it. "She was something else," he said more to himself than the others.

Episodes like that, and there were plenty, had strained the marriage as much as the faithlessness and the lies and the whiskey-soaked nights. But what eventually broke it—years later—was the night Jack got arrested for underage drinking and hauled into the county jail in Fairleigh. Once again Mike had been no help, unreachable, probably screwing around while his son was being worked over in a holding cell. By then Alice's uncle was long retired from the police department and in a nursing home, so she'd had to call her father to intervene, and while she waited for him to get the chief of police on the phone at two A.M., she'd sat on that bench and endured the sound of fists on bone and the smack of open palms striking her boy over and over again. When Jack had come home bruised and bloodied for "resisting arrest," all Mike had to say was, "You ought to know better than to smart-ass a cop."

If I had to point to the moment I lost the last shred of feeling for my husband, that was it, Alice thought. I turned a blind eye to everything else, but there was no way to love him, or even like him, after that.

His voice back to its normal register, Paul said, "Remember when I got into Georgetown, but Dad and Grandpa were pushing me to go to BC just because they'd gone there? We were all sitting around the living room—Theresa, you were there—and Mum'd had a good few drinks. I didn't even think she was listening. They were just banging on me about it, remember, T?"

Theresa nodded. She lifted her chin and pursed her lips in an expression the shocked Alice recognized immediately as her own, and perfectly mimicking her mother's trilling, slightly sloppy, whiskey voice said, "LSAT, GUL, BCL . . . *S-h-i-t!* What goddamned difference does it make whether he goes to Georgetown or Boston or Whatsamatta U? It's *his* life and Paul can do what he pleases. Now leave him alone. Conversation closed."

Theresa was listing slightly, her elbow resting on the mantelpiece with her hand, palm up and shoulder height, holding a make-believe Virginia Slims cigarette between her elegantly splayed fingers just as Alice had all those years ago. With her other hand, she shook the empty thimble glass she still held as if it were a bell. "Now, Mike, be a dream man and get me a drink, won't you please—just a halfsie."

It was such a pitch-perfect impression of Alice in rare form that even Alice herself recognized it. *I had no idea. She's brilliant, really quite the actress. How is it I never knew?*

Theresa's siblings chuckled. Clearly they'd seen this before. "Oh Alice, what a piece of work. God, but she could be funny," Molly said, wiping away the single tear that ran down her cheek. "I'm going to miss her." The others looked down, no one spoke.

The oak-paneled room was quiet as Alice and her children huddled together, each lost in thought. Outside, the blue winter twilight surrendered to black. The stars began to flicker and the moon began to rise, first peeking over the harbor, then floating up past the rooftops of Bridge Point, and finally breaking through the spiderweb of barren branches to the night sky above.

The minutes ticked on, and Alice listened as her children shared stories and swapped reminiscences so that, one finger at a time, they let her go, and as they did, the smoky fetters loosened and untangled themselves. Alice lingered just long enough to gather up all the things she should have known, and with her last thought, she gave herself over to the smoke, blended with it, became it, wafting, whisper, wisp, gone.

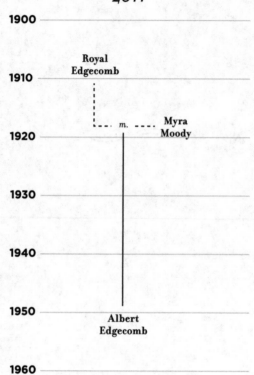

2011

1900

1910   Royal
Edgecomb

1920   *m.*   Myra
Moody

1930

1940

1950   Albert
Edgecomb

1960

TRINITY

The ghosts in Albert Edgecomb's house don't seem to notice the time and bang around at all hours. Lately they've been keeping Albert up at night: Mother rattling the kitchen pots, Uncle Hartwell stomping around the attic where he shot himself, and that homely red-haired girl in her bloody pinafore, just standing at the foot of Albert's bed, picking her nose. At least she's quiet. There are others, too, but these he either can't identify or prefers not to think about. Albert used to roll over and cover his head with the pillow when it got noisy, but lately he's started shouting at them to quiet down. Sometimes it works.

This day in July starts like every other, with the midsummer sun arriving on schedule, accompanied by the rooster's bare-scrape alarm and the tease of cool air drifting in with the tide. Last night was particularly raucous, so Albert didn't get much sleep. He squints against the glare, licks the salt that has accumulated on his lips, lumbers to his feet, and makes his bed. After he washes and dresses, he yells, "I've had about enough of your deviltry, so you'd best behave tonight and let me sleep." Then he tromps down the narrow stairway, slightly sideways. It is important not to brush against the walls. If he does, he'll have to go back up and start again from the top.

At the foot of the stairs, Albert pauses to look at the snapshot that sits next to a vase of blue plastic daisies on the TV he never watches anymore. "Good morning, Mother," he says. In the picture, the newly married Myra Edgecomb shies away from the camera. There is a tangle of earth-clotted carrots overflowing the basket on her hip. Still slim behind her checkered apron, she is two months pregnant. "You're there, Albert. I just didn't know it yet," she told him when he was a little boy. "Your father took that picture, so he was part of it, too." This is Albert's one family photo.

In the kitchen, Albert taps the water spigot three times with his right index finger before opening it to fill the kettle. He spoons equal parts Nescafé and sugar into his mug. Then he peels off three strips of bacon, puts them in the big black skillet, and lights the burner. When the bacon is just shy of burnt, he lines up the strips on a sheet of newspaper to drain and cracks two eggs into the pan. He flips them carefully so as not to splatter.

"Now close the flame and count. One Mississippi, two Mississippi . . ." Mother recites the numbers with Albert all the way to ten, which is when the eggs are done. Albert likes the ten-Mississippi eggs well enough, but it's Mother's voice that fills him up. He worries that if he switches to oatmeal like Doc Norden said, she might not come back. Or one of the others might take her place.

After breakfast he steps outside and surveys the plot of land his family has farmed for five generations. Across the road, on the shore of the reach, the tide is going, leaving the slabs of slick gray rock that lie halfway vertical to dry in the sun. Ellsworth schist, the stone is called. Albert remembers his mother telling him that, her finger tracing the wavy folds of waxy stone like sagging flesh (like his own flesh now) that had been heated and deformed, then pushed up through the ground by volcanoes millions of years ago. She'd read a library book about it before she married his father, long before Albert was born, but she'd remembered that and more, things about rocks and trees and clouds and birds, and she'd tell Albert about them at bedtime. He can't remember everything she said, not even much of it, but he remembers the rocks like folds of old skin and his mother's smooth face and her voice lulling him to sleep.

Albert breathes deep. The pink perfume from the beach roses curls into his nostrils and vines around the lingering smells of fatty bacon and lemon dish soap, then squeezes until they're gone. Summer is Albert's favorite season. Good things happen in summer: the ocean breeze is warm and sweet, the sun heats the earth and his garden grows, he wakes to birdsong every day, and even the cranky old chickens seem happy. Days like this, winter is less than a ghost, unreal, benign, a memory that can't touch Albert, can't harm him. In winter things die from the lonely cold, and even the house, already listing under the burden of time, moans with the weight of it. Albert nods his head three times to clear it, pushing thoughts of snow and ice and the sharp-toothed dark from his mind.

At the chicken coop, he fills the feeder and changes the water, then opens the door to let the hens out. He counts them as they hop down from their roosts. One two three, one two three, one two three. All nine present and accounted for in waltz time.

Wednesday is weeding day, so Albert steers his wheelbarrow over to the garden. His knee bones grumble as he crouches between the rows to clear out the interlopers and harvest his crop. By lunchtime he's filled Mother's basket with more pimply kirbys, yellow squash, and green peas than he'll be able to eat all week. The pole beans and tomatoes aren't ready, so he passes them by and dumps the weeds over the banking on the way back to the barn.

"What do you think, Mother? Run the extras over to Father Morrill?" he asks, knowing full well he should spend the afternoon replacing the hinges on the cellar hatch, scraping the barn doors, or taking care of any of the dozen other repairs that need his attention. When she doesn't answer, he takes it as permission to go visiting and sets the basket in the truck bed, then he goes to the kitchen for a cucumber sandwich.

After lunch, Albert is walking to his truck when he feels a cool shadow, a bird passing overhead. He looks up at the mottled white underside and black wing tips of a red-tailed hawk ascending, something small and bloody writhing in its talons.

A second later the creature wiggles free and plummets to the lawn. Albert doesn't really want to, but he approaches the bloody mess, a small rat, torn almost in half, barely alive, its black eyes bulging in panic and pain. Albert hates rats. The big ones get into the henhouse, break the eggs, and suck them dry. Sometimes they kill his birds. Once he found two chicks with their throats torn out, not even eaten, just mangled and left in the dirt.

It's plain nothing can save the rat and he considers leaving it there, but it's just a small one, probably never did any harm. Albert crosses the driveway to his truck and returns with the shovel from the emergency toolbox.

"The longer I wait, the more you suffer," he says just before he closes his eyes and brings the blade down squarely on the quivering animal, ending its pain in one blow.

Albert raises the shovel and shakes the carcass off, then wipes the rat blood on the grass. He wonders if animals have souls and is thinking maybe he should say a prayer when his thoughts are interrupted.

"Getting pretty good at killing things, aren't you, boy?" the voice snarls, then singsongs, "Pretty good, pretty good, pretty good."

Albert closes his eyes so as not to see the raw red scrapes across Royal Edgecomb's knuckles. He tries not to breathe in the stench of blood and liquor that always follows his father. His heart is slamming against his chest, his mouth bone-dry.

"Get out of here," Albert shouts. "Get out, get out, get out!"

Usually the three-magic beats back the darkness and silences the voice along with its hateful ghost, but not this time.

"Who threw out my whiskey? If it was you, I'll thrash you good," his father growls.

Albert runs for the truck and clambers inside. He grinds the shift into reverse and tears out of the driveway. Halfway to town, he steers the truck into the lay-by and drops his head onto the steering wheel, breathing slowly in and out like Mother told him. When he has stopped shaking, he thanks the Lord three times, blesses himself, and continues down the road to church.

Father Gideon Morrill is overdue for a call on Albert Edgecomb but can find any number of excuses for not going. He is considering the possibilities when the man appears at the front door of the rectory, arms full of his garden. "Hand of God," Morrill murmurs.

"I was just thinking about you, Albert. You must be heaven-sent," he says too loudly, and invites his visitor into the kitchen for a glass of iced tea.

Albert wipes his feet three times on the welcome mat. The priest's house has always been ghost-free, but you can never be too careful. He sets his offering on the counter and sits.

The priest says, "Thank you so much. You're always so generous with your harvest."

Albert smiles and sips his tea. He wishes the drink were sweeter but is afraid it might be extravagant to ask for more sugar.

Morrill asks how things are going on the farm.

"Could use a little more rain," Albert says, then talks at length about his garden: which vegetables are ripe, what looks good this year, and when he thinks the blueberries will be ready for raking.

Father Morrill smiles and nods, but he's only half listening. He's wondering how to broach the subject of Albert's mental state. One time, he asked Doc Norden if he thought Albert might be delusional, but the doctor dismissed the possibility. "Obsessive-compulsive, sure," he said. "And he's not exactly the brightest light on the Christmas tree, but crazy? I don't think so."

After Albert finishes the crop report, Morrill asks, "Things okay with you? Any visitors lately?"

"Ayuh," says Albert. "Been keeping me up at night."

The priest notices the creases between Albert's eyebrows look deeper than last time they spoke. He nods when he can't find words to fill the silence.

"I been wondering, Father, does God make ghosts, or are they the devil's doing?"

"God makes everything, Albert, good and bad, including the devil, so in a way it's both, I guess." Morrill is on shaky ground. His faith in God has never wavered, but the truth is, he has always had doubts about certain church teachings, such as the notion of tormented souls haunting the earth and demonic possession. Though he accepts the existence of Satan in a vague way, he's never seriously considered the possibility of encountering him, or his minions, and prefers not to think about such things.

Morrill knows there is no place for cafeteria Catholics in the clergy and reminds himself it will not help poor Albert to see doubt in his priest. "Do you think maybe it could be your mind playing tricks on you, Albert? From loneliness, perhaps, or sadness."

Albert taps the rim of his glass three times. "Maybe, but this morning my father showed up again." He is talking into his lap. "I wish he'd go away." He isn't sure the priest believes him, but there's no one else to tell. "I know it's a lot to ask, Father, but you think you might come out to the house? Try and drive him off? He'd have to listen to you."

Albert's cheeks are burning. He's never asked anyone for help before. Mother always said don't involve other people in your problems, keep your counsel. That's why he doesn't go to Confession, why he can't take the Holy Communion.

The last thing Gideon Morrill wants to do is cart himself out to the Edgecomb place for a midweek ghost hunt. He feels unequal to such a task, even if the possibility of finding anything evil is remote, but says of course he will, first thing the next morning, before he leads the elder ladies' choir practice.

In his examining room, Doc Norden has determined that the mass underneath the bottom fold of Naina Tremont's belly is a hardened accumulation of dead skin, grease, and dirt, probably years in the making, and not a fatty tumor as she feared. Her mother, she says, died from a fatty tumor, and she's convinced they run in the family. The doctor suggests that more frequent baths, with a scrub brush, would be a good way to avoid such scares in the future and sends her on her way. Having opened the window and sprayed the room with Lysol, he washes his hands and splashes his face for good measure.

Even though he is seventy-four years old and semiretired, many people in town still refer to him as young Doc Norden. He inherited his practice, and patients, from his father almost forty years ago, but days like this, he is less grateful for the windfall than he might be.

His daughters, he thinks, were smart to become teachers and move downstate. They are lucky not to have to scrape filth from gelatinous flesh, lance plum-size boils, or relay a death sentence to someone twenty years their junior, as he has done today.

Out front, the receptionist tells him his last appointment just canceled—a small mercy, so he closes the office early and returns to his desk. As he does at the end of every workday, the doctor traces his finger along Sarah's smiling mouth in the photo of her taken ten years before on the dock of their place at Bell Lake, back when she still knew who he was.

Today, he'll get to the nursing home in time to feed her dinner while he tells her about his day. Once they'd have laughed about the fatty tumor and commiserated over the injustice of lives foreshortened while they sat on the screen porch sipping gimlets and listening to the loons on the lake. Today his wife will stare vacantly at him between spoonfuls of pureed beef stew and reluctant slurps of vanilla-flavored dietary supplement. Today he will speak to her as if she understands his words, and today he will fail, once again, to cover her face with a pillow and put an end to her suffering, as she always promised she would do for him.

"Plenty worse things than death," he mutters, not for the first time, and throws his lab coat into the hazmat bin.

At the rectory kitchen table, Father Morrill cuts the cards, then indicates the heap of damp vegetables on the counter with a tilt of his head. "Had a visit from Albert Edgecomb today," he tells Doc Norden. Over the past two years, their Wednesday-night cribbage tournament has evolved from habit to ritual. The doctor brings crabmeat rolls and onion rings from the Dairy Bar take-out window; the priest, having divested himself of his collar, supplies the beer. They never drink more than two in an evening, the doctor because he's driving and the priest because he's a priest.

"Albert still communing with the spirits?" Doc asks.

"Says he'd like them to stop answering back," says the younger man. "Asked me to go to the farm tomorrow and try to clear them out." Morrill is trying to seem confident, like there's nothing other than an aging, lonely dirt-farmer out there or that he drives away demons as a matter of course.

"You talking about an exorcism?" Doc asks as if he were inquiring about Morrill's plans to join the circus.

"Not really. Houses don't have souls, so it's not an exorcism per se. A simple blessing'll probably do. Kind of a placebo for Albert, you know? Of course, if he's really having chaotic visitations, that's another thing. . . ."

After Albert left, the priest dug out some of his seminary textbooks to bone up on the litanies, invocations, and procedures for dismissing spirits and/or cleansing demons from homes. As he read, he recalled the subject being covered in his classes. At the time, he paid about as much attention to the lectures as he did the emergency evacuation pantomime on an airplane.

"And here I was thinking I had the worst job in town," Doc says.

They play the hand and peg the score. The doctor wins in a skunk to take two out of three, leans back in his chair, and drains his glass. Morrill retrieves the second round, and Doc accepts the bottle, saying, "Last call," though he knows otherwise.

"Think you'll find the devil out there on the East Point, Padre?" Doc asks.

"Never know where he'll turn up," the priest says. It occurs to him that the doctor might actually believe in ghosts, and if so, he's probably not the only member of the Church of Saint Paul the Bleeding Apostle who does. The priest doesn't kid himself about such things. He's a spiritual man, but he's also a realist.

"Whatever happened to Albert's father?" Morrill asks.

"Speaking of the devil . . ." Doc Norden sighs. "Royal Edgecomb, he was a right nasty piece of work, awful handsome, though. Boozer, brawler, used to knock Albert and his mother around pretty good. Married Myra Moody kind of late in life, for around here, anyway. She must've been about thirty and he was probably ten years older. Story goes, Royal came home late one night, drunk as a lord, *as per usual.*

Dead of winter. Parked right in the middle of the front yard. I guess he passed out after he got out of the truck. Sherriff found out he'd been in a fight in town earlier that night. Anyway, my father used to examine the bodies after he certified them, no M.E. back then, you know. Turned out Royal had a collapsed lung, loaded with cancer. Coughed up blood all over his truck and out in the yard, but it was the cold that killed him. He was stiff as a Popsicle by the time they found him next morning."

"Good Lord. How old was Albert?"

"Fifteen, sixteen, maybe. Anyway, I don't think anyone quite believed Albert and his mother never heard anything, or thought to look out. Then again, it wasn't much of a loss, except maybe for the bartenders in Fairleigh, and the whores. Excuse me, Father."

"I've run across the term before. You think they just let him die?"

"Couldn't say. No one ever asked, really. Good riddance and all that," Doc Norden says with a shrug, then drains his glass. "Funny thing, Myra died ten years later to the day. Heart attack, in her sleep. Never woke up. Albert found her, of course. Called me out to the farm. That woman was the least peaceful-looking corpse I ever saw."

Doc picks up a text from his buddy backing out of their Thursday-morning golf game, so he offers to go out to Albert's place with the priest the next day, figures he should probably check Albert's heart and blood pressure anyway. They decide to meet for coffee beforehand at the diner near the East Point Road.

When Doc gets home the house is dark, but he knows the glass and gin bottle are where he left them last night, on the lamp table next to his recliner, so he doesn't bother with the lights. He kicks off his shoes, settles back in the chair, and stares out the picture window at the night sky, but owing to the full moon, he can't see many stars. On the lake, the loons wail back and forth in a mournful call-and-response, their cries flowing in waves across the water, the sound softened and rounded by the contact. Sarah loved listening to them, said their three-tone calls were loonish for *where ARE you.*

Across town, on his knees, Gideon Morrill begins with the Hail Mary and the Our Father. He considers asking for guidance in leading the dwindling, geriatric flock he inherited from Norman Barbizon and for help bolstering attendance at Mass; instead, he gets to his most pressing concern.

"Lord, I ask You for clarity so that I may see the way back to the true faith that will armor me against the deceptions of the devil, wherever I find them. Give me strength and courage so that I may walk in the light of grace and be worthy of the challenges You set before me. I ask this in the name of the Father, and the Son, and the Holy Spirit."

He genuflects but continues kneeling, worried that he hasn't spent enough time in prayer but lacking anything more to say. Morrill stands and turns out the light to begin what he assumes will be another wakeful night, wanting desperately to sleep, to dream of archangels and sanctifying grace, but fearing he will again be forsaken.

Out at the Edgecomb place, Albert's mother sits by the front window, watching for lights on the road, as she does every night. Sometimes the others keep her company, but never Royal. She makes sure he stays outside where he belongs, with the creatures of the night. Lately he's gotten bolder, saying ever more hateful things to Albert. She isn't sorry for letting Royal die, even if it has cost her immortal soul; she'd do it again.

Her regrets are all for Albert. Her son was always different, but the counting and tapping got much worse after Royal passed. She wishes she could have spared him the torment of knowing his father suffered like he did and the guilt he feels for it.

Tonight Myra vows to make things right; she'll stay put when she sees the headlights. She won't make any noise or wake Albert. Tonight he won't hear her rummaging in the kitchen or see her standing over Royal. She will not force him to turn his back on his dying father; for once, she will make sure her son sleeps through the whole thing.

But this night, like every other, Myra Moody Edgecomb is compelled to get up from her chair, to search the kitchen cabinet for a weapon, to hold it over her lawfully wedded husband even as he labors for breath and shakes with cold, and finally to leave him outside to die. Now as then, she understands she cannot save Royal from his darkness, cannot save his soul any more than she can save her own. But she can end this violence, this despair. She can save her son.

Two A.M. Albert hears the usual commotion, but tonight, instead of hollering for silence, he gets out of bed. He is exhausted, desperate for sleep, and blind with rage at being denied. Halfway down the stairs, his right shoulder brushes the wall, but tonight, like that night so many years ago, he doesn't stop or count to three or turn around.

"Mother?" Albert calls. When he sees nothing, feels nothing of her presence, he shouts again, more sternly this time.

In the kitchen, the cabinet door hangs open. Before bed, he checked it three times to be sure it was latched tight. He decides to nail it shut after breakfast.

Albert walks back to the front room and peers out the window. He remembers doing the same thing that horrible winter night. Forty-six years ago it was.

Just like before, he sees his mother in the yard and runs out the front door, hears Myra's voice, harsh and cold. "You will never hurt us again, Royal Edgecomb."

Tonight the air is warm and still, but in the moonlight Albert can see it all: the snow, his mother, rolling pin in hand, leaning into the truck, pocketing the keys, leaving the door open and the dome light on, then striding toward the house. She tells Albert to come inside, but just like before he runs to his father. On the ground, Royal is coughing up blood, the snow around him speckled red.

Now Mother is shouting at Albert, calling him back to the house, but this time Albert will not turn around. He doesn't have to look back to know Uncle Hartwell is peering at him through the attic window or that pinafore girl is watching from his bedroom. He can feel them around him, and the others, too.

Albert looks down at the spot where his father lay that night. He sees Royal's shivering body splayed next to what's left of the rat he smashed earlier but couldn't bring himself to bury. For once Royal is silent, unthreatening. Albert says, "I'm sorry. I should never've left you out here."

He begins to cry, standing in the place where his father died alone, slowly, in freezing agony. "I could at least've made it quick," Albert whispers.

At that moment a jolt, jagged as lightning, hot and cold at the same time, passes straight through Albert and brings him to his knees. After the shock comes fluttering warmth, like a blood bloom, spreading up from his belly to his chest and down his arms to his fingertips. It is pleasure so intense it is nearly pain, and though Albert is frightened, he gives himself over to it, not knowing whether he wants the feeling to stop or go on and on.

From high above, the night sky reaches down to collect Albert's last breath as the white moon paints all that lies beneath in black and blue, haze and shadow. The silence thrums, absolute, and Albert's last pump of blood dissolves into the endless vibration of forever.

Just before five A.M. a clatter of crows wakes Father Morrill from the callous, fitful sleep that has been toying with him for the past hour. He wipes the crust from his eyes, briefly considers rolling over, forces himself out of bed and into the shower. He has work to do—God's work—and whether or not he is equal to the task, he will do it.

In the house by the lake, Doc Norden comes to in his recliner, grasping for the ghostly wisps of his dream about Sarah. He listens for the loons, but the lake is silent. Remembering that he offered to go out to the Edgecomb place with Gideon Morrill, he groans. The priest, he reminds himself, has offered plenty of moral support since Sarah got sick, so Doc figures he owes him. Besides, the guy is the most god-awful cribbage player he's ever met, and the doctor enjoys schooling him every week.

Out on the East Point Road, Albert Edgecomb rises. The tide is at rest, neither coming nor going beneath a bank of summer fog that hovers so dense and low on the reach, only the mountaintops are visible on the far shore, disembodied peaks floating on a cloud sea. Above the fog, the sky is streaked with purple slowly fading to pink. Albert drifts across the lawn to the front door and passes through. He is home.

Above the Edgecomb farm the red-tail soars, scanning the ground for prey. When she spies movement in the garden, she tucks her wings and dives, capturing a young chipmunk in her talons, then flapping skyward. It is dangerous to be so near the ground, but she is safe now. She tightens her grip on the writhing creature and banks south toward the nest, back to her mate and their greedy hatchlings. There she makes quick work of the chipmunk. The creature suffers only a moment, and it is over.

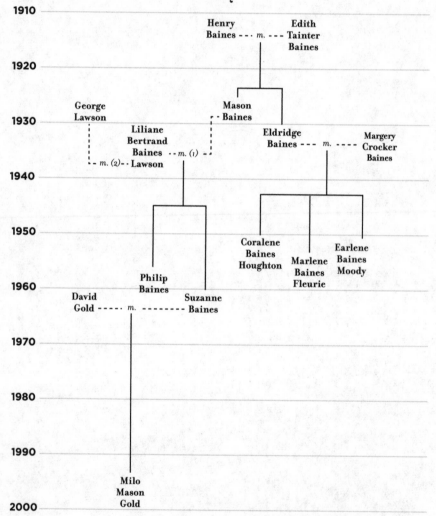

2017

1910

Henry
Baines - - - *m.* - - - Edith
Tainter
Baines

1920

1930

George
Lawson

Mason
Baines

Liliane
Bertrand
Baines - - *m.* (1) - -
- - *m.* (2) - - Lawson

Eldridge
Baines - - - *m.* - - - - Margery
Crocker
Baines

1940

1950

Coralene
Baines
Houghton

Marlene
Baines
Fleurie

Earlene
Baines
Moody

Philip
Baines

David
Gold - - - - - *m.* - - - - - - - - Suzanne
Baines

1960

1970

1980

1990

Milo
Mason
Gold

2000

REQUIEM (FOR THE UNBURIED)

SUZANNE BAINES

The ladybugs are all dead, red pebbles scattered everywhere: the floor, the windowsills, the kitchen counter. They crunch when I step on them. Good luck, that's what Maman always said they were, but now as I sweep them into a pile, I wonder whether being dead makes them bad luck, or no luck. Doesn't really matter, I guess, but still I feel compelled to bury them. I worry they'll haunt me if I don't.

Behind the cottage, the black earth is corpse-cold under tender blades of newborn spring grass. With only the chittering red squirrels to bear witness, I sprinkle the bugs over the hole I dug and replace the patch of crabgrass on top. From scraps of high school Latin and memories of the occasional funeral, I try to cobble together a prayer for the dead. *Requiem in pace? Requiesce?* "Rest in peace," I say instead.

My gravedigging complete, I return to the task at hand: opening up the cottage after the long winter. First there's the water, which has been off since last fall. After starting the well pump, I listen to be sure the water heater is filling. Next I flush away the antifreeze in the upstairs toilet and reattach the showerhead. I think what an unimaginable luxury this endless, effortless supply of hot water would have been to my ancestors when they arrived here in Maine nearly three hundred years ago, how inconceivable a daily shower would be to them, how mine is only the third generation to pee indoors on anything but a chamber pot.

I'm turning the mattresses when, outside, the rumble of an engine rises, then stops. A car door slams. Through the bedroom window I see my favorite cousin, Earlene, Tupperware bowl in hand, striding from her pickup toward the house. At sixty-four she's nearly ten years my senior, and though her back is as pike-straight as ever, she's thicker around the middle and grayer than last time I saw her, two years ago it would be. I run downstairs bird-calling her name.

"Earlie Earlie Earlene!"

She's through the screen door before I get to the bottom of the stairs. Her hugs still smell of spray starch and drugstore toilet water, a blend of stiff and soft I trace all the way back to the nights she babysat for my brother and me. On the way to the kitchen, something crunches under her sneaker.

"You had ladybugs wintering here, Suzy." She bends down to clean up the remains with a tissue from her sleeve. "They always find a way in, but seems like they never can get out."

"There was a whole houseful, all dead." I don't mention I buried them. She'd think I was out of my mind.

"Too bad. If there's one thing this family could use more of, it's luck," she says.

I put the beef stew she brought in the fridge, which is empty but for half a dozen wine bottles and a tub of chocolate pudding. Peering over my shoulder, Earlie says, "Still eat like an eight-year-old boy, I see."

"An eight-year-old with a drinking problem," I reply. This makes her smile, even as it occurs to me how often there is more truth than humor in a joke. I offer to split my can of room-temperature Diet Pepsi with her, and we take our glasses outside to the picnic table under the beech, where we settle on opposite benches. The tree won't leaf out for another few weeks, so the sun picks its way through the buds and bare branches, the light broken and weak. Across the reach, to the south, the rounded hills of Acadia roll across the land like swells on the bay. It's warm for Maine in May, but cold by any other standards, so I zip my fleece up to my chin. Earlie, in shirtsleeves, dismisses my offer of a sweater.

Most people would ask how I've been doing since the divorce, but Earlie dives right into local gossip and Baines family updates: she starts with her husband. Millhouse is working too much, as always. Their third grandbaby's due any day. Victoria Moody had a tumor the size of an avocado—California, not Florida—removed from her ovary, but she's fine and being looked after at home. Who knew Dougie Lemay would turn out to be a half-decent husband after all? Poor Sarah Norden (young Doc's wife) died last year and Doc followed not three months later. Broken heart, what else could it be? Sheriff Largay finally retired to Daytona Beach and took his deputy, Stumpy LaVallee, with him, peeling one hundred and forty years off the collective age of the local law enforcement staff and finally confirming the existence of the love that dared not speak its name after decades of the whole town whispering it. Besides a touch of sciatica and the occasional bout of heartburn, she says, "I can't complain, but sometimes I do anyway."

It's my turn, so she waits. I tell her about my son, his job in New York, his horrible beard, and the eyeglasses that look just like the ones our grandpa Baines used to wear.

"Milo's become a hipster, has he?" Earlie says. I shouldn't be surprised she's familiar with the term. The whole wide world, hairy or smooth, brought to this remote corner of Downeast by cable TV and the World Wide Web.

I give her the skinny on my brother, Philip, his wife and kids, which I picked up recently during an extended visit with them in Paris.

"And you?" she asks.

"Okay, you know, not bad for an old broad."

"That's good," she says, tells me the family is glad to have me back home, which I know is not uniformly the case, and asks how long I intend to stay. I tell her the truth, that I have no idea, no plans beyond the summer. What I don't say is this: I've run out of places to run, there's nowhere to be but here.

Before leaving, Earlene helps me unload my crated paintings from her truck and carry them into the living room. I had them shipped up from Brooklyn two years ago, after we sold our place there, and they've been cluttering up her attic ever since.

Back behind the wheel, she invites me to her house for the annual Baines family Memorial Day cookout. "You're looking a little peaky, Suzanne, but we'll get you fed up. Promise me you'll eat that beef stew, now." I do, and she waves, throws the truck into gear, and backs down the driveway, disappearing around a tangle of hawthorn in a splatter of gravel.

After Earlie goes, I make good on my vow, heat up the stew and take the steaming bowl to the sofa, where I plop down without bothering to remove the sheet that covers it. New England soul food, my dad called meals like this: baked beans, fish chowder, Jell-O, macaroni and cheese. My French mother never made such things, looked down her nose and called it "nursery food," but I always loved having it when I visited the relatives. Earlie's stew is just like I remember, root vegetables and beef cooked almost to mush, thick broth, plenty of salt, no pepper.

Under the kitchen sink, I find more ladybug corpses and brush them into a paper towel. Lacking the energy to dig another hole, I fold it up and slide it into the pocket of my jeans, grab a beach chair, and walk down the long slope of lawn to the shore. The slate-blue bay shudders beneath a gusting wind, foamy whitecaps breaking here and there. The high tide has just started to turn, and in a few hours, the waterline will have retreated twenty feet from where it is now, leaving behind a wet moonscape of barnacle-crusted boulders, mounds of ocher seaweed, and even the odd starfish clinging to rock. When we were kids, my brother and I would "rescue" them at low tide by pulling them off the exposed rocks and pitching them out into the deep water. It occurs to me that between our manhandling and the impact, we probably killed more than we saved.

As I'm about to settle into my chair, I remember the ladybugs in my pocket and fish the paper towel out. At water's edge I drop them into the reach, a burial at sea.

Buried at sea, just like my father, except he wasn't dead when he went in. He wasn't oblivious to the frigid water or sewn up cozy in a sail and slipped overboard with prayers and a salute like in the movies. Not buried at all, he was lost. Lost in a winter squall that sucked him, and my grandfather, overboard. Somehow Uncle Eldridge, the third man on the boat that day, managed to hold on to the hull, but my father, or what remains of him, is still out there in the bay, unburied at sea with dead ladybugs and murdered starfish for company.

Thoughts of my father pull me back to the house I grew up in, a barn-red saltbox two coves up from here on a knoll overlooking the water. It's February 1976 and my mother is sitting at the kitchen table, frozen in place despite the heat from the furnace and the scream of the kettle. My dad's oldest friend, Caspar Titcomb, ancient and palsied in his too-big clothes, is making hot whiskey: a quarter of a lemon studded with cloves, a double shot of Jameson, and boiling water. The untouched cups of hot chocolate he made for my brother and me have already gone cold.

Aunt Margery just called to say the coast guard is airlifting Uncle Eldridge to the hospital in Bangor and that they're still searching for the others. Philip and I are in our usual chairs between the table and the wall, but nothing is usual tonight. My brother is holding my hand, something he hasn't done in a very long time. We are teenagers, long past such things, now suddenly not.

Agnes Juke sits across from us. Her arthritic hands cover my mother's clenched fists, and I'm struck by how much they resemble the ball and claw feet on our dining room table. She murmurs something I can't make out over the clatter of dishes. A cup appears in front of Maman and Agnes tells her to drink, but she says she can't. Philip and I translate because she's speaking only in French. For her this is the language of grief and loss. Many years later she will tell me that in her mind she was back in 1940 with her own mother at their house in Saint-Rimay, reliving the moment they got the news that the Battle of Sedan had claimed her father, that the Luftwaffe's bombardment had been so heavy, the devastation so complete, there was no body to return to them. Her father had been blown to bits and scattered along the Belgian border, the first member of our family to be left unburied. Soon after, France would fall, ushering in four grueling years under the Nazi jackboot.

Caspar says, "There's still hope, Lil. The tide's dead low and if they found Eldridge, they can find Mason and Henry." Agnes agrees, says our father and grandfather are tough SOBs, that they know every inch of this bay, every buoy, ledge, and harbor.

For a long time it's quiet in the kitchen. Finally Maman speaks. Her voice is low, lacking inflection or emotion, which scares me more than if she were hysterical. *"Il est mort, j'en suis certaine."* I choke out the translation: "He is dead, I'm sure of it."

Silent tears run down Philip's face. I open the quilt I dragged off my bed and cocoon him, my arms around his neck. She is right, we all know it.

We begin the next day in darkness, to sunflower-covered drapes drawn over the living room windows where my father liked to stand, looking past the ramble of rugosa and Maman's tidy vegetable garden to the water, staring at it in a way he never did my mother or us. Maman will not open the curtains again.

Bad luck, the investigators tell us, that's all it was. Our father's lobster boat was in the wrong place at the wrong time. Not luck, but "that murderous bitch of a bay he loved more than me," Maman says. The following summer, when Philip tries to take *Orion* out for a sail, she runs screaming to the dock, grabs my brother by the scruff, tells him she'll set fire to our father's little sloop if either of us ever gets near it or that bloodthirsty ocean again. The next day, Reynard Fletcher shows up towing a boat trailer behind his pickup and winches *Orion* out of the water. It's the last time we ever see the boat that was our father's great joy.

As grief-mad as Maman is, our grandma Baines is worse. With her husband buried and her son lost, she sits and stares out the window for days at a time, hardly speaking, inert, crumbling, a skeleton with a cigarette in a dirty brown cardigan. I want to run away from her, from this, and in less than a year we do. As soon as Philip goes off to college, Maman sells everything and the two of us move south to Portland, where she has friends, a small group of fellow expats, and George Lawson, who will become her second husband.

In our new house, I comfort myself thinking that I will never see the like of that again, never have to wait for news that doesn't come, never hold out hope when there is none. And I don't, not until many years later: twenty months after the dawn of the new millennium, under the New York City sky. In my beach chair I shudder despite the warmth of the sun; I am powerless to halt the tide of memory.

Holding the line against gentrification and newcomers like me, the old Italians in our Brooklyn neighborhood make wine from the grapes they grow in their backyards and fly homing pigeons from rooftop coops.

It isn't uncommon to see the birds flocking overhead, their pinfeathers shimmering white in the sun.

This fine September morning in 2001, I am on the way home after dropping my son at school, rushing and fretting about the deadline my client just moved up. To pay for preschool when Milo was a toddler, I started peddling my art in the lucrative, ridiculous world of greeting card companies. At some point, the goof became what passes for my career. I still paint seriously, just not very often.

We returned from our summer vacation in Maine at the end of August and are settling back into city life. Ten years before, as a wedding gift, my husband, David, bought a couple of acres on the southern end of my family's property in Wellbridge with the goal of building a cottage one day. I've always had mixed feelings about the place; neither my mother nor my brother ever went back after my father died, but I always felt a pull from my hometown. It matters to me that my boy grows up knowing as much about where my people came from as he does the East Village where his father was raised and France where his cousins live.

There is a warm kiss in the September air that day, a chambray sky, the promise of a little extra summer. I am about to turn onto our block when I notice a flock of pigeons high above, flying not in the usual flowing swoop but randomly, in chaos, with no apparent direction or leader. On the corner, a neighborhood guy in an undershirt, suit pants, and house slippers is standing, eyes skyward. He tells me a plane just crashed into one of the World Trade Center towers.

I don't understand. How could anyone make such a stupid mistake? I look from him to the sky and am about to ask when I realize those aren't birds, but swirling papers, hundreds of them that have drifted across the East River from lower Manhattan. David's office is there, on the twenty-fifth floor of a building on Liberty Street, a few blocks from the Trade Center. Every day my husband walks through the subway concourse under the towers on his way to work. I'm trying to calculate his travel time, to figure out whether he might be there now, but can't make my brain work. In the distance sirens scream, and I run for home. When I get there, I try to call David, but the circuits are jammed, overloaded by people like me trying to reach office workers, tradesmen, cops, and commuters. On TV, the news swirls in a sickening kaleidoscope. When the second jet flies into the South Tower, the news announcers are frantic, hysterical, and I sink to the floor, fetal, whimpering. I'm dialing David's office over and over but cannot get through. I lie on the living room rug holding the phone like a life buoy. The announcers say there are more planes in the air, then report one has hit the Pentagon. The phone rings. David shouts, "I'm okay, Suz. They're telling us to stay put." Over and over he says this as I scream into the phone, begging him to come home, to run. He says he can't, tells me to take Milo out of school. He can see the whole thing from his office window. "Oh my God, the tower," he moans. I hear his colleagues wailing in the background. "It's collapsing. Go get Milo! *Now, Suzanne, now!*" The phone goes dead. The school is between David's office and our house, in the path of the noxious smoke I see on TV. As I run, all I can think about is getting my baby back, and David, my little family, to keep them from being blown up along with our neighbors and friends, all those people going to work or flying home, the parents, the children. Oh my God, the children. How many will there be? All in the wrong place at the wrong time.

Back home, Milo plays in his room, unaware of what has happened to our world, too busy with his Transformers to ask. Or maybe he's shutting it all out. His school was smoky, so I tell him there's a fire downtown but Daddy is okay, which seems to be enough for his seven-year-old brain. So far he has seen nothing. Before we got home, a fourth plane crashed somewhere in Pennsylvania, now the second tower falls and I smother my sobs in a pillow. I can smell the smoke from Manhattan, so I close the windows against it, nauseated by the thought of breathing in the ashes of the dead.

At eleven o'clock the mayor orders the evacuation. David calls again to say he's leaving the office and will walk home to Brooklyn. I am terrified there will be snipers on the bridges or bombs set to go off once the exodus begins. My hands shake so violently I can barely pour the brandy into a glass. Never in my life have I actually needed a drink, not like this. Our backyard is full of papers now, some burnt, others pristine, the towers' many fallen birds.

David walks through the door an hour later, covered with ash, in shock, giddy and dazed at the same time. He hugs me hard and long, but I am the only one crying. Just before a dinner of peanut-butter sandwiches and tomato soup no one but Milo will eat, I find him in our boy's room, asleep on the floor next to an elaborate tower of red blocks. When Milo knocks it over, David lurches awake, screaming a single word: no. It will be years before he tells me what he saw: the fires, the falling buildings, the rubble, the people jumping from a hundred stories up, hand in hand, choosing to fall together rather than be cremated alive.

Even though I grew up in Maine, New York is the only place I've ever felt I belonged, where, despite the bigness of it, the anonymity, I fit in. I move easily along its streets, enjoy the tap of my heels on the pavement, the great mirror skyscrapers and garish neon pulse, the feeling that everyone is different, and difference is the norm. Even so, in the weeks that follow September 11, I beg David to leave, to get away from the targets on our backs, the endless grief, our neighbors crying openly in coffee shops and on the street, the tattered, hopeless flyers asking, "Have You Seen This Person?" tacked up everywhere by families who will never get back even the smallest scrap of the people they've lost, never bury them. The cruelty of this is relentless, unendurable.

"Where the fuck would we go?" David shouts at me after days of arguments. "Maine? You hate the winter. France? Milo and I don't speak

French, and even if we did, what would we do there, sponge off Philip, or your mother and George? No place is safe now, Suzanne."

It's clear the thought of leaving New York makes David, now barely able to get out of bed, even more upset, so I let it go; instead, I try to toe the bullshit party line that says if we hide or flee, the terrorists win. But no one is winning here. No one.

As a compromise, David agrees to start building our cottage on the land up north, and we head to Maine the following May to watch the builder break ground. I had expected to feel relieved at leaving the city, but instead the grief wells up with each mile and crashes over me at the state line. We pass the salt marshes of the southern coast, the sandy beaches, the rolling green of fields and fir. With Milo asleep in the back seat and David behind the wheel, I sob so hard we have to pull over to the breakdown lane so I can vomit.

On the beach, I watch a tiny green crab scrabble across the pebbles and shells. How can something so small do such damage? I wonder. In the past few years, they've invaded the shore and eaten up everything the mussels used to feed on, or at least that's one theory; whether it's fact or fiction I can't say. I do know that where once the shellfish were abundant, easily picked, now there are almost none, and I imagine them starved to death by these tiny interlopers, this cancer on the natural order. The crabs don't know they survive at the expense of others, and why should they care? This is how life is: my feast is your famine; your freedom, my prison.

The tide ebbs, but the memories flow, some vague and fleeting, others immediate and clear. I recall being back in France. It's 2010 and Philip and I have come to Antibes to watch our mother die surrounded by jasmine, lavender, and olive trees in the crumbly limestone farmhouse where she and her second husband retired. George is already six years gone. The same lung cancer that took him has come for her. I imagine them passing death back and forth with every kiss, like a virus in a wisp of smoke. Starved for air, she labors to breathe, her gasps getting wetter and shallower every day. She has told us no feeding tubes, just drugs; she was very clear about it. Compared to this, my father's death doesn't seem so horrible. In the days before she dies, when she breaks the surface of the morphine sea, she keeps telling me to find someone to love me. "But I have, I'm married to David. Remember, Maman?" I say. She rolls her eyes. Eventually I stop answering.

During the days I spend with Philip in the house above the Mediterranean, I have time to think and I come to understand that 9/11 was not the beginning of the end for David and me. Yes, we were damaged, but every day people endure tragedy, and they manage to stay together. My brother's third child died just two weeks before she was to be born, and his poor wife had to go through labor and delivery, knowing she would give birth to a corpse. They went on to have two more children, found a way to keep loving each other and believe in their future. The truth is, David and I got married to be married. We are a house built on sand and buttressed by our son. I hope it will be enough, but my hope has no wings; a flightless bird, it is tethered, earthbound.

When Milo goes off to college, David and I lose our buffer, the cartilage between the two bones, he and I. Living together is lonely, for both of us, I think. We work longer hours, fight more often, then stop bothering to fight at all. For a few more years we hold on, and when the end comes, I'm more relieved than sad, and probably he is, too.

I shift my chair out of the lengthening shadows and into the last patch of sun to try to stay warm, extend my time on the shore with the brine in the air and the lap of the waves. There's movement in my peripheral vision, and I watch as a big sloop rounds the headland, beating to windward. It's unusual to see anything but kayaks and the occasional motorboat in the reach. There's no navigable outlet other than the approach, which shrinks to a tight, shallow trench at low tide. Why would they come here, especially with the tide going? Maybe they're looking for safe harbor.

My husband never felt safe here. A city boy, born and raised in Manhattan, David always said it was too quiet, that there was no one to hear you scream if something dangerous—a bear, a pack of rabid raccoons, toothless guys with chain saws—came out of the woods. When I left him, he told me to take the cottage, said he'd never come back to this place, that it had never been his.

For me the divorce was an act of self-preservation, a lifeline, selfish but necessary in the way such things are. Though he was twenty-two at the time, Milo was devastated when we split up, said it was my fault because I was the one who left, and didn't speak to me for three months. That was the worst part. Every silent day in my miserable sublet I waited for his call and thought about dying, longed for it the way you do an old lover or lost faith, but I lacked the courage to see it through and instead slopped along until the morning David showed up with our boy, and Milo shouted, cursed, and sobbed his way back into my life.

It's still not right between us, not like it was before, and maybe it never will be, but this was the kindest thing David ever did for me. He didn't have to. He could have kept on holding the moral high ground, but he was better than that, better than us, and I am grateful.

After the rapprochement with Milo, I tried living in France. My work is portable, requiring nothing but an iPad, Wi-Fi, and a middling amount of creativity, so I decided to go to Paris for a while, try to start over. Philip lives there with his family, I speak the language, and I have always been a city person. After six months, I was still unsettled; it wasn't home, and I knew it never would be.

From my saggy chaise I watch the tide recede, carrying the martyred ladybugs past the anchoring sloop and out to sea. I wonder how far they'll go, imagine them floating east, nearly weightless on the surface of the Atlantic, drifting around the tip of the U.K., into the Channel, and upstream on the Seine to Paris, a gift from my dead father and me to my brother.

Philip always hated Maine, the cold and the snow, the isolation and the people. "Inbred and frozen in backwardness," he calls them, and has instead embraced his French half, the part that came from our mother. He and his wife teach at the Sorbonne; their kids bring the grandchildren over for dinner every Sunday. When we talk on the phone Philip keeps to French, answering my lazy franglais with professorial grammar, complicated syntax, and obscure vocabulary. Just to tweak him, I call him Pip, like Maman did. He says he hates it, but I know he doesn't, not really.

The beach lengthens as the tide ebbs, dragging the shadows along with it; I can almost see them stretch. Soon the sun will drop behind my cottage, stealing the last bit of heat and the final dregs of daylight. I recall one low-tide evening, the summer we built this place, when the setting sun shone gold and bounced off the water, gilding the seaweed-covered rocks across the reach in a paroxysm of light that transformed our world into a Turner painting, glowing luminous color in liquid swirl. It lasted only a minute or two as David and I watched, together, silent, holding hands. I've always wanted to be able to paint that scene, to re-create that moment, that light, on canvas, but I work better in shades of dark.

Today the sunset disappoints, just slips below the horizon and dims the sky to deeper blue, and so I fold up my chair and wedge it behind a rock, safely above the high-water mark. I think about pulling my boat out of the garage and rowing over to the sloop, now sitting at anchor in the middle of the reach, where the water is deepest. I imagine the boat owners, a happy family gathered belowdecks, having dinner and playing cards, and I wonder what they'd make of me, if they'd smell my desperation and avoid me or offer me a drink and invite me aboard. Probably neither, it would just be uncomfortable, a forced interchange, and we'd all be glad when it was over.

I pass by the toolshed David and I converted to an art studio and remember the paintings in the living room. Some are complete, but most are unfinished. In the cellar, I find a crowbar and carry it upstairs, where the crates lean against the wall. The temperature is dropping, but soon I am sweating with the effort of prying them open. Once I've uncrated the canvases, I line them up around the room, a rogue's gallery of old friends and a few enemies. I try to remember the last time I picked up a brush.

One painting in particular takes me back to my studio in Brooklyn. I couldn't get it right and it was giving me fits right up until I packed it away. It's a winter landscape, based on an old photo of the Baines farmhouse that was taken in the forties, when my father was growing up there. In the picture, the house, where my cousin Cora lives now, is surrounded by snow, its black roof straight as a ship's prow in a sea of winter white, broken only by the pole of a clothesline that pokes skyward like the periscope of a submarine. I was trying to capture the bleakness of the half-light and the heavy clouds but succeeded only in creating a scene that's more suitable for one of my clients' "I'm sorry" cards than a gallery wall. Technically it's not bad, but it lacks soul. I still don't know how to fix it, so I turn it around to stop it mocking me. In the kitchen, dinner awaits: pudding and wine. It'll do.

The next morning my head aches and my mouth tastes like the inside of a bait barrel. It's after nine, and in my mind I hear Grandma Baines, always appalled by louche behavior, admonishing me for being a filthy stay-abed.

I pick up a half-empty wine bottle, carry it downstairs, and shove it in the fridge, rather than dumping it down the sink and tossing it in the bin beside the one I emptied before it. Waste not, and all that. In the pantry there's a can of chicken noodle soup that won't expire for another week, so I nuke it and carry it to the sofa, trying to figure out whether it's worth a visit to the grocery store to avoid subsisting on peanut butter and stale crackers.

Today the weather is dank, the fog thick as paste. The sloop is either invisible in the mist or already gone, leaving me alone with the lady-bugs, the crabs, and the dead. I wonder if it was ever really there at all and figure that since a walk around town and a little human contact are the last things I want, they're probably just what I need.

I shower to warm up and am surprised at the lurch in my stomach when I see David's robe hanging on the back of the bathroom door. The cottage, though all mine now, is still full of his things, which makes me even lonelier than the weak gray light does, so I call him to ask what to do with it all—his clothes, photos, and books, the birthday gifts Milo and I gave him at the parties we threw for him every August.

My ex-husband sounds surprised to hear from me. "Would you like me to pack everything up and send it to you?" I ask, and realize I don't have his address. We were together for almost thirty years and now I don't even know where he sleeps.

"Just donate it or junk it. There's nothing I need," he says, delivering a gut punch I never saw coming.

"Not even the photos, or the books?" I can't bring myself to mention the presents: Milo's little handicrafts, the stainless-steel wineglasses I got for picnics in the rowboat, the "Fish Gut Lane" T-shirt we had made the year the cottage was finished.

"If I haven't missed them by now, I never will. Anything you think is worth saving, you can give to Milo. Gotta run. Good to hear from you, Suzanne. Take care, now."

With a click he disappears back into his new life, the one that doesn't include even a thought of me. David never was attached to things, places, never kept anything or dragged it around for long. I can't remember him holding a grudge for more than a few minutes; even his grief was short-lived, efficient, complete in reasonable time. When his mother died, he was devastated, but it was clean, uncomplicated pain: he loved her, she loved him, she was gone. We sat shiva, buried her, and moved on. How I envy his unencumbrance.

I think there might be things Milo would want but am overcome by the desire to get rid of it all, to unencumber *myself*, so I grab some garbage bags from the kitchen and start emptying drawers into them, not stopping to sort or fold, thinking I'll drop everything at Goodwill on my way to the Foodland.

I draw the line at David's underwear, carry the small drawer to the kitchen, and turn it out into the trash. The socks and boxers fall, but the last thing that drops is a picture. Taken a lifetime ago, the photo shows Milo perched on David's shoulders. His blond curls tumble down his three-year-old neck; he's laughing so hard his eyes are shut, and his mouth is wide-open. David, waist deep in Long Lake on a fine summer day, holds Milo's ankles in one hand while the other reaches up to save his boy from falling backward into the water. David is laughing, too, his shoulders more broad than bowed, not a trace of gray in his hair. I remember taking that picture. I remember David being young and cheerful and Milo wanting nothing more than to spend the day being thrown into the lake and passed from David to me and back again.

In those days David thought I was interesting, said he'd never met a girl who could gut a fish *and* navigate a gallery party. I thought I'd found my soul mate in a corporate lawyer who read poetry for pleasure and could recite every line of *Duck Soup* from memory. During visits to the Baines family farm, before we built our place, he'd weed the garden and shovel horse manure with the kind of enthusiasm only a city boy could muster. The day I taught him to drive the tractor, he said it was the best of his life.

And yet here we are, no *we* left. Like the sloop in the reach, David has moved on, turned around and sailed away to a safer harbor, remarried and content, but I am landlocked, my wheels still spinning, sinking in the mud of the past sucking me down, deeper and deeper, in the swamp of memory. Trapped in a marriage long dead but still unburied, the bits and pieces of it scattered and rotting all around me, unable to find my way out, I am haunted: by killer waves on gray water, burning papers like swirling birds, the unburied dead, the unfinished past, the unyielding everything.

I open the door to my studio, set down my jar of turpentine, and place the winterscape on the easel. I know what's wrong with it now. Instead of standing straight and square under the white snow sky, the Baines homestead should be half-buried, collapsing in on itself with the weight of all that surrounds it and all that has gone before. With a whispered prayer for inspiration, I squeeze black paint onto my palette, next to it some white and a touch of blue. I dab my brush and begin the delicate task of bashing in the roof.

Requiem aeternam dona insepultis eis, Domine.
(Grant the unburied eternal rest, O Lord.)

ACKNOWLEDGMENTS

Much of the production of this book happened during the most harrowing months of 2020, amidst the suffering and death of a worldwide pandemic as well as ongoing racial injustice and political unrest in the United States. I cannot fathom how, in New York, the people of Flatiron Books got out of bed in the morning, let alone stayed focused and kept working. And yet they did, professionally, compassionately, and well, on my book and many others. It was a marvel to see and a joy to be part of.

For taking a flyer on a quiet book about small lives and helping it become a real novel through hard, dark times, thank you, Megan Lynch. Special thanks as well to Callum Plews, Katherine Turro, Claire McLaughlin, Lauren Bittrich, and everybody at Flatiron and Macmillan.

Deepest thanks to Stephanie Cabot of Susanna Lea Associates for plucking me from the slush and believing in this book. Thanks, too, to Ellen Goodson Coughtrey and Sophie Pugh-Sellers. Thank you, Roma Panganiban, my first reader.

I also want to thank the entire publishing industry—authors, agents, editors, publishers, printers, shippers, truck drivers, and booksellers—for soldiering on to keep the world of words and ideas alive when we needed books so much.

I owe so much to the great storytellers I have been lucky enough to

know. Over more years than I care to count, they have shared their stories, jokes, and observations and in the process taught me the power of
words to uplift, amuse, challenge, and irk. From them I have borrowed
many stories and excellent turns of phrase. For those still living, I hope
you don't mind. Thank you: Roy E. (for Easy) Pierce, Pauline Tetzlaff
Hinman, Sue DeMarco DiSalvio, Janet H. Fitzpatrick, Baxter Jones,
Lillian Arlene Burpee, and the unforgettable Mrs. Dorothy Quinn.

A thousand thanks (and that's not near enough) to Robin Grunder at
Blue Egg Strategy for taking my chaotic scribblings without complaint
and rendering the messy world of my characters and their relationships
clearly and elegantly in all those family trees. You reign supreme.

I am indebted to my trusted group of readers for their patience in
looking at things (over and over again), for their insight, and for their
support through thick and thin: Rosalyn Hoffman Feldberg, Karen
Plummer Winslow, Cristy Carrington Lewis, Stephanie Lewin, and
Nick Ferrone.

Thank you, Kathi Hansen, genius writer, most astute reader, fierce
champion, spit sister. Where would I be without you? My gratitude is
endless and my debt unpayable, but I will keep trying.

Thank you, Betsy Parsons, for introducing me to literature all those
years ago. (I know you're still reading, because heaven is surely a library.) Thanks to Shelly Oria for telling me I could write, and Sarah
Blake for reading. At NYU, thank you, Helen Schulman, Darin Strauss,
and Deborah Landau. I will be ever grateful to the brilliant John Free-
man for his kindness, for believing in this project, and for knowing what
I was trying to do even when I didn't.

Thanks to my mother, Barbara Kimball, for believing I could do
anything and insisting it was true. I am eternally grateful to my grand-
mothers, Florence Burpee and Susan Bean, and my grandfathers, Albert
Kimball and Harvey Winslow, who are everywhere in this book and
my life. Thank you, Dad—and all the Winslows, Kimballs, and Pierces

in this world and the next—for putting up with me, for being funny and difficult and clever and tough, but mostly for being there.

I owe more than I can say to my lifelong friends who long ago became family. Thanks for sticking with me, Mary Quinn and Frank Hodgkins, supreme raconteurs and two of the finest, funniest, smartest people I have ever known. Without you this book would not exist.

Always and ever, Max Dietshe and Grace Winslow Dietshe, thank you for being the most patient kin, my miracle and my life. You are just everything, and then some more.